SNAPSHOTS

Michael O'Higgins

NEW ISLAND

SNAPSHOTS

First published in 2015 by
New Island Books
16 Priory Hall Office Park
Stillorgan
County Dublin
Republic of Ireland

www.newisland.ie

PRINT ISBN: 978-1-84840-466-3
EPUB ISBN: 978-1-84840-467-0
MOBI ISBN: 978-1-84840-468-7

British Library Cataloguing Data.
A CIP catalogue record for this book is available from the British Library.

Typeset by JVR Creative India
Cover design by Anna Morrison
Printed by ScandBook AB

New Island received financial assistance from The Arts Council (*An Chomhairle Ealaíon*), 70 Merrion Square, Dublin 2, Ireland.

10 9 8 7 6 5 4 3 2 1

For Trish

Part One

Summer in Dublin, 1981

prologue

Dick Roche parked up in the corner of the back yard of the Hunter's Lodge. He was waiting bolt upright, constantly checking his rear- and side-view mirrors. This place was out of town, suitably off the beaten track. But you could never be too careful – it was popular with couples in the first flush of dating, or lads who were playing away. A cop in the company of a criminal here would stand out. There'd be serious, probably terminal, consequences if word got out.

In due course the passenger door opened and Jimmy Daly, or Source 17, District 6, as he was officially known, sat in. Daly was a thin reedy man with a receding hairline who Roche suspected was prone to ulcers. He always seemed to be chewing spearmint gum or Bisodol. He was a dapper fella – his shoes were always polished and he smelled of cologne. Daly scrunched himself down into the seat to make himself smaller with his hands in the pockets of his bomber jacket.

Jimmy made a living providing hardware and other logistical backup to serious criminals. He also made money on the side being a tout, Roche's tout. Sure, his motive in providing information was usually suspect – jockeying for position or to settle an old score. He was no altruist. But he was tried and tested. He'd been the first informer that Roche had ever recruited and he'd run him with great success down through the years.

Daly had recently sold Christy Clarke two short arms for a job. Clarke had stipulated that the weapons had to be still in the box. This was to ensure ballistic analysis of any spent casings or bullets wouldn't yield a forensic history. He'd dump the guns afterwards. The target was believed to be a payroll drop at a tyre factory. Harry Brown and Liam Kinsella – Clarke's lieutenants – had been spotted timing the security van on the day of a drop. Clarke himself had been seen in the vicinity in the small hours, head down hoodie up, his outline a wispy silhouette on the horizon. Roche had been staking out the yard for the last few weeks.

'Morning boss,' Daly said, 'anything for me?'

Roche handed him an envelope containing five crisp £10 notes, paid out of the Secret Services Fund, the name given to the slush monies paid to touts. Every week, Roche completed the form in triplicate, had a Chief Superintendent countersign it and waited three working days for the monies to be sent by special courier from the Department of Justice. From the start of their arrangement, Daly had insisted on being paid up front. Roche approved: it lessened the need to perform.

Daly held the envelope lengthways in his hand, tore a strip off the side of it, concertinaed it, and squinted so as to satisfy himself that he was looked after. It was a ritual.

'It's getting close, that's all I can say,' Daly kicked off.

'What's that mean?'

'Harry Brown and Liam Kinsella picked up the two shorts from a hide yesterday.'

'Go on.'

'That's it. Nothing more. But you know yourself Christy doesn't put his boys at risk unless there's a pretty good reason for it.'

Roche considered the information. It was hard and specific. His cop's nose told him that Daly was probably right. Something was about to happen. Brown and Kinsella didn't have the brains or vision of their leader, but they were serious street thugs. It'd be a coup to take them all out of circulation. Maybe Clarke was just moving stuff around. He trusted no one. But sometimes the reason for things was more prosaic: if it looked like a duck, walked like a duck and quacked, it was probably gonna fly in some shape or form.

'Thanks Jimmy. Thanks for that. Talk soon.'

one

Roche crawled into the roof space of the Ford Commer van. He withdrew his Smith and Wesson .38 revolver from his shoulder holster, let off the safety catch, and placed it by his side, muzzle pointing away from him. He pulled back the leather peephole cut into the roof – the single modification that justified the vehicle being known as the surveillance van – and confirmed that the entrance to the wages office was in his line of sight. He took a few moments to compose himself and settled down to wait.

Boredom was the enemy now. He'd impressed upon the younger men that Christy Clarke had the knack for picking a moment when complacency had set in. But he wasn't sure he'd made them understand how nasty and dangerous a little fuck Clarke was.

Clarke had plugged a security guard in the chest at close range with a sawn-off shotgun during a previous robbery. The entry wound, the size of a golf ball, was as big as a grapefruit by the time it had exited through his back. He'd haemorrhaged pints of blood into his lungs and suffocated. He'd died in less than a minute.

They'd come across Clarke puffing and panting a short distance away wearing only his underpants, washing his hands and face in a dirty puddle of rainwater. Clothes were strewn around the ground. He'd arrested Clarke and brought him to the station. Clarke had steadfastly ignored all questions put to him during interviews.

They'd swabbed his hands for residue. Tests had failed to detect any traces. Particles consistent with firearm residue were found on the cuffs of the shirt abandoned close by.

Pat Flannery, who'd been heading up the investigation, lost patience. He'd moved the interrogation down to the locker rooms. There, he'd repeatedly ducked Clarke in a bath of ice-cold water. Flannery had apologised in advance but said that he had to protect society from people like him. At first, Clarke had just laid back on the floor of the bath, his cold blue eyes staring back at them. But when he couldn't hold his breath any longer he'd kicked like a donkey.

Flannery had roared at Roche to help, and so he'd leaned with all his weight on Clarke's chest to pin him down. They were soaked through, but Roche could tell the wet rings under the arms of Flannery's shirt were sweat. Clarke had called them a bunch of cocksuckers and, looking at Roche, had stamped the ground and muttered, 'Cockroach.' He'd sprayed graffiti on the station wall after he'd taken up his present posting: 'Sgt CockRoche is a Dick and a pervert.'

It'd been obvious to everyone that Clarke had killed the security man. Flannery had meticulously assembled the case against Clarke into an investigation file and send it off to the office of the Director of Public Prosecutions in Merrion Street. No charges were directed. The pen pusher who was in charge of the file concluded that there was no evidence to connect Clarke to the shirt with residue on the cuffs. Like some other robber might have thrown it there and it was entirely normal for a middle-aged man to be in his jocks washing his face in a puddle in the middle of a cold November afternoon.

Roche had been a rookie back then. But he hadn't been too judgmental – he'd understood how easy it was to blow some poor fucker to kingdom come when the adrenalin was coursing through your system. He'd shot people himself in the intervening years. You were only allowed fire when your own life was at stake. It'd been drilled into him on the range to fire at the upper torso, into one of the vital organs, but he had still shot people in the legs when it came down to it. Today, he'd be following procedure to the letter. One neat shot to the head would do the trick.

He closed his eyes and pictured Clarke lying supine on the ground, blood congealing around his mouth, his cheeks the dull pallor of a dead pig. He'd just be an inanimate object then, and you'd be left wondering what all the fuss had been about. The thought of it made him want to believe in an afterlife. It didn't seem right that everything would just stop without any repercussions. But what were the chances that there was a man with a tail and a fork ready to roast him for eternity?

The distinctively coloured navy blue armour-plated security van drove into the yard.

He saw the proprietor scurrying across the yard into the factory. Roche had paid him a courtesy call to warn him that they'd intel that Christy Clarke and his crew were targeting his payroll. A small fat man, he'd stared quizzically across at Roche from his big desk, his nose twitching in disapproval as he explained that it'd be safer to pay staff by cheque. He'd assured Roche that the firm would happily write cheques in the morning. It'd free up half a dozen people making up the wage packets for starters. He'd then said something about a lot of the workers not having bank accounts and that it wasn't practical.

There had to be more to it. And sure enough, when Roche had poked and prodded, it had emerged that the union would only allow it if staff were allowed half an hour off to cash their cheques.

'Have you any idea how much that would cost us?' the man had asked incredulously. Roche didn't, but he'd still wondered how many tyres would be lost in half an hour's production that would have this man risk his own life and that of his staff. He'd noticed that the man made sure that he was always on the factory floor whenever the wages were due.

A security guard jumped out of the front passenger seat and walked to the rear of the vehicle. A chute opened from the back door and he picked up a bag containing the money. It was surprising how £83,000 fitted into such a small bag.

Roche strained his eyes to follow the security guard's progress as he walked across the yard, in the door and up the stairs to the cash office. He watched the gate at the entrance to the yard. Every man in the unit was watching, waiting, hoping.

The security man returned less than a minute later, empty-handed. He stepped into the front passenger seat of the van and it drove on to its next drop.

And that was it. Roche reversed out of the roof space. He put the safety catch back on his revolver and re-holstered it. The static from his radio crackled as units were told to stand down. He'd be back next week. In the long run the odds favoured the guards over the career criminal. Clarke's greed would inevitably get the better of him: he'd be standing in front of his van, five foot eight of sinewy muscle, a pistol in his hand, looking around for his prey and Roche would be there within a split second. He'd be justified in topping him. He wouldn't be found wanting when it came down to discharging his duty.

two

Fr Brendan quickened his stride. The noise from the bell was shrill and incessant. He was right on the edge of a temper by the time he got the door open. Lillian Clarke stood before him, a pack of John Player Blue and a plastic lighter clasped in her left hand, and a pair of pink-rimmed sunglasses tucked into her ample cleavage. He noticed faded bruising on her arms, a signature tune no doubt hammered out by Christy when he came in full from the pub.

You could see that she'd been a bit of a looker in her day. She'd have lit up the flats alright: a pretty Scouser must have been as rare as an exotic bird back then. She was still attractive in a coarse sort of way. But childbirth, a hankering for cod in batter, and living with a psycho like Christy had taken a toll.

Wayne was stood beside her, hands in his pockets, face set in its permanent look of defiance. With his cherubic face and long hair he almost looked a bit girly. But he was the Under 12 champion at the local Francis Xavier boxing club and played cornerback for St Joseph's GAA team, who hadn't lost a match in years.

He motioned them across the threshold with an exaggerated wave of his hand. They trooped down in single file to the living room. They all stood for a moment in front of the empty marble fireplace, unsure where to sit down. She began to fuss over her hair on seeing her reflection in the large gilded mirror over the mantelpiece.

A large colour television, which had been given to him as a present by his parents when he'd been moved here, sat on the cabinet in the corner. He'd been watching an episode of *Jim'll Fix It* and had decided to invite Savile to do a fundraiser here when the bell had rang. He went to turn it off but Lillian said that it should be kept on for Wayne. He suggested they go into his study but she made a gesture with a shake of the head that it was unnecessary.

Instead, they sat down in armchairs facing off against each other.

'Bastard!' There was no need to explain that she was referencing Christy. In Scouse it almost sounded like a term of endearment.

'Sorry about the language, Father. He's doing my head in.'

Invective gave way to diatribe: Maurice spent his time blagging with Christy and it was only a matter of time before he was caught and got a big sentence. Orla wasn't going to school and didn't listen to a single word she'd say. The wardrobes and ceilings were covered in a black mould. Wayne was getting one chest infection after another. She'd sued the Corpo and got £1,200 in damages.

'Well that must have made things a bit easier?' he said in an attempt to quell the wave of negativity.

'You must be joking! When he found out, he took the money off me, and then gave me a hiding for not telling him about the case.'

She took a cigarette out and tapped it off the pack to compact the tobacco. He'd only seen men do that before, auld fellas at that. It looked odd to see someone with such petite hands doing it. She lit up, blew the smoke upwards and her shoulders sagged. He pushed an ashtray under her nose. He hated smoking, especially in the presbytery. Fr Peter had told him to stop being so precious and to get a life when he'd complained to him.

'But where do I stand, Father? I really need to know. Do you get me?'

Yes he did, but they both knew that the answer was part of the problem. Christy, it had to be acknowledged, was a ne'er-do-well, a recidivist robber. Banks, payrolls, and cash in transit were his favourites. He also had a hatred for authority. Unusually – in Fr Brendan's limited experience career criminals were extraordinarily inept – he excelled at it. Not that it made any lasting difference to how they lived. What Christy didn't spend in the pub he soon lost in the bookies or at the dog track. But that didn't mean that she was entitled to turn back the clock just because she'd made a bad bargain. They were man and wife, joined not by the hip, but by God himself.

'The solicitor says that I can get a barring order and that the court can rule a separation agreement.'

'The solicitor says that, does he?'

It was happening more and more: left-wing politicians, newspaper columnists, and vocal minority interests were relentlessly pushing their own secular agenda. If the priest in the presbytery couldn't hold the line, the game was up.

'Well I don't know a huge amount about the law. But I do know that marriage is for better *and* for worse.'

'Fuck that! He's melting my brain.'

'Now, Lillian, if you are asking me to give my blessing to breaking up your marriage?'

'Christ! So, the next time he is sticking my head down the toilet I just go with the flow?'

Again, the answer was perfectly clear. She should call the gardaí. But the last time he had given that advice the errant husband had confronted him on the church steps and told him that if he ever stuck his nose into his business again then, priest or no priest, he'd batter him.

'The Church runs a perfectly good counselling service. Maybe the pair of you could try to talk it out.'

Lillian snorted and he saw Wayne smirking, no doubt rehearsing how he'd play it all back in the schoolyard. He'd already overheard Wayne doing a very passable impression of him lecturing on the importance of treating girls with respect and 'not turning them into shop-soiled goods'. Wayne had squirmed his nose up for effect when he'd trotted out that line.

'Look, Father!' and here she paused, and ostentatiously looked over at Wayne. Whatever was she going to say that could be any worse than what had gone before? Jimmy Savile was fixing it so that a boy with leukaemia could drive a Formula One racing car. Wayne was sitting up straight, hands clasped together down between his thighs, chewing gum, feigning disinterest in the conversation going on behind him.

Lillian leaned forward right into him and whispered: 'I caught Christy coming out of Orla's room twice last week. He's *at* her. When he has got drink on him and wants to do *something* he can't be stopped.'

Her warm moist breath gently ruffled the hairs in his ear. The intimacy of it caught him off guard, and even though the sensation wasn't exactly unpleasant, it caused him to involuntarily shudder.

'Yes, well, that's an appalling state of affairs. But it's not enough to bring about the dissolution of your marriage,' he replied brusquely.

'What about an annulment? I was sixteen, up the duff, scared shitless.'

'Well, maybe if you had made that case back then. But what is it now, twenty years?'

There was a lull in pace but then she came alive again. Lately, it turned out, Christy had started staying out all night, and she couldn't get a straight answer out of him.

'He saunters in at twelve o'clock in the day smelling of some cheap tart.'

He was struck by the fact that the irritation previously noticeable in her voice had given way to bitterness.

Despite her apparent directness, he'd known it'd take time to get to what was really bothering her. She could put up with the beatings, the drinking, the chaotic living, even that he might be interfering with her daughter. But she wasn't prepared to tolerate Christy being with another woman. The real bugbear had now been vented. The meeting, he sensed, was drawing to its natural close.

He saw the pair of them out. Lillian, he noticed, was buoyed by the chat even though he knew that he had said nothing that could be of any practical assistance to her. Sometimes, articulating frustration acted as its own release, even if the listener was an adversary.

'Wayne is doing a grand job with the piano,' he remarked.

Fr Brendan had taken up his post as a curate and vice-principle of the school on the day of the annual concert. The performances had been woeful. But Wayne had brought the house down, taking off Máistir Lillis, right down to rubbing his snot into the hair of his charges. And the memory of Wayne falling to his knees waving out to the audience as the curtain fell still made him smile.

One of his first initiatives had been to start up piano lessons. Fr Peter had, as usual, scoffed but Wayne had been his vindication. Wayne only had to be shown how to play any piece once. In class, Wayne was disruptive, easily distracted and adept at winding up his teachers. But he could happily spend hours working out how to play his favourite pop song on a guitar.

Fr Brendan hated pop music. It was so empty and venal. He was teaching Wayne sheet music, guiding him through the works of Beethoven, Wagner, Brahms and Mozart in the hope he'd instil something in him. He hadn't charged him a penny: seeing a real talent like his was payment enough.

'Let me tell you, Father, that one is my future: Wayne's as bright.'

She spoke with that unmistakcable pride which a mother reserves when talking about her favourite.

'Will you come on, Ma?' Wayne said impatiently, catching her arm. But behind his obvious embarrassment there was a hint of a smile breaking through. That he could smile at all while living in the midst of such dysfunctionality was a testament to the resilience of human nature, Fr Brendan thought.

three

Wayne watched his Ma spread the jersey out on the counter so that Kenny Dalglish's autograph, written in blue marker just below the number 7, could be fully appreciated. It was the one he'd been wearing when he'd scored the winning goal in the European Cup Final and was his Da's pride and joy. Liverpool had squandered so many chances that night. And then Graham Souness had taken the ball down on his chest right on the edge of the box, slipped it through the legs of the Bruges defender to Kenny, who'd then chipped the keeper. His Da, who had been close enough to see spittle around Kenny's mouth, often said that it had been the happiest moment of his life. Wayne didn't doubt this was actually true.

His Ma then stacked a large pile of match programmes alongside. They included pre-season friendlies with oddball teams, which were collector's items. His Da had paid a grand for the jersey at a charity auction. The other bits and pieces had been accrued over a lifetime. To him they were priceless.

'£475. Take it or leave it, Ned,' Lillian said.

God loves a trier, was all Wayne could think. The time his Ma had come with the bag of sovereigns, left to her by her Nan, you could see that he'd been itching to get his hands on them but the negotiations had still gone on for days. Ned Gearty skinned everyone. The chrome and glass cabinets crammed with jewellery, cameras, Walkmans, televisions and hi-fis were testament to his knack for knowing how to best capitalise on the misery of others.

'Done, Mrs Clarke.'

He counted the money out in twenty-pound notes and a single fiver. He ran his bony finger along the terms and conditions stencilled in neat black ink on the back of the ticket.

'You can redeem the items within ninety days if you repay the money plus accrued interest.'

They all knew that wouldn't be happening. Gearty followed Leeds United. He was fanatic. He wanted the stuff for himself. He was just making sure that Wayne's Da would have no comeback when he found out. Clearly Gearty didn't know his Da very well if he thought that he'd be the slightest bit impressed with words written on a bit of paper. If the stuff were still on the premises his Da would simply walk in and take it. If it wasn't, he'd probably burn the place down.

Outside, his Ma put the money in her purse, patted it before putting it into her bag and said they were heading into town.

They strolled along in silence.

'Da will beat you,' he said.

'Your Da is a prick, son. He might be stronger than me, and a bully too, but he is gonna rue the day he crossed me. Just you watch.'

'Get it back, Ma. Now. You'll be sorry if yah don't. We all will.'

She wasn't for turning. But Wayne kept at her, begging her to be smart.

'Here, look at this,' she said.

They stopped to look at the display window of Waltons music shop on Parnell Square. There was a grand piano, a load of fiddles or maybe violins, he didn't know which, a couple of double basses and a drum kit surrounded by loose sheet music strewn haphazardly around the floor. He saw banjos and bodhráns and electric and acoustic guitars on display on the shop floor. This was a shop where the customers all probably knew how to read music, a place parents brought their children to buy cellos or recorders. They probably sold guitars to showbands and didn't do rock 'n' roll.

'Come on!' she said to him. He followed her in the door. Wayne stopped in front of a rack of guitars. He ran his fingers along the steel strings.

'Can I help you, madam?' The man's accent was snobby.

'Set up that guitar and amp for him,' his Ma answered, pointing at a Gibson Les Paul. It was dark red with flashes of orange around the F holes that looked like seahorses. The fretboard was decorated with mother of pearl inlay on the third, fifth, seventh, ninth, and twelfth frets.

The assistant eyed her up suspiciously like they didn't belong here. But the steel resolve in her voice made it hard to refuse.

The care and veneration with which the assistant held the guitar both impressed and intimidated Wayne. He spent a bit of time adjusting the guitar around Wayne's midriff. He plugged in a Marshall amp, leaned over Wayne's shoulder strumming strings and adjusting the bass and treble. After what seemed like ages, he gave Wayne the thumbs up.

Wayne strummed a few chords to warm up his fingers. The sound was crisp but very full too. His whole body was tingling at the idea of letting it rip.

'Do your stuff,' his Ma said.

He played 'Hurricane' by Neil Young. Its length meant he could have more time on the Gibson. The notes in the lead guitar sequence shot forth all effervescent like bubbles in a fizzy drink. Customers had, by then, stopped what they were doing and gathered around him in a circle. He saw his Ma glaring at him when his face contorted into machinations.

'No orgasms,' she silently mouthed.

When he finished there was a warm spontaneous round of applause.

A man who must have been manager of the store stepped forward. 'How old are you, son?'

'Eleven,' Wayne answered.

'That's quite a talent your boy has there,' he said, turning to his Ma. 'Nurture him.'

'At £650 for a bloody guitar and amp? Are yah havin' a laugh or what?'

He stroked his chin with his hand and then asked, 'How much have you got?'

'£450.'

'Take it. If he does well don't forget us.'

They paid up as quickly as they could in case he changed his mind. They were a sight going up the road, she carrying the guitar and him pushing the amp. The wheels jarred on the uneven pavement; he hoped they wouldn't break.

She still had £25 leftover. His Ma insisted that they stop for a celebration drink. It was still early and the fresh sawdust scattered around on the floor gave off a sweet cloying aroma. The air smelled sour and musty from beer, piss and fags. He saw Tony and Maud sitting in the corner; he drinking whiskey, she brandy and port. They were brother and sister and lived on the balcony below them. Tony drank mostly on tick and the story was that he'd drawn up a will that made sure the publican would get paid when he died. Others were drinking alone, filling in dockets from the bookies next door. They'd periodically get up and leave and return a few minutes later, all smiles if they'd picked a winner.

His Ma ordered a vodka and lime. He had a Coke and a packet of Tayto. He didn't enjoy it. Being the principle beneficiary of her crime made him feel like an accomplice. His Ma sat there, very quiet, smoking and rubbing the twenty pound note between her thumb and forefinger, already anxious to get in another round.

'Another vodka 'n' lime,' she shouted to the barman, 'and whatever the young fella is having.' He could never understand how his Ma and Da, usually so tight, were prepared to shell out for endless bottles of Coke and crisps provided it was in the pub.

The barman put the drinks and Tayto up on the counter. A man sitting on a stool wearing a dirty raincoat stared at Wayne when he went to collect it. He was drinking a glass of Guinness and a small one. He had wavy oiled hair with red tufts growing out of his ears.

The man looked over at his Ma and smiled, revealing a set of yellow and black teeth. He insisted on paying for their drinks and then sitting at their table. He winked at Wayne and produced a ferret from the inside pocket of his raincoat. First, he allowed it to drink a bit of the stout that'd spilt on the table. He then picked it up by the scruff of the neck and dangled it in front of them. Its cold pink eyes glowered with rage as its legs threaded air. Wayne noticed a small hammer-shaped black blemish under its left leg. He saw a single long white hair growing out of it.

Its fur was the same colour as the ceiling in the living room at home, stained yellow by all the smoking. 'She's a good un,' the man was saying, 'put her down a rabbit hole and you'll have the whole place clear in no time.'

It was obvious the moment he spoke that he was a knacker.

Wayne was shocked that his Ma not only accepted the drink from him but also was now chatting away, asking him questions about the ferret. She always referred to tinkers in her thick Liverpool accent as 'pikeys'. His Ma was rightly acting the maggot.

Wayne was glad when after a while his Ma said that he should go home. His Da would freak if he heard that she had been drinking with some geezer. But if his Da ever found out that she'd been drinking with a knacker, and did so in Wayne's presence, there'd be war. Tony and Maud had surely picked up on it and Wayne hoped and prayed that one of them didn't say anything to him.

Wayne picked up the case containing his new guitar and slung it over his shoulder. He lined up the wheels of the amp facing the direction of the door and whispered to her, 'Thanks Ma – love yah.'

'You learn everything you can from the priest, do you hear me? He's your passport out of here.' She poked his chest for emphasis. 'Do yah hear me?'

Wayne didn't like the priest. But he knew that she didn't like him saying that, so he said nothing. He just nodded.

He hurried home and got playing. By bedtime his fingertips were raw. The endorphins blocked out any pain. It'd felt like he could measure the exact level of tension in each string to the nearest millimetre, feel every separate individual coil of steel, and each vibration of sound reverberating around the fretboard. He'd read that some of the world's greatest guitarists had stopped playing a Les Paul for fear that it would end up playing them. Having felt the connection with it, he understood why.

He heard his Ma come in. She'd be well-oiled and he was glad that she went to bed before his Da came home.

How long would it be before he sussed out his stuff was missing? And what would he do?

Last Christmas was the worst. Christy had arrived in full of vim and stout. His Ma had complained that he should have come home earlier. He'd grabbed her left arm and, using it as a lever, repeatedly bashed her face into the doorframe. The action was so mechanical he hadn't even removed the fag from his mouth.

Ma had spent Christmas in the Mater with her jaw wired shut. She'd lived on Knorr soup and Bird's custard for six weeks, sucking it up in a straw. His Da didn't seem embarrassed. He said that he'd never known such peace and quiet. But he also told her she wasn't to set foot outside the door. So maybe he'd cared more than he was letting on.

What would happen when his Da actually had a real reason to be angry? Wayne felt tightness in his chest just thinking about it.

four

The shop assistant parcelled up his shirts in brown paper that she tore from a large roll, bound it with string and tied it off in a handle. 'Have a good day, Father,' she said as she handed it over the counter. As a child he had traipsed around here after his mother for shoes, communion outfits, curtains and furniture. Back then, he had found it a forbidding place but the sense of familiarity and continuity an old-fashioned department store like Clerys offered was now very reassuring.

Outside, men and women stood in front of the large display windows. Some looked up and down the street; others tried to look nonchalant. People had been meeting on dates under Clerys clock for as long as anyone could remember.

The pharmacies, jewellers and banks that had been the backbone of O'Connell Street had all moved out to the new shopping centres in the suburbs. The discount stores selling garish knick-knacks and slot machine arcades with their neon lights were ruining what remained of the ambience. Even the Gresham Hotel had opened up a nightclub that drew in the dregs.

Outside the GPO, he saw four young men and a woman standing to attention in front of posters of dead hunger strikers. Fr Brendan silently mouthed the names: Bobby Sands, Francis

Hughes, Raymond McCreesh, Patsy O'Hara, Martin Hurson, Joe McDonnell, Kieran Doherty and Thomas McElwee. Mickey Devine was at death's door.

The Iranians had already renamed the street in Tehran where the British Embassy was housed as Bobby Sands Street. But that was just get-up-your-nose politics. How many would be able to name Sands' compatriots in years to come? People still remembered Terence MacSweeney, the former Lord Mayor of Cork who had fasted to death in 1920. But the three other men who died with him barely registered a footnote in the history books.

The gang of five wore black berets, white shirts, skinny black leather ties, drainpipe trousers and shoes. Any expression of humanity that might have existed was masked behind dark sunglasses. Even though large tricolours bookended the group and softened up the monochrome effect, he still thought the term 'colour party' a misnomer.

A man refrained through a tinny megaphone: 'Thatcher is a murderer, support the five demands.' Activists fanned out, handing leaflets to passers-by. One attempted to thrust one into his hand. Fr Brendan put his hand firmly up to indicate both his disapproval and rejection of the offer. The man defiantly stared straight into his face to emphasise his lack of respect for the cloth, and then moved on without even formally acknowledging him.

Fr Brendan recognised him from the flats behind the presbytery. He didn't go to Mass. He hung around the stairwell drinking cans and smoking fags. Today he was somebody and anxious to let the world know it.

Hawks, like Adams and McGuinness, had ousted the old-style republicans Ó Brádaigh and Mac Stiofáin. The secularisation of the State was now as much part of their campaign as a thirty-two county socialist republic. The new breed of volunteers openly despised the clergy and there was a hardness about them.

Mrs Hendricks had left him out a tray with corned beef sandwiches with neatly trimmed crusts. The heat had turned the scrolls of butter runny and yellow. A freshly starched white napkin stood out like a miniature tepee. The nickel silver plating on the Edwardian salt- and peppershakers had worn away, probably, he concluded, from Fr Peter grasping it with his greasy fingers.

He liked having the presbytery to himself. It had originally been built as a townhouse by a wealthy linen merchant who had then promptly lost all his money after the Act of Union put tariffs on trade between Ireland and England. Soon after, the great Georgian houses in the area had descended into tenements. The house had apparently once operated as a busy brothel when parts of Dublin boasted the largest number of prostitutes per square mile in Europe. The dark-stained parquet flooring and insipid cream-coloured walls broken up by religious paintings and icons combined to make the place dreary. He'd installed a little writing desk in his room where he liked to sit in the evenings writing letters and homilies. For all its faults the house was tranquil, a cocoon, a place in which he felt protected.

Afterwards he did his post. A letter from the executive council of Life Before Death, a pro-life group, informed him that he had been appointed to a steering committee chaired by Cora Jameson to agitate for a referendum to outlaw abortion. Cora was a heavy-hitter: he must be doing something right. The news that he'd been paired with her cheered him up no end.

Pro-life groups were portrayed by the media as being a right-wing rump, the thin end of the wedge of fascism and intolerance.

Nothing could have been further from the truth. This was a grassroots organisation. There was far less ideology than the media reports suggested. Members were for the most part law-abiding middle-class types with a social conscience. In his experience meetings were lively gatherings where people were wholly engaged with an issue that troubled them. For him it was a relief to mingle with others who shared the same sense of commitment and foreboding as he did.

The dangers of secularisation and the hush puppies in Sinn Féin who fronted for the men of violence were underestimated. He'd mentioned it to Fr Peter several times. Fr Peter had initially urged him to concentrate on issues that were relevant to the parish, and had then become quite angry when he persisted, warning him not to bring politics into the presbytery.

Meantime, Sinn Féin was getting organised; they were onto the Corporation over every broken drainpipe. Organising marches on drug dealers' houses, and then, Ku Klux Klan-like, going about evicting them. Insinuating themselves into the community by osmosis. And slowly but surely it was transferring into votes. It was just a couple of council seats so far. But the momentum was with them. The Church would get left behind if it were not careful.

five

Wayne followed his Da up the back stairs onto the roof of the block. Maurice brought up the rear, dragging along a couple of pigeon boxes. Today was Chinwag's first race. His Da had paid mega money for her from a champion breeder in Yorkshire. He'd a big bet on. There'd be trouble if she didn't perform. His Da would go off on one and Ma or someone else would pay.

Some owners paid for their birds to travel in the transporter that was hired by the Dublin-based clubs but his Da liked to be there at the moment they were released. Wayne marvelled at the way the birds flocked together and flew hither and thither for several minutes before striking out for home. His Da said that they were checking out the earth's magnetic fields so that they could work out which was the way home. When they got closer to the city they'd go their own ways. His Da said at that point they used things like railway lines or big buildings as visual aids to make their way back to the lofts.

Wayne did a three hundred and sixty take on the view from the rooftop. He could see the copper dome of the Four Courts in the distance and the Cusack and Hogan stands in Croker. Many was the time he'd watched from Hill 16 Heffo's Army beating the culchies, even though Kerry had got the better of them in the last few years.

He walked over to the parapet and stared down. The sight of the ground so far below always made him a bit queasy and he took a step back. He often imagined himself jumping off and what that moment would be like when he hit the ground. Sometimes he'd think about his funeral and what everybody would be saying. 'A great lad, Wayne, a powerful boxer and he was mean on the guitar,' they'd be saying, 'I was so sure he was destined for great things.' He'd picture his Ma crying and his Da feeling bad about the way he'd behaved. It was sick but he couldn't help it. Sometimes he wondered was he right in the head.

He could just make out the tiny plume of smoke coming from a woman smoking a cigarette below. He spotted the Cassidy girls, linked together, heading over to the Mater hospital. Marie, their mother, was riddled with cancer, and had gone as thin as a matchstick. The word was that she wouldn't see out the weekend.

He saw a group of lads weighed down by their kit bags boarding a minibus. It'd be great to play for a team that travelled in their own bus to play matches. You'd feel like a proper footballer then.

'Fucking bastards – cunts!' The voice belonged to his Da.

The sheer venom of the invective told him that something was terribly wrong. He saw his Da emerging from the loft dangling a ferret by the scruff of its neck. Maurice was looking into the loft, shaking his head in disbelief. Wayne ran over to get a proper look.

The ferret was a nicotine yellow colour, except for its mouth, which was covered in a ring of fresh blood. His cold black eyes darted rapidly in all directions seeking an escape. He'd probably have recognised it even without the confirming hammer-shaped black mark under his left leg. It threaded the air even more intently than the last time he had seen it, correctly sensing that its whole existence was at stake.

The floor of the loft was covered in pigeons, their still eyes staring out from limp necks. There were lots of loose feathers floating around. They must have come off when the birds panicked or were caught by his sharp teeth. The ferret hadn't needed to kill all of them for food. He'd nibbled on a couple, taking lumps out of their throats or chunks out of their bellies. There were drops of congealed blood where they'd bled from their wounds. But he'd just kept going until he'd gone through the lot like a regular killing machine. He wondered why no one had heard the squawking and how long it'd taken to wreak this carnage.

Wayne picked out Chinwag in the corner. In life you could tell by the way Chinwag had comported himself that he came from a good line. His eyes gave off a beady inertness now but the brightness of his plume still cut him out as regal.

His Da walked to the edge of the roof and flung the ferret off. Wayne waited for the splat like in a cartoon. But the ferret actually hit the ground running, scarpered out the gate across the road and then ran under the gate of the builders' yard. That made his Da even madder: he jumped up and down, his face contorted into a spasm of rage.

'Who did this? It's fuckin' one of Roche's crew!' He had his fists in the air, looking upwards. 'I'll fucking kill whoever it was. Pig or no pig! Do you know anything?'

Maurice shook his head and shrugged. 'No, Da, I haven't a clue. I left out feed last night around eight and they were grand.'

Wayne walked into the loft making sure he kept his back to his Da. He was planking. What if his Da asked him did he know anything? His Ma had come up with a story that the priest had loaned him the guitar. That had shut down any further inquiries for the time being. He was sure that his denial wouldn't be convincing. His Da would sniff it out of him. And that would set off a chain reaction. His fear wasn't just on his own account: the ferret and the knacker would inevitably lead back to his Ma and from there to the pawn.

His Da began stuffing the pigeons into a black plastic bin bag.

He'd a way with animals. Once during the snow they'd come across a pup on the back stairs. It was only a couple of weeks old, far too young to be weaned. Wayne had bent down to touch it. It was ice cold to the touch. No breathing. He'd just touched his first dead thing. He was upset and had wanted to cry.

His Da had took it up in his hand and cupped it under his jumper. When they got home he'd sat down in front of the fire and put the pup on the hearth. He'd stroked the back of its head with the underside of his forefinger. Wayne thought his Da was mad. But within a short while the dog stirred. Then it opened its eyes and after a few minutes was sitting up drinking a saucer of milk. Wayne had heard all the stories about his Da and seen his viciousness at first hand. But what had struck him so forcibly during the whole event was how gentle his Da had been. Wayne had no doubt what he'd witnessed was a miracle.

His Da knew the personalities of every one of his birds. They reacted to his presence and his voice. He let out a string of curses when he came across Chinwag. He stuffed it in the bag with the others and kept at it.

six

The bell rang shortly after midnight. Fr Brendan was in bed reading his scriptures. He put on his dressing gown and went downstairs to answer the door.

'It's time, Father,' Siobhain Cassidy said.

'Come in.'

She hesitated, anxious no doubt to get back to her mother's bedside, before stepping into the hall.

'Has she spoken to everyone?' he asked.

She nodded and then added, 'Except Darren. The Governor said that he'd get him over first thing in the morning.'

'I'll put in a call to the chaplain, see what he can do.'

Her face softened and the impatience knit into her brow receded.

There were plenty of young men from the parish in choky. He'd made a point of calling down to Fr Harris when he'd first come here to find out whether any of the lads were in need of a visit. The older priest had appreciated the gesture. Fr Brendan got through to Fr Harris within a couple of rings. He explained the dilemma. Fr Harris said he'd ring the Governor and get straight back to him.

The Cassidys were a big Republican family. Old man Cassidy had fought in the 1956 Border campaign and been interned in the Curragh. Seamus had served time for IRA membership and being in possession of an AK-47 and bomb-making equipment. He'd also been a spokesperson for the wing in Portlaoise prison. Rumour had it that he'd been involved in kneecapping various drug dealers. Seamus had spoken at a number of rallies called to promote the five demands of the hunger strikers.

Darren had got into gear in his mid-teens. He'd gone on a spree of jump-overs in every shop in the neighbourhood and beyond. Seamus's stock had soared after he went to prison; Darren's robbing to fund his habit hadn't gone down as well. But Marie stilled doted on him. He was the special one.

Siobhain's chap was serving a sentence in Mountjoy for armed robbery. He remembered Fr Peter saying that Siobhain had convictions for shoplifting. You'd never have guessed it. He'd seen at first-hand how well Siobhain and her sisters had looked after Marie throughout her illness. They were a credit to her. In the short time he'd been here, he'd been deeply impressed by how much better the poor coped with death. There was less melancholy and melodrama. They were much less attached to possessions. There was less fear too. Life and death weren't seen as competitors here.

He got dressed, gathered up the oils for the sacrament of extreme unction and said a few prayers that Marie might have a gentle passing, while they waited for Fr Harris to ring back.

He answered the phone on the first ring.

'That's great news, Fr Harris. We're indebted to you.' He smiled at Siobhain to communicate the call had been a success.

'How long do you think that'll all take?'

'Well it'll take as long as the officers want it to take. He could be there in half an hour if they put their mind to it.'

But what if they didn't? he wondered. He'd found the prison unneccesarily bureaucratic during his visits. Certain officers revelled in following the rule book. He decided there was no point in articulating his concerns to Fr Harris or to Siobhain.

They hurried down on foot to the hospital.

Marie was propped up in the bed by rigid pillows that had the consistency of sandbags. Her lips were cracked and dry. One of the girls had been keeping them moist with cotton buds when they'd arrived. She'd been put into her own room so that she could have a bit of privacy. Wordlessly, the family left the bedside as soon as he entered.

'I know now why the old bag put me in here, Father,' Marie said, in reference to the matron who'd authorised her transfer off the ward. Fr Brendan didn't reply: people had a right to engage with their own death without someone queering the pitch with false hope. It wasn't as if she wasn't prepared. She'd lived in the parish for over forty years but still wanted to be buried with her parents in their plot in Donycarney after requiem mass. He was disappointed, even if it meant less work for him. Siobhain had explained on the way down how she'd called them in earlier and divided up her bits and pieces.

'A lot of love in this room tonight, Marie.'

'And why wouldn't there be? They're only giving back what I gave them over a lifetime. They owe me.'

Her breathing was shallow, but he was glad to see that she wasn't in any pain.

'I'd kill for a cigarette.' She turned her face away. 'Maybe tomorrow I'll be smoking in hell?'

He held her hand. It was limp and clammy.

'That's where I want to be anyways if you can't smoke in heaven. Do what you have to do, Father, and get the girls back in.'

He anointed her forehead, hands and feet with oils. The bishop had sanctified the oils on Holy Thursday. When it came to confession she gave an impatient wave of the hand and said, 'The usual.' Usually, the remission of sins provided spiritual aid and comfort. For the most part she'd stared off into the distance. But when he started to pray over her he saw her eyes illuminated intermittently by flickers of fear and what looked like resentment. He finished up with communion. He worried that she wouldn't get the wafer down but somehow she managed.

You could get knocked down crossing the road. Or get a cancer. But his own death seemed so far away he couldn't really visualise it in any meaningful way. He wondered how so many people could keep fear at bay knowing that they were stepping forward into the dark, how they avoided panic and kept their dignity. He was sure that he would let himself down by snivelling that he didn't want to die.

You were entering a process that was irreversible, that spelt redemption, condemnation or simply passing into the void of a black hole filled not even with silence but with a nothingness of which you would not even be aware. The most committed believer must have doubts when it came right down to the line.

When the family returned he led off with a decade of the rosary. The girls knelt down on the floor with their hands on the bed. The men stood with their backs to the wall, their lips moving uncertainly and inaudibly over the words.

He enunciated the words slowly, his tone rising at the commencement of each Hail Mary and hitting a bass cadence on the words 'thy womb Jesus'. Down the country he'd alternate every decade in Irish. Here in the metropolis, hardly anyone under forty even knew the Gloria in English. The Cassidys weren't regular churchgoers as such. Even Marie. But he pressed on. He'd performed this ritual often enough to know that the rhythm of a familiar prayer was a comfort even to those who had long lost their faith.

seven

Wayne awoke to the sound of loud voices. The tension at home had been unbearable since the Chinwag pigeon massacre. It wasn't just the loss of his precious birds, it was the realisation that someone had wanted to do him down, to knock him off his perch. Not knowing who was responsible was doing Christy's head in.

At first, he'd been happy to work on the assumption that it was the guards. If Roche hadn't done it himself then he'd put one of his rookies up to it. The way Flannery had pulled Roche's strings in the old days.

Back then guards would give any up-and-coming fella or even a stalwart like Christy himself a bit of a hiding to remind him who was boss. These days the guards wore well-cut suits and fought the battles with their heads. Roche worked by sussing out a fella's weaknesses – money, woman trouble, queer, drink – and traded on them.

But in every other respect Roche ran a tight ship. He'd put a stop to verballing fellas in the interview room. And he was blessed with plenty of patience. It'd paid dividends. Lads who were careless were being detected and banged up. Viewed from that perspective, the attack didn't make any sense.

He'd racked his brains trying to think up someone who was out to get him and, more importantly, why. That was what had set Christy off on one. That's when the paranoia got going. Was it some buck firing an unprovoked shot across the bows to unsettle him before taking a potshot at him? Or someone else who was trying to set him up? The not knowing was gnawing away at him.

Initially, he'd gone around asking the usual suspects to keep their ears close to the ground. When that hadn't worked he'd made known his disappointment and warned that there'd be repercussions. He decided that he needed a show of strength. He'd gone to see the Hickson brothers. They were up and coming. They'd do.

He'd taken a red-hot clothes iron to Gerry Hickson's face.

Wayne could hear Harry and Liam in the kitchen below trying to talk him down.

'You're ruffling a lot of feathers, Christy, bringing down a lot of heat on people. I'll be honest with you. I don't like it. It'll end in tears and someone getting killed,' he heard Harry saying.

'Look it,' his Da replied. 'My birds are dead and some cunt is goin' to pay. Do you get that? I'm the one who is going to make sure that some cunt is goin' to pay. And I'm not even fussed what cunt pays the tab so long as some cunt does. Do you know what I mean? I can't let this go even if I wanted.

'And I don't. Can you imagine if the word went out that Christy Clarke had turned into a soft touch? I'll crucify a few good men before this thing runs its course if that's what it takes.'

One Good Friday his Da had knelt on the arms of a suspected tout while he nailed his hands to the floor of his lock-up. But he'd refused to admit to giving the police information. His Da had been so impressed by this that he suddenly decided to believe him. He pulled out the nails, bandaged his hands and drove him to A&E, and advised him to make a claim against the State for compensation to the Malicious Injuries Board.

These were the stories that gave his Da such a fearsome reputation. But to Wayne they pointed out his biggest weakness. Sure, his Da understood how people's minds worked, and who was likely to be lying. He was mostly intuitive, and mostly right. But when he got it wrong he could get it very wrong. And there was no talking to him.

'Christy, have you lost it or what? Who the fuck do you think you are?' Wayne could tell that Liam was getting tired of his Da.

'I know who I am. Question is do you know who you are? You want out, you know where the door is.'

'Oh spare me. You want someone who is goin' to tell you what a fuckin' genius you are all the time just say the word and I'm out of here. We're only trying to keep yah right. But maybe you don't want that. Maybe you want some mad fucker to do Roche's work for you and blast you out of it with a shotgun? Is that what it is?'

'Would you listen to that prick, Harry? Thinks he knows it all. He does like fuck.'

'You're the prick, Christy. Harry's right. Go off and get yourself a few yes men to sit around with you. We'll both go.'

He'd wanted to talk to his Ma about putting the ferret into the loft. But he didn't dare. He was afraid that his Da would ask him had he heard anything and he'd have to lie and be found out. He'd watched his Ma closely from a distance. He thought she'd be planking herself. But there wasn't a bother on her. He'd even seen her sneak a smile whenever he started ranting about what he was going to do to whoever did it.

Downstairs the talking went on. The same old shite. Harry and Liam spoke in quiet, measured tones. But his Da wasn't listening. He'd drink on him for one thing. And his dander was well and truly up. That was the way it'd remain until some bigger crisis came along. Alternatively, he might wake up one morning and find that his mind had miraculously consigned the angst and paranoia to a far distant recess in his mind. And everyone would breathe a sigh of relief and smile again.

Meantime, everyone was on a war footing.

eight

Fr Brendan was making his way back from the coffee vending machine when he heard a commotion on the corridor. He saw that the Cassidys had surrounded a prison officer. Darren was tethered to the officer's wrist. The girls were in the thick of it. Siobhain was poking the officer's chest with her finger. His brothers were blocking the officer's path, which he noticed was leading away from Marie's room. Seamus was squaring up to him.

'Have some respect for a dying woman. Do you hear what I am saying? He can't go in there with the cuffs on.'

'That's not going to happen,' the officer responded. 'Now if you'll excuse me, we're heading back to the prison.'

Fr Brendan walked right into the middle of them. Two other prison officers who formed the escort were standing back a few paces with their arms folded. He sensed that they disapproved of this carry on, thought their colleague had overstepped the mark, but Fr Brendan had been around institutions long enough to know that if it came down to making a choice they'd still back him.

'What's your name?' Fr Brendan demanded of him.

'ACO Reynolds. And yours?' The tone was disrespectful.

'That need not concern you. Could I ask you to demonstrate some compassion and decency please?'

'Tell that to the old lady he jabbed with a syringe full of blood and then told her he was infected with the virus.'

There were so many things that Fr Brendan wanted to say that would put this pup in his place. Reynolds was used to confrontation, probably thrived on it. He'd return Darren to the prison in a heartbeat. Reynolds was one of those irritating men who enjoyed having his bit of power and always needed the last word. No, he'd write a very full letter to the Governor later, but for now he needed to get people down off the mountain.

He spoke in a softer, more conciliatory voice.

'We're on the fifth floor. It's not as though if you take the cuffs off that he's going anywhere. I will go with him. You can be standing here on the door.'

He paused to let Reynolds think a moment.

Reynolds looked over at the other two officers. They looked away, a bit embarrassed now, disgusted even, that it had got this far.

'He's got twenty minutes. I'll be in to take him out again. Everyone else stays outside.'

There were mutters from behind him as the family went into conclave. Provided Marie didn't actually die when he was in there, it was workable. Seamus said they'd go with it.

Fr Brendan sat in the corner and read his breviary. Marie and Darren didn't say much, they just kept squeezing their hands together. Darren hadn't seen Marie for a few weeks. He looked haggard and hurt to be presenting to her now in this state.

'Wise up and get a life,' he heard her say.

'I will, Ma. I will. I promise.'

Marie got very upset when Reynolds came into the room and cuffed Darren before taking him away. Darren looked back at the door, but he was jolted forward by the pull of the cuffs. She'd barely lifted her hand up from the bed in acknowledgment. He heard the family effing and blinding at Reynolds as he led Darren down the corridor. Siobhain's voice was the loudest. He admired her spunk. Marie pursed her chapped lips in frustration and clenched her fists.

The family gathered around the bed. A short time later, Marie's eyes rolled up into her head, leaving only the whites. The descent into death had begun. Fr Brendan started the five glorious mysteries. Marie was in a coma, but who was to say she couldn't hear and get succour from their prayers?

Siobhain recounted a time on holiday when they had been out on a boat.

'It was really rough, Ma. The waves got bigger and water started to come in over the side. We were all panicking and crying. But Ma, somehow we made it back.'

Her voice was breaking.

'I was so frightened, Ma. But we got through that day, and we'll get through this one.'

Tears fell out of the dull whites of Marie's eyes.

The conventional wisdom was that hearing was one of the last things to go. It was why young priests were always warned to be careful when speaking around a dying person. Well he'd seen it now with his own eyes.

The gap between breaths gradually grew longer. Then, her frail body suddenly heaved up in a spasm and sank back down again, her face held in a tight silent grimace before one final breath spluttered its way out. The majesty of the death rattle brought a moment of awestruck silence before the girls cried out in grief. 'Ma, Ma, Ma,' they kept saying. Siobhain intertwined her hands together and sobbed quietly. He always felt privileged to bear witness.

The nurses swung into action. One stuck what looked like a mini crutch under Marie's chin. The top was soft and black. It forced Marie's face back into shape again. Another pressed down

Marie's eyelids and held them in position until they stayed. She said that Marie might burp if there was any air trapped in her lungs and not to get a fright. It was businesslike but there was compassion too. The girls stayed to help the nurses lay out the body.

Fr Brendan sat on a bench in the corridor. Domestics pushed trollies up and down laden with breakfast cereals and gigantic metal pots of tea. The smell of toast and greasy fried food neutralised the antiseptic air. Just then, Siobhain touched him on the knee and asked him if he wanted a cup of tea. The contact sent a tingle surging through him. What was it about death that made him feel so totally alive? he wondered.

nine

Dick Roche parked up in the corner of the back yard of the Hunter's Lodge and waited. After what seemed like an age, Daly stepped into the car. The two of them chatted away while Daly crumpled the torn envelope to check his readies. They talked about the long hot summer and how there was a chill in the air in the evenings before getting down to the business in hand.

Daly was what was known as a 'collated person'. A guard was obliged to note his every move and file it back at the station. Part of the brief was to single out criminals like him for attention. Street searches under the Misuse of Drugs Act, constant demands to produce tax and insurance, prosecutions under public order offences. It was the force's way of keeping serious criminals, if not on the back foot, at least on their toes.

The policy had other uses. Eventually, a serious criminal got done for a proper crime. A judge handing down sentence to a man with an endless stream of road traffic convictions wasn't long reading between the lines and he sentenced accordingly. And the constant contact – even the in-your-face variety – often opened up lines of communication that sometimes branched out in unexpected directions.

Back in the day Roche had done Daly for drunk driving. The sample had come back three times over the limit. Still, he hadn't been confident of getting a conviction. Drunk driving cases were notoriously technical, and judges, most of whom liked a jar and didn't see drink driving as a real crime, would throw out a case on the most frivolous of grounds.

Roche had been taken aback when Daly had pleaded guilty. And so he had cut him some slack – played down the level of intoxication and talked up his cooperation in meeting the case. The judge had imposed the minimum fine and disqualification the law allowed and invited Daly to reapply to have his licence back after six months.

A couple of weeks later he'd bumped into Daly on the street. They exchanged a few pleasantries and went about their business. Their paths crossed intermittently after that. Roche had supported his application to have his licence restored when it came back before the court.

Not long after, he'd been doing a drugs search of Daly, shooting the breeze, when out of the blue Daly gave him information about an armed heist that was going to take place at Kilmartin's bookies on Grand National day. Roche had been sceptical. Daly was the sort of guy who was always working an angle. Nonetheless, he reported the information up the line.

An armed task force was assembled. Undercover detectives from the Serious Crime Squad posed as punters making bets. The raiders – all dedicated hard chaws under their balaclavas – were confronted the moment they stepped onto the premises. Shots were fired and one was fatally injured. The two surviving gang members received lengthy sentences.

Roche was covered in kudos. He was the first to admit that it felt good, that it came with an adrenalin rush that he recognised could be very easily addictive.

It'd taken Roche a while to get onto Daly's wavelength. Daly was cute enough to know that he couldn't please all of the people all of the time. But like anyone obsessed with looking after number one he kept himself right with as many people as he could. The information came slowly and erratically. Eventually, Daly had come on the books officially.

There was very little moving around town that Daly didn't know about. But he was sparing with information. The stuff he gave Roche was rarely enough to even ground an arrest. Roche had to work it up to the next level. Roche approved – that methodology protected Daly and kept the relationship going. It also meant that he'd had to keep working as a policeman. He'd seen good guards go to seed because they'd become too dependent on a tout to do their job for them. The relationship was fraught with danger for all parties. Touts were grassing up people who trusted them. They were inherently unreliable. The biggest problem was that you could never be sure what a tout's agenda was. Roche had learned well after the event that Daly had given up the lads in the bookies because they had failed to pay him for guns that he'd provided them for an earlier job.

You had to be careful to keep the lines cleanly delineated. It cut both ways. A careless tout ended up face down in a ditch with a hole in his head. This way everyone was winning.

Over the next few minutes Daly filled him in on what was happening on the street.

Christy Clarke was accusing all sorts, Roche included, of putting the ferret into his pigeon loft. He was beating up fellas all around him. Some said he was using it as a cover to attack rivals, and people were getting very pissed off.

Roche let him rabbit on. On one level it was garbage really. But this sort of intel was a snapshot, an essential building block in the battle to lock up villains. You needed to know your enemy.

'He's still very sore about his birds,' he was saying. 'He put a red-hot iron to the face of one of the Hickson lads and announced that he was there "to iron out some problems". The roars of him could be heard for miles.'

It did sound like Clarke was losing it.

'Is retaliation against him a real risk?'

'Nah, he's cute enough to pick on people who don't matter. But he's no diplomat and he'd want to watch out.'

The story about Clarke and the pigeons was fascinating. But not something that was going to go anywhere. He didn't want to be the one to bring up the factory payroll. The danger of prompting a tout to say what you wanted to hear was too dangerous.

'He seems to have gone to ground otherwise, then?'

In reply, Daly arched his eyebrows. Roche worked hard to stifle any expression of interest. You didn't lead a tout. Not with words anyway. He simply nodded back at Daly in a way that invited a reply.

'He's busy enough at the moment anyway.'

'How busy?'

'Busy enough to be trialling a high-powered bike.'

'A payroll?'

'Nah. Don't think it's that. He's mixing it with the Provos. Beyond that I know nothing.' He had pronounced the last three words in a mock-Italian accent like Marlon Brando in *The Godfather*.

Roche didn't push him: this was as much as he was going to get. Daly had probably heard that Clarke was looking around for a couple of bikes elsewhere and was sore that he wasn't in the loop.

Still, this wasn't the time to start looking a gift horse in the mouth. Top brass was paranoid about a big rise in support for the IRA as the emotive effect of the deaths of each hunger striker built. It was growing exponentially. Orders had come down from high to monitor and report every piece of intelligence that was linked to paramilitaries. Daly had advanced the information in good faith. It hadn't been contrived. It had a ring of truth to it. And he'd mark it. And make something of it.

'Anything else?'

'Marie Cassidy died yesterday. The family is very upset about the way a screw treated Darren when he was brought to the hospital to see her. Seamus wants the 'Ra to take direct action.'

Notwithstanding the family's Republican pedigree, they'd be waiting, Roche thought. Right now, the Provos were too busy manipulating the fallout from the hunger strikes; there was no way they were going to distract from that by attacking a member of the Irish Prison Service. This spat would pass whether the Cassidys liked it or not.

ten

Marie was laid out in the dead centre of the room. The coffin was a white-lacquered glossy job with half-doors and a deep cushioned red velvet lining; the top door was open. She wore a red and white polka dot dress. Her fingers were entwined around a gold cigarette lighter where rosary beads ought to have been. Sometimes a body retained little of the person that had inhabited it, but she was a good-looking corpse. The lines in her face accentuated her character and transcended its otherwise sense of lifelessness. The pain and distress so evident in her last agonised breath were dissipated. She looked at peace.

The couch and chairs had been pushed back to maximise space. Extra seats were lined up against the walls. The air reeked of perfume and smoke. There was a bonhomie, and a sense of wickedness even, in the air. Fr Brendan had only intended staying for the one drink so as to pass himself. As the priest who had officiated at her bedside this was expected. But several mourners had come up to congratulate him for facing down Reynolds and he was by now on his third (or was it the fourth?) 'one for the road'. He was quite the celebrity, and was enjoying it.

Siobhain snuck her arm tightly around his waist and leaned in more closely than was necessary. 'How are you doing, Father? Are you settling in alright?' She was carrying a bottle of wine by the neck in her other hand with two empty glasses hanging by the stems.

'Sit down,' she said, pointing to the couch, which out of nowhere had space for the pair of them. She poured the wine and offered him a glass.

'It's taking a while but I am getting there.'

A sparkle in her eyes belied the sadness of the occasion. He chatted away. She was simpatico, and in no time he found himself giving out about Fr Peter and how some people thought he was stuck up. Siobhain airily dismissed his concerns, gently gripping his elbow for emphasis and topping up his glass from the bottle.

'Don't mind them. You'll be grand, Brendan. You're going to be great. You're already great.'

He liked the way she'd casually switched to calling him by his Christian name, the way she pronounced 'great' in her flat Dublin accent and was so tactile.

'I do my best,' he muttered lamely.

He was prickly when criticised but he never knew what to say when he received a compliment.

'We really appreciate what you did for Darren.'

'It was nothing really. But I'm glad he got to see Marie. That was so important for both of them.'

She delved into her handbag and produced a packet of fags. She lit up and exhaled high into the air. She rested the edge of her free hand on his knee. It was an innocent enough gesture, asexual he was sure, but he was uncomfortable with it and wondered what to say about it without causing offence.

He saw Seamus Cassidy making a beeline for them from across the room.

'Father, would you come outside for a moment please? I need a word.'

He turned on his heel without waiting for an answer. Fr Brendan followed him through the crowd. There was something about the lad's tone that he hadn't liked. He hoped that Seamus didn't think that he was getting a bit fresh with Siobhain? That would be mortifying.

Seamus led him down to the end of the balcony where a group of men were gathered.

The balcony was lit up but it still took a few seconds to get his bearings. Christy Clarke was standing to his left, his elbows positioned over the back of the balcony wall and his right leg cocked against it. Beside him was Eamonn Crosbie, a Sinn Féin councillor. He recognised a fellow with the Eire Nua tattoo on his arm as a member of the colour party he had seen outside the GPO earlier in the week. Another man he didn't recognise stood facing them with his hands in his jeans pockets. There was nonchalance and energy about him. The deference the others showed him marked him out as the most important man in the group.

Seamus introduced him to them, but not vice versa he noticed, and then withdrew.

Councillor Crosbie did the talking.

'Evening, Father. That was a great thing that you did up in the hospital.'

'It was the right thing to do.'

'Will you tell these gentlemen exactly what happened? We've heard so many different versions.' He said it with a chuckle.

Fr Brendan ran through the sequence of events again. When he was done, the man he did not recognise asked him some questions. Fr Brendan had to strain his hearing to decipher his strong Belfast accent. Had the officer been gratuitously disrespectful to the family? Did the officer really believe that Darren might run away? Was it his impression that the officer was abusing his position?

For a fraction of a second he wondered why he was being asked these questions. But he didn't push it. Nor did he shirk what he saw to be his responsibility. He was among men. It was proper that this should be articulated openly. Besides, if he was honest, he was enjoying being the centre of attention.

'Where was Darren going to go? Jump out the fifth floor window? Reynolds was being a bully,' he replied. 'I'd be the first to acknowledge that being a prison officer isn't an easy job, that you can't be everyone's mate. But what happened was very wrong.'

'Thanks, Father. That's how we thought it was. We just wanted to hear it from the horse's mouth,' the Belfast man said.

'I wrote a strongly worded letter of complaint to the Governor calling on ACO Reynolds to apologise to the family.'

The men smiled at each other knowingly, the way you do when someone who is naive says something stupid. It irked him. Normally he'd avoid people like this. Yet here he was, showing off, trying to ingratiate himself with them. It must be the few drinks. He was about to reassure them that he intended to follow up the complaint at a higher level, but before he could get his words out the Belfast man spoke again.

'Marie had been ill for a long time. It was a release in the end. A sad day for the Cassidys all the same.'

The manner in which the words were spoken left him in no doubt that the case was closed, the discussion had run its course and that he was now being dismissed.

He made his way back inside. Siobhain was nowhere to be seen and the numbers had thinned out. The alcohol was repeating on him, leaving a sour taste in his mouth. He'd have heartburn later for sure. He suddenly felt quite tired and got an urge to leave.

As he left the flats complex, two burly men approached him purposefully and blocked his path. They introduced themselves as detectives from something calling itself the Serious Crime Squad and flashed warrant cards under his nose. One said Detective Sergeant Dick Roche. He didn't get a chance read the name on the younger detective's card.

'A good turnout for Marie, Father?' the younger one said.

Roche then spoke. 'That was very exalted company you were with tonight.' Fr Brendan's antennae immediately went up but he made no reply.

'We saw you talking to Liam Reidy. Did you know he was OC for Belfast? He shot dead an unarmed constable last Christmas Eve while the poor man held the car door open for his wife carrying the presents. That's our Liam. He has stepped back from all that now, of course.'

So they had witnessed the conversation on the balcony.

'Yeah. He's Army Council, you know. He and a few others meet once a month and dictate what the IRA is going to do next. Bombs in London and Manchester, blowing up a few more horses, shooting milk men and bread men supplying to the barracks, that sort of thing,' the younger one added.

Fr Brendan's first instinctive reaction was to say that if IRA policy was to be decided by the likes of Christy Clarke it must be on its knees, but thought better of it. They wanted to shock him into giving them a response. Well they could bloody well wait. A strong sense of self-preservation warned him against being drawn into conversation.

'What was he asking you?' Roche enquired.

Did these buffoons really believe that he was some sort of a fellow traveller? Again, he was sorely tempted to give them a piece of his mind. But he knew that any answer was going to lead to more questions and he'd had quite enough of that for one night.

'Ah, just talking about how big a loss Marie was,' he answered.

'Is that right?' Roche said, making no attempt to hide his scepticism.

They stood there impassive, waiting to see if his embarrassment would get the better of him. As if.

The younger one spoke again. 'Night, Father. Safe home. We'd offer you a lift but it's against regulations to have anyone in the car unless they're under arrest or something. Besides, the walk might do you good.'

They well knew he only lived around the corner. Fr Brendan hurried off, smarting at the snide remark about his alleged state of inebriation.

eleven

Fr Brendan awoke to the sound of bin lids banging on the ground. His head hurt. The digital clock radio glared 5.28 at him in neon red. Daylight peeped through the curtains. 'Mickey Devine, may the Lord have mercy on your soul,' he said aloud. His brain tried to unfurl the blur of the previous night's events. Images came in snatches and in no particular order. He cringed thinking about how he had been so effusive with the men on the balcony. The detectives had been quite put out that he'd not given them any information. He wished that he hadn't been so evasive with them. He hadn't done anything wrong with Siobhain other than being a little indiscreet about parish matters. Thinking about his behaviour, there was nothing he could put his finger on that was out of order but he still felt guilty.

He got up and went to the window. It overlooked the courtyard belonging to the flats. There were around a dozen women with bin lids clasped like battle shields in their hands. When Bobby Sands had died there had been hundreds and the din had been deafening. Still, on a Sunday morning, with the city being so quiet, the sound would travel for miles.

The flats were built in anonymous storeys constructed in grey, precast concrete, fronted by balconies clad in pebbledash. The only concession to colour was a dividing line, between floors, of mosaic tiles of trains, horses and other generic images. Three-dimensional graffiti written out in a staccato font in red, black and silver colours intermittently adorned the walls. Motörhead, Kraftwerk and something called REO Speedwagon were sprayed on the balcony where he'd been the subject of an inquisition last night.

A mock road sign, painted black on a yellow background, depicting an IRA man clad in outsized military fatigues and a balaclava was captioned 'CAUTION – SNIPER AT WORK'. Below it a heretic had written, 'What's Bobby Sands phone number?' and the answer '8 nothing, 8 nothing, 8 nothing'.

He watched Wayne Clarke dribble a tennis ball around three players until he was one-on-one with the keeper. His body leaned one way, his foot tapped the other. The keeper was rooted to the spot without time to dive even the wrong way. Wayne ran out, flanked by his teammates, arms aloft swinging first to the left, while his hips swung to the right, and then vice versa. The exuberance of the movement had a dance-like rhythm about it, and for those few moments the boy transcended the drabness of his surroundings.

Shirts and trousers hanging on clotheslines blew gently over the remnants of a rusting, burnt-out car. The council had promised to take it away weeks ago and he made a mental note to get onto them later in the morning.

Devine was the ninth hunger striker to die, and the announcement of each death this way was now a ritual. The practice had originated in Republican ghettos as a way of warning of British Army raids. Now it had been resurrected, not just to mark a death, but as a post-hypnotic cue to call the masses to riot. And no doubt the streets of Derry and Belfast were right now full of callow-faced masked youths wreaking havoc under the watchful eye of the IRA, who cynically misrepresented the mayhem as spontaneous demonstrations of popular support. And dozens of TV crews obligingly beamed it around the world without any analysis whatsoever.

Fr Brendan admired Thatcher's resolve but any fool could see that her dismissal of the strikers as criminals starving themselves to death was playing right into the IRA's hands – turning thugs and non-entities into martyrs. Bobby Sands had already been elected to the House of Commons. Kieran Doherty and Paddy Agnew had won seats in the Dáil. The election of the two men had played a big factor in denying Fianna Fáil an overall majority, and Haughey was now locked into a weak minority government that was dependent on the support of independents.

Downstairs, he made tea and toast. He washed the food down with a pint of water and couple of aspirin. Soon, he heard Fr Peter clattering down the stairs. The man would be late for his own funeral.

He bounded into the room sweeping a mound of blond hair over his forehead. Fr Peter was a good few years older than Fr Brendan but, with his clear complexion and athletic build, he was in great shape. The mane of blond hair and blue eyes gave him a Germanic appearance. En route to the back door, he picked up one of the crusts Brendan had cut from his toast. He spread it thickly with butter and popped it into his mouth. Jesus, Devine had fasted for over sixty days without food and this ludraman couldn't even observe the hour rule.

'It's alright, padre.' Fr Peter cupped his hands piously. 'Bless me father for I have sinned. I ate some crumbs from a rich boy's table and did not observe the hour fast period before celebrating the Eucharist. Absolution, please!'

Fr Brendan had grown up on a farm. A big one. As a family they'd lived well but never ostentatiously. He and his siblings had been given the best education money could buy, in his case

Clongowes Wood run by the Jesuits. That was the deal. After that it was up to each of them to make their own mark. He hated the silver spoon analogies.

'Eh, before you go,' Fr Brendan called after him. 'I was wondering, maybe, whether we could do a meet and greet on the steps after our Masses. Mickey Devine died last night, and it would be a good time to maintain a presence.'

'I have been meeting my parishioners all week. I'm not one of those Sunday priests.' The tone was light, gently mocking.

Three weeks out of four, Fr Peter served the eight and nine o'clock Masses – he was halfway down the North Circular Road already clad in his civvies – jeans and a sweatshirt – before some of the old biddies were even off church grounds. Where was the spirituality in that?

'It's just – things are moving. The Church is dead in the water if we aren't seen to respond.'

'The Church has survived very well for two thousand years, thank you.'

Subtext: we got on fine before you came.

'And will continue to do so for a very long time,' he called out cheerfully.

Subtext: And we will be fine when you're gone too.

twelve

Fr Brendan tapped the mic and it gave back the reassuring thud. Having to serve twelve o'clock Mass was one thing that he liked about Fr Peter heading off early. Many of the malingerers that gravitated around the porches would leave at communion, but for now it was standing room only.

He gripped the lectern on either side and cleared this throat.

'On Friday last, a member of Mickey Devine's family brought his two chuildren, a little boy and a girl, into the prison infirmary on the H blocks to say goodbye. For weeks she had watched his knuckles getting thinner, his cheeks going sunken, his hearing and sight failing. She took his hands and guided them onto the heads of his children, "weans" a woman who was interviewed about the visit called them. Sadly, his offspring didn't recognise who the man in the bed was. At the end of the visit she stood at the door and looked back. She saw tears running down his face. Afterwards she told a friend that it was the hardest thing she has ever had to do.'

The congregation looked up, their attention rapt.

'That is a haunting picture. Just the sort of black propaganda that the IRA is so adept at engineering. Or is it? You see, I can't work out whether the image is for or against the strike. Sure, it makes the Brits look bad. But the inability of children to recognise their dying father, you might think is at least equally, if not more, of a potent metaphor.

'Outside the H blocks, journalists maintain a presence that turns into a vigil with each impending death. Unsurprisingly, the Unionists are very unhappy. They argue the saturation coverage is at the expense of the victims of IRA violence. Peter Robinson, the deputy leader of the Democratic Unionist Party, has angrily denounced the hunger strike as "a suicide stunt".

'That's unfair. It takes courage to refuse food for over sixty days. Resolve to lie in bed with your organs failing to the point where your own children do not know you. Conviction to extract a promise from your loved ones not to interfere when you lapse into unconsciousness, the first stage in the descent to death. But sometimes bravery of a different sort is needed. There comes a time when it has to be articulated that a point made several times over is just repetition.

'It was not for Mickey Devine, or those who follow in his footsteps, to find that courage. That is for Gerry Adams and Martin McGuinness. To have the courage to call a halt and end needless further suffering. And to do it sooner rather than later.

'Mickey Devine. *Ar dheis Dé go raibh a hanam.*'

He paused to let the words hang, to allow space for a little reflection.

'Let us stand for the creed.'

He led off. The congregation immediately joined in, and soon the pitch and rhythm of the single unified voice perfectly carried the prayer.

In death a hunger striker was instantly transformed. His past misdeeds were erased. The orchestrated riots had an importance and symbolism that went beyond the carnage and destruction. He had no doubt that the effects of this hunger strike would reverberate for a long time: there was no telling where it would all end. What Thatcher and the Unionists had not yet fully realised was that the power lay in the deed itself. Now was history in the making. He knew they were going to pay a terrible price for their failure to appreciate all of this. That was why he'd been careful not to undermine the significance of the event or the sacrifice.

There was plenty of tacit support for the IRA campaign here. They didn't see anything wrong with a milkman who delivered to the barracks being gunned down in front of his family as a collaborator. They understood the Provo's classification of him as a legitimate target. It was an extension of the castle and big house mentality. Behind the veneer of friendliness, bordering on obsequiousness, there lurked resentment and hatred towards authority. His parishioners thought Mickey Devine was a martyr.

The fact that the strikers had willed their own deaths, and been allowed to die with a greater dignity than many of their victims, was conveniently overlooked. They weren't interested in complexities or niceties. Not while there was a war to be fought.

In the meantime the congregation needed guidance and it was his duty to provide it. As he brought up the offertory gifts to the altar, he could feel the adrenalin coursing through his system. What a pity Roche and his rookie weren't present to hear his homily. They might be a little less free and easy with their innuendo.

Fr Peter would be annoyed with him when he found out what he'd said from the pulpit. He abhorred politics. He didn't like the Church being embroiled. He was the ultimate man of least resistance, against anything that caused even a vague ripple.

Fr Brendan placed the wine and host down on the altar and blessed them.

When he looked up, he saw row upon row of half-empty pews.

thirteen

Bricktappers, the name Fr Brendan gave to the voices that wanted to turn him, were out in force today. He'd gone over to Fr Peter's Mass to help with communion. His sermon had been a hackneyed address about snobbery, which he said went beyond money and status. Clever priests, he said, often looked down on their less scholastic brethren and parishioners. Fr Brendan knew straightaway that particular piece of improvisation had been directed at him. Fr Peter would be delighted when he heard about the walkout and he would lambaste him for his poor judgment. The thought made him miserable.

He'd put on a pair of jeans and a T-shirt after lunch and headed to the Phoenix Park. It was unusual for him to not wear the collar on a Sunday, particularly when he had an evening Mass to serve. He'd told himself that he'd done this not because he'd already succumbed to the bricktappers, but because he couldn't be in clerical garb if he did.

The fine weather never failed to bring out the crowds. There were people drinking tea from flasks and eating food spread out on chequered blankets. Hawkers moved among the crowds selling sweets and chocolate. The All-Ireland semi-final was playing in the background on transistor radios. Offaly were getting the better of Down. Kerry was already in the final and neither side looked capable of stopping them win five in a row.

Kids kicked balls. There were groups of teenagers wandering about, and if you looked closely you'd see certain boys and girls gravitating towards each other, wanting for this to be noticed by the others but then also praying that it wouldn't be. Sunbathers lay down on the grass snoozing, newspapers covering their heads. The ambience was insouciant.

Couples seemed to be everywhere. Fr Brendan was glad that priests didn't marry. He'd never had a long-term relationship or wanted children.

But it was days like this, when he felt down, that brought it home to him that he'd always be on the outside looking in. He'd often heard couples say that they were so ingrained into each other that they finished each other's sentences. How wonderful, he thought, it must be to be able to confide all your worries to a loved one, to ascertain how their day had gone, and to offer and receive words of encouragement. That couldn't happen without reaching a closeness he'd never have.

He passed by a man and a woman exchanging sharp words, the way people do when they have lost respect for each other but don't know it yet. Was it natural to bond with one person for life? Even the secularists encouraged regularised unions. Was marriage merely a convention that only survived because Church and State feared that society and morality would otherwise disintegrate?

He'd been struck by the number of mature women who complained under the cloak of anonymity of the confession box that their husbands had lost interest in having sex with them, and yet they never threatened, much less took any steps, to leave their man. It could be explained, in part, by their respect for their vows. But he was also sure that fear of being alone, and the unknown, was the glue that kept some marriages together long after good looks and the sex had waned.

Fr Peter had headed off to his brother for lunch and wouldn't be home before midnight. That was the official version, anyway. A few months ago, something urgent had come up, and after a ring around he'd run down a contact number for the brother. After the brother told him that he was not there, he'd added, politely but firmly, that he had not seen or spoken to him in years. Clearly, Fr Peter was spending time with a friend. Maybe he had met her in the confession box.

Fr Brendan rested up by the Papal Cross. It was hard to credit that a million people had come here to hear the Pope say Mass. He'd sat for hours with hundreds of other people on the floor of a goods train that morning, stuck on the tracks behind countless trains ahead of them waiting to get to the park. There'd been loud cheers when the driver had announced over the crackly intercom that the Aer Lingus flight carrying the Holy Father was overhead. No one had complained. People were in great form and couldn't do enough for each other. It transcended age and class.

The logistics of the visit had been huge. The dean had directed all seminarians to help the regular building contractor to build the altar for the Mass. They'd all worked around the clock. There'd been a great sense of camaraderie and the craic had been mighty. The cheerfulness had been infectious. He couldn't remember a time when everyone had got on so well.

One evening during a tea break he had gone for a stroll. A short distance away a well-dressed man in his forties had propositioned him. He'd walked right up to him and pointed at bushes a little distance away and asked him: 'Would you like to come in here for sex?' He'd got irritated when Fr Brendan had asked him what he meant. The approach had startled him. Several others followed suit. He'd heard whispers about this sort of thing going on in the Phoenix Park but he'd never believed it.

Eventually a bloke his own age came along. He was a good-looking man with a strong Dublin accent. 'Are yah up for it?' was all that he said. The casual nature of the enquiry undid his innate sense of caution.

He'd walked behind him like an automaton. He was excited, but also terrified someone he knew would see him. The anonymity, the taboo and excitement had been utterly intoxicating. Fear wasn't going to stop him.

The two of them went in behind some trees. There'd been a heavy shower of rain a few minutes earlier. Fr Brendan pulled up his trousers and kneeled down in the soft mud. It had felt warm under his knees. He had then given the man oral sex. The man had grabbed his hair and amid grunting and cursing ejaculated into his mouth.

Afterwards, when he was fixing himself, he had told the other bloke (he had never even got his name) this was the first time a man had come in his mouth. The man had replied matter-of-factly that he'd always remember it so, and without any further acknowledgement walked off in the direction from which he had come.

The encounter itself had been sweet and uncomplicated.

But the recriminations started as soon as the man had disappeared from sight.

He was appalled at his own conduct and overwhelmed by it. He'd believed that he could control his feelings and desire. It had been part of the reason why he'd entered the seminary. He'd hoped that the feelings would go away and for a long time they had. Why had he engaged in something unnatural, and promiscuous, and so deeply sinful? Some of the literature suggested that it was possible to contract AIDS from swallowing semen. He believed that he should get it as a punishment. He was mired in guilt and promised to God that he'd never do it again.

He'd left the caked-in mud on his knees for days as a memento in spite of his self-loathing. The touch and sight of it aroused him. Over the years he'd been drawn back there again and again by the same force that brought a binge drinker to a certain sticky carpet pub – an allure so powerful it blocked out the aftertaste. Usually he came under cover of darkness. The night sky added to the subterfuge.

You never knew whom you might meet. Big or small, fair or dark, same age or older? The seediness of the encounters only acted as a spur.

The bricktappers were on the go again today. He had arm-wrestled with the voices but he'd known in his heart that it was only a cover to heighten what lay ahead. A charade to be played out until he was ready to be picked up.

He walked down towards the place. A man in a car passed him by twice, slowing down each time. He passed a third time. Some men came right out and were brazen. Others came so far, so tantalisingly close, and pulled back at the last moment over and over.

As the man drove on he spotted an unmarked patrol car signal him to pull in. The man pulled in to the side, alighted from the car and stood there with his arms folded, leaning on his car door. He was well dressed and looked like a businessman.

Fr Brendan's heart was in his mouth. If he turned around and walked away they'd surely think he was hiding something. On the other hand, if he walked past they might just pull him over and start asking awkward questions.

One guard was asking the man questions. The other wrote everything into his notebook. His registration details were called out in an unnecessarily loud voice.

The man was squirming under the scrutiny of the policemen. This was much worse than being beaten or robbed. There was now an official record held by the State of being in this place. His details would be recycled around the garda locker room and maybe make its way up the line if he was someone in his own right or well connected.

Every time he came here he'd braved being recognised, or contracting the virus or a plain old-fashioned STD, getting rolled over, or just beaten up by some lads who hated queers. Punters didn't run to complain to the gardaí.

Fr Brendan passed by without being stopped. His heart was beating so hard he thought it would come out of his chest. He turned and headed for home. He'd be back. That was the depressing thing. The bricktappers would always get men like him to come here, even in broad daylight where the risk of exposure was greater, looking for illicit sex while trying to look nonchalant.

fourteen

Wayne crossed the room on his tiptoes. His Ma and Da were both stretched out on the couch, the remnants of a few carry-outs on the floor. They had their rows, even bad ones like this morning, but she'd still sit down with him and drink and make up, provided there wasn't a new row when they got going.

He gingerly pulled down the handle of the hall door, but the noise from the coil in the spring still seemed deafening to him. He prayed they wouldn't wake. His Da would surely send him out for another six pack. Fr Brendan might have doubled the rate for altar boys to a pound, but he also sacked anyone who was late.

Once clear, Wayne ran the whole way to the church.

He robed up in the sacristy and checked that everything was ready to go. Fr Brendan hovered around, making sure that he had adequate stocks of wafer for communion. The priest double-checked that he had put markers in the pages for the reading and handed the tome to Wayne to place on the lectern. When he came back inside Fr Brendan was kneeling down, eyes closed, saying a prayer. Normally the priest was all chat but he seemed preoccupied today.

Wayne concentrated hard during the service. He collected the offertory gifts and carried them to Fr Brendan at the steps of the altar. He listened carefully to the consecration and rang the bell when Fr Brendan held up the big host, the chalice, and when he put his hands over the wine. He followed him down the communion line, helped him keep the platter below people's mouths in case a wafer dropped and stood beside him at the altar while the priest tidied up and handed him the tray containing the balance of the wafers and wine. Fr Brendan liked everything done just right and got annoyed if anyone made a mistake.

Wayne sat down on the altar steps to wait out the couple of minutes Fr Brendan allowed for people to say their post-communion prayers. The priest busied himself toying with the missal sheet, absentmindedly turning it over and over in his hand.

Earlier, his Da had been giving out shite that Fr Brendan had been preaching against the Provos and that people should complain to Fr Peter. Even his Ma, who wouldn't hear anything said against him on account of the music lessons, said that he was too precious for his own good.

He heard the priest addressing the Mass goers, giving out Mass times during the week and details of the next novena. After the final blessing Wayne walked ahead of the priest into the sacristy carrying the wine and the wafers. Once inside, Wayne heard the lock turn. Fr Brendan said they had to do that in case robbers came. What kind of a scumbag would do that? he wondered. Wayne knew lots of robbers. His Da, for one. He'd never sink so low to steal the plate money. Junkies maybe. But he didn't think even they'd do that.

Fr Brendan took down a mahogany box. Inside, it was lined with green felt and there were hundreds of communion wafers packed into recessed lines like poker chips. He replenished the chalice with fresh supplies for the morning. He topped up the wine and placed it back onto the offertory tray.

Then, the priest changed his mind, picked it up and handed it to Wayne.

'It's OK,' the priest said seeing his hesitation and thrust it into his hand.

Wayne was sceptical: his Ma had made him take the pledge for his confirmation and that meant he wasn't allow take drink till he was eighteen.

'This is God's nectar. It's not like ordinary wine anymore. If it was, how would alcoholic priests ever serve?'

Everything within Wayne said he ought to refuse. But a priest was a priest. Especially when he paid a pound for serving Mass. Besides, he didn't want to run the risk of annoying him. His Ma would go mental if the priest cancelled his precious music lessons.

Wayne took a sip and put it back down.

'Throw it into you man, it won't kill you.'

The remark was supposed to make him feel better. It had the opposite effect. Wayne heard his irritation and the slight menace underpinning it. He was scared and his ability to resist gone.

He put the glass to his lips and downed it in a single gulp. After a few seconds he felt a bit light-headed; he also felt a warm glow in his chest. Was this it then? If so, it was hard to see what all the fuss was about. It didn't even taste nice. They sat in silence for what seemed like a long time.

'You must be at an age now when you have an interest in girls, no?'

What a weird thing to say, he thought. He almost smirked. Who did the priest think he was? The wine had increased his sense of well-being. He felt confident enough to ignore him and so did not answer. He was still nonetheless taken aback by the priest's next question.

'How are you developing?'

Wayne didn't know what to say. The priest was actually asking him about his thing. The older lads in school gave him jip about this sort of thing. But no adult, let alone a priest, had ever asked a question like this before.

'Pull down your pants. Come on! Come on!'

It was said in a way that didn't brook discussion. It was the sort of thing that he would have refused to do if he thought about it at all. The problem was the part of his brain that involved thinking wasn't working right now. It wasn't even accessible. Thinking about this made him feel bad. Wayne dropped his pants.

The priest took his mickey into his hand and ran his fingers up and down it. Wayne smelt the wine from Fr Brendan's breath. He wondered how that was, given that the wine had been changed into Jesus's blood during the consecration and the priest's earlier claim that it was no longer drink.

The priest cupped Wayne's balls and stuck his free hand up under his jumper and began to rub his tummy in an anticlockwise circular motion. The sensation was pleasant. Wayne felt himself going hard.

'Lift up your arms.' He did as instructed.

Fr Brendan took off Wayne's altar boy smock. He then went behind Wayne and rubbed his hand over where the hair had started to grow. Wayne felt like he was in a bad dream when you couldn't run or speak up no matter how much you wanted to. He remained rooted to the spot.

'You have started to get hair there then. Good!' Fr Brendan went about his examination in the same workmanlike way Dr Connolly had examined him the time he had been kicked in the goolies by one of the piebalds up the back fields. This was vaguely reassuring.

'Close your eyes and I want you to breathe long deep breaths.'

Then the priest moved the skin on his mickey up and down. Wayne jerked hard against the motion but the priest held him firm around his midriff as if in a vice grip.

Wayne often played with himself at night. The lads in school were always slagging him that the helmet in his thing would fall right out if he pulled the skin too far back. A thousand times, and more, he had pulled the skin back to the brink and stopped.

The priest was moving his skin back and forth faster. The helmet did not fall. Suddenly, he felt a rush between his thighs. It went up through his mickey and spread outwards around his groin. It felt like he was going to burst or wet himself. Then he felt something shoot through his piss hole, and saw white sticky stuff that looked like milk of magnesia spurt out – it must be spunk, the stuff he had heard the older boys in the schoolyard sniggering about.

Fr Brendan flicked his hand in the air and Wayne saw tiny specks of it landing on his green surplice hung up in the wardrobe.

Fr Brendan handed him a handkerchief. 'Clean yourself up.'

The priest looked down at the ground, avoiding eye contact. Wayne reached out for it and the priest instantly turned away from him. The priest then went over to the collection monies. He dipped his hand in and grabbed a pile of change.

'Put your hands together.' He trickled the money into the well. 'That's between us. This is our thing. Not everyone can understand it. Do you get me?' Wayne didn't but nodded anyway; it was the sensible thing to do to get out of there.

Back home Wayne went straight upstairs to his bedroom and counted. There was nearly six pounds. That part felt OK. The stuff he'd cleaned up did not. It was cold to the touch and it made him feel dirty. His mind was flooded with bad thoughts. Why had his thing got hard? Did this make him into a queer? He'd sensed the priest's worry that he might tell anyone. Why that too? The moment when the stuff had shot out had been nice. But the last thing he was going to do was actually tell anyone. He'd have cheerfully died first.

He picked up his guitar and strummed a few chords to distract himself. After a few minutes he threw it down on the bed and stormed out, slamming the hall door that earlier he'd opened so carefully. He reflected that a lot had changed since then. Things might never be the same again.

fifteen

The first thing Fr Brendan did when he got back to the presbytery was to go upstairs to the bathroom. It was dark but he didn't turn on any lights. Fr Peter wasn't due back for hours but he locked the door all the same. He was feeling bad about what he'd done to Wayne and knew that very shortly he was going to feel even worse. What had got into him?

But the self-recrimination would have to wait. He had to attend to other more immediate needs. He was still in the flush of excitement of what had occurred.

He dropped his pants, sat on the toilet seat, closed his eyes and visualised kneeling in the soft warm mud for the first time in the Phoenix Park. He'd never seen that man again. He could still play the images in his head like he was watching a movie. It never failed to give him a charge.

He didn't last long.

There were few things in his experience that were more fleeting than ejaculation. Even the intense ones that were mired in seediness and accentuated by the excitement that he might lose everything if he were found out. It was usually at this juncture that he'd ask himself was it for this momentary spurt that he'd been going up the walls? Last Christmas Day he'd watched the movie *Dr Strangelove*. Colonel Jack D. Ripper had been convinced that the fluoridation of the water was a Commie plot to induce a feeling of emptiness after ejaculation. He'd readily recognised, identified even, what he'd been on about. Did that make him mad too? Or did it mean that he'd just appreciated the satire?

Just then he was hit by an even more powerful realisation. He recognised that no matter how bad the post-orgasmic low, it was never going to fall below a point that it would stop him acting out. The bricktappers would come again in their own good time, impervious to prayer or guilt. The desire always returned with renewed fervour.

He sat there alone with his thoughts. In the blackness that enveloped him he tried to make sense of what he'd done.

None of this would have happened if he'd have gotten his rocks off up in the park. The sudden appearance of the gardaí had thwarted him and left him feeling deeply frustrated. It was a mark of how wound up he was that he'd done it. He couldn't help himself. He'd needed some form of release.

He'd never touched a child before. The feeling of revulsion that now descended upon him was borne out of the innate badness of the act. That came not just from having broken a taboo, or breaking a law that provided stiff jail sentences. It came from within. His intuition screamed 'this is very wrong'.

And who better to know?

His own sexual initiation had occurred in the potting shed when he was around Wayne's age. Jim, the gardener, used to touch him on his private parts, until he'd make his penis hard. Things had progressed quickly from there.

He'd felt dirty for having engaged in something that his intuition had told him was some heinous form of moral turpitude. He'd felt inadequate sexually and in other ways later on in life, and suspected these feelings stemmed from what he'd done, or had been done to him.

But he also knew that analysing it in those simplistic terms was facile. Had it really been so bad? He'd enjoyed the attention, the soccer magazines Jim had given him as unsolicited gifts and the chance to drive the ride-on mower. The sensation of arousal felt good and there wasn't any way of getting away from the fact that he enjoyed the act of coming. Always.

Even now, while stuck in the morass of self-loathing over what he'd done, a part of him was still tingling with excitement. He found it all very confusing.

What would happen if Wayne told? Fr Brendan would never have dreamed of telling anybody what Jim the gardener had done to him. Maybe Wayne was different. He was plucky and had the father's unpredictable gene.

There'd be dire consequences. He'd be prosecuted. His parents would die of mortification. He wouldn't be able to face them or anybody else. He'd commit suicide first; try to make it look like an accident. He remembered from his own schooldays how despised teachers who touched up students were. Would he get a name for it among the boys?

He was snapped out of his reverie by what sounded like a barrage of hailstones hitting a window at the front of the house. He pulled up his pants and went to investigate.

He stood in the porch outside. He saw a number of coins scattered on the ground in front of him. He went out to the gate and looked up the street. He saw Wayne running away like the clappers. He picked up the money, counting it as he went along. It came to just under six pounds.

He went back inside and put the kettle on. He wet the tea and put a couple of biscuits onto the saucer. He went into the living room and sat in the armchair, dunking his biscuits. It'd been a very long day and he was tired, exhausted even.

More bad thoughts were crowding him. He was now beset by a new worry: what would Christy Clarke do to him if he found out that he'd molested his little boy?

sixteen

Cora Jackson firmly tapped the table with her index finger to indicate that the matter was now closed and called out the next item – 'media monitoring'. The elderly solicitor in the grubby cord jacket, who insisted on speaking in Irish, raised his hand.

Cora pursed her lips and ignored him.

'The print media is a doddle. But who will monitor what's being said on the airwaves? It's much more time consuming. Any volunteers now, please?' Straightaway, three hands shot up in the air. The gaeilgeoir took his hand down pronto. Fr Brendan stifled a grin.

Forming the 'Campaign for a Living Life' as an umbrella group to coordinate a national strategy for the diverse pro-life groups had been Cora's idea. Fr Brendan had fretted that the group would operate as a magnet for every right-wing loony and end up discrediting them all. Time would be taken up distancing themselves from their crackpot views while the real work went undone. He'd initially been tepid on hearing of the proposal.

But Cora knew better than anyone how things worked. And was blessed with boundless energy. First, she'd hijacked the Fianna Fáil party machine and used it to build up a network of support. Pubs and small hotels provided their function rooms for meetings like this. She'd also tapped into unrest within Fine Gael and sections of the Labour party. The group was well populated by experienced politicos. Next, she made sure only her people got into positions of authority, and set about marginalising the misfits by deploying them on time-consuming tasks where they could do no harm.

On the road, she launched a charm offensive, cajoling local worthies into seeing that there was a real danger that abortion would be introduced by the back door if people sat on their hands. She also made it clear that anyone who was not with her was against her. They'd got acres of newsprint. Even the *New York Times* had gone big on the story. Donations were coming in from far and wide. Cross-party support had ensured that they couldn't be ignored any longer. There was a groundswell building.

Not everyone was pleased. The parliamentary parties recognised that any referendum was going to be divisive and were ducking and diving. Cora predicted that they'd come to heel once they realised that the momentum they were building was unstoppable. Politicians needed to be re-elected and they'd follow their noses in the end, was her prediction.

Cora had lineage. Her father had stood as a successful candidate for Sinn Féin in the general election in 1918 and had been a member of the first Dáil Éireann. Subsequently he had fought with the anti-treaty forces in the civil war. He had later joined Fianna Fáil under De Valera.

As a child she had sat up beside him on the makeshift platform on the lorry that went from church to church of a Sunday morning. She heard him lambaste W. T. Cosgrave for imprisoning and executing the same IRA men who only a few years before had fought for Ireland's freedom.

Cora was secretary of her local *cumann* and had been the constituency director of elections for as long as anyone could remember. She was one of the first women tallymen, and could tell at a glance how votes were being transferred down the line under the complicated proportionate representation electoral system, and accurately predict the result long before the final count. By examining votes and transfers from ballot boxes in smaller townlands, she could work out which families had defected, or which she'd pulled over the line.

Today she was working her way down through the agenda, effortlessly rolling out their campaign, working out, on the spot, how logistics were to be best deployed. Fr Brendan was more than happy to defer to her.

Next, regional PROs were appointed.

'Now, I want members to draw up lists of people who are influential in the local community. Sound them out. Build up a database of support. We need lists of persons in favour of abortion, tacitly or otherwise. Any information about them that lessens their standing in the community is useful. Local knowledge is invaluable here. Funnel it to the local and national PROs who can deploy it to undermine their views.'

That was as polite a way as Fr Brendan had ever heard muckraking described.

'This referendum is as big an opportunity as we will ever get,' she said as she wound up the meeting. 'The coalition government is hanging by a thread. Fianna Fáil is so desperate to get back into power it will do anything to get a vote. The media is wary of us, but soon they will accept that this is an issue people really care about. We've to exploit all these factors. Put maximum pressure on your elected representative. Leave no stone unturned.'

The meeting broke up on a high. On the drive back to town (Cora was, by now, his unofficial chauffeur) she talked excitedly about how she was pulling out all the stops to get a meeting with

Charlie Haughey. Fr Brendan had enjoyed clocking up the miles. She'd a keen interest in Church matters, knew the personalities involved and was acutely aware of all the potential problems simmering away below the surface. She was one of the very few people who actually saw how vulnerable the Church was right now and recognised the need to fight back.

'You'll have to come down for Sunday lunch soon.'

'I'd be delighted, Cora. Maybe you could invite a few people over and I'd say a Mass.'

'That would be great, Father. We'd be honoured.'

It still felt odd to be addressed as 'Father' in such deferential terms by someone who was so much older and experienced in the ways of the world than he. Not that he was complaining exactly. It reinforced his sense of place and gave his life some meaning, especially in troubled times such as these.

The campaign had been a blessing. He'd thrown himself into the work and in time the episode, as he now termed the touching up of Wayne, had receded into the background. He'd gone to confession in another part of town to a priest whom he knew gave a sympathetic hearing to this sort of thing. That'd made him feel a bit better in himself.

He'd been petrified that every knock at the presbytery announced the arrival of Christy Clarke to settle with him. Stark denial was his strategy but he didn't think Clarke would dwell on the formalities of asking for his side of the story. He was not known as a 'route one' man for nothing.

In the days that followed he'd contrived a few incidents during music lessons to pull Wayne up on. He'd sent a strong letter home to Lillian saying that he'd cancel further lessons unless Wayne pulled up his socks.

A letter was high-risk. Maybe Wayne would break down when confronted and tell her what had gone on in the sacristy. But he might do that anyway, and he'd be sounding very credible too in the absence of any motive to do his music teacher down. Either way, he had the letter of complaint written now and he'd cite Wayne's annoyance over the letter as the reason why the boy had made up a story.

seventeen

Wayne watched his Ma, out of the corner of his eye, nibbling on a bar of chocolate between drags of her cigarette. All the women on the landing smoked, but none produced as much smoke as her. It came gushing out her mouth and nose simultaneously for three or four breaths. He liked it when she blew the match out with the smoke from her mouth. It was funny to think of smoke quenching a fire. She broke off the serrated strip from the corner of the box and picked at her teeth while she smoked.

She'd got very annoyed when he'd tried to bring up putting the ferret into the loft, saying she hadn't a clue what he was talking about. He was afraid that she would punish him for knowing too much. It was nice to watch TV together just the two of them. That hadn't happened in ages.

The movie they were watching was called *Midnight Express*. Billy, an American guy, got caught smuggling hash out of Turkey. The prisoners lived in squalid rooms in multi-storey blocks built around a courtyard. There were no locks. It was more like the flats than a regular prison. Rifkey, the prison stoolie, could provide anything: hash, heroin, even a boy, for a price. With his ingratiating manner and long greasy hair, Rifkey was universally hated but untouchable.

Occasionally, prison officers raided for contraband. Violators had their ankles tied together and then were hoisted up on a rope. The guards beat the soles of their feet with a baseball bat. Rifkey eventually snitched once too often and Billy bit his tongue out (the frames were played in slow motion and it was gross). His Ma said Rifkey was a tout and it was good enough for him. Wayne thought the way she said 'tout' in her Liverpool accent made her sound very hard.

A big fat guard beat up Billy and then went to take off his pants to rape him. Billy ran at him, head-butted him in the stomach and pushed him backwards. It was a great moment when the back of his head was impaled on a coat hook on the wall. Billy took the keys off the gaoler's belt and made good his escape.

Wayne had his very own dirty little secret to worry about. He'd hung his head in shame and mortification the other day when he'd walked in and saw his Ma standing beside the washing machine holding his bed sheets up to the light.

It was the pervert priest who had shown him what a proper wank was, and now he couldn't stop. He wasn't put off about the slagging about going blind or his eyes narrowing like a Chinaman but even if he had it wouldn't have made any difference. He was hooked.

He only wanked off to girls. It wasn't his fault that he'd gone hard when the pervert priest touched him. But it bothered him when the lads in school said a standing cock had no conscience. He didn't have a girlfriend yet, and he was sure that if people found out what he'd been doing he never would.

Billy had been scared shitless but that hadn't stopped him standing up for himself. Why hadn't he told the pervert priest to go and fuck himself? He'd asked himself this a thousand times. Instead, he went along with him doing things that were disgusting and unnatural. The thought of his hand on his prick nearly made him sick.

Mr Walsh, his teacher in fourth class in primary school, used to be at the boys. He'd announce every now and again that he'd work to do and that the class should do homework. He'd get at least half of the class out on the line for talking or messing. He'd give them six of the best. The boys who had been biffed would lie face-down on their desks crying. All the while Walshie would have little Barry Crosby on his knee, saying aloud, 'Would you listen to all those cry-babies, Barry,' while he had his hand down his pants.

All forty-one other boys bore witness. But no one said anything at home or to Mr Crowley the principal. No one said anything to Barry either unless they were pissed off that they'd got slapped and he hadn't coz he was teacher's pet. They'd call him a powder puff, and make jokes about the master touching his willy.

He wondered about the remark his Ma had made to the pervert priest down at the presbytery, about his Da going into Orla's room late at night. He'd asked Orla about it and she'd told him to fuck off. Rita, her best mate, had taken him aside afterwards and told him Christy had never laid a hand on her. Rita said that his Ma was out to get his Da because Christy was whoring around, and his Ma was also jealous of Orla – she was young and good-looking, footloose and fancy free, all the things that his Ma wasn't anymore.

Now, his Ma was many things. And she'd many faults. But the idea that she was jealous of Orla or anyone else for that matter seemed daft to him.

There was no point in saying anything to her about the sacristy. In his Ma's eyes the pervert priest could do no wrong in his dealings with him. She'd already boxed his ears after she got a letter from him complaining that Wayne wasn't trying hard enough.

She'd only tell his Da and he'd surely kill them both. But not before he gave Wayne the third degree, demanding to know why he'd gone along with it. How could he explain to his Da that he'd got a hard on?

eighteen

The staggered deaths of the hunger strikers ensured wall-to-wall coverage in the newspapers. Roche had never seen anything like it. The *Indo* was doing its best to quell populist opinion. It was heavily critical of the IRA. The IRA leadership, who'd initially opposed the strike, was now ruthlessly exploiting the men for political gain. And it was working. Hunger strikes struck a chord within an Irishman. The atmosphere was very charged. It was just like the aftermath of Bloody Sunday after the Paras had shot dead thirteen civilians attending a rally in Derry. A mob had burned down the British Embassy on Merrion Square. A repeat could trigger anarchy.

The provisional IRA murder campaign had just got under way in the North when he'd graduated out of Templemore. The IRA green book outlawed attacks on Free State forces. But within a couple of years Provo active service units were robbing plenty of banks in the south and they frequently shot dead anyone who got in their way.

By then Roche had been transferred to the Subversive Surveillance and Intelligence Unit under the wing of Sergeant Pat Flannery. The men and women they targeted were obviously guilty of serious crimes, although hard evidence was difficult to come by. Improving the case by verballing up a false confession or tweaking forensics was seen as no more than evening out the score. If the accused wasn't going to acrtually admit what they'd done it was acceptable to put a throw-away line into his mouth, which was consistent with his guilt. Suspects were sometimes given a few clatters or beaten up, or, like Clarke, given the ice-cold bath treatment. That was par for the course, tacitly understood by the suspects and investigators alike.

In court, accused after accused gave evidence of alleged ill treatment. Initially, the Court rejected the allegations and ruled confessions admissible. Nonetheless, a small section of the media highlighted a pattern of alleged brutality. There was talk of a 'heavy gang' operating within the force, which was focused on results and wasn't too fussy how they were obtained.

At first, Roche hadn't lost any sleep. If the accused hadn't committed the actual crime before the Court, he'd been involved in lots of others: there were no 'innocents' at this level. This was a war they were fighting and everyone was in it together.

The belief that they were the frontline troops guarding against the country descending into anarchy, the constant surfeit of adrenalin coursing through the system and the stress of the work all took its toll. But Roche couldn't help noticing that behind all the camaraderie and the macho talk good men were fraying at the edges.

How else could you explain why so many lads went home full of drink and beat their wives? In time he'd realised what the real problem was. Cops and robbers: the law was what differentiated them. It was a distinction that was ingrained in a policeman, even the bad ones. Once you crossed the line you entered into a no man's land. It'd been exciting to begin with. And like a lot of allurements it was habit-forming and difficult to break. Most of the men had been operating for so long on the margins that they couldn't play it straight anymore even if they'd wanted to. Their moral compass no longer had a fixed point of reference.

For Roche the binge drinking, the crankiness and the high incidence of depression were all merely symptoms of a more sinister malaise that was eating the men up. It wasn't so much the work getting to them as the methodology.

Eventually the Court of Criminal Appeal had set aside a number of convictions as being unsafe. The judgments were often highly critical of interrogation methods. The IRA propaganda machine went into overdrive. RTÉ and the mainstream newspapers now gave their claims airtime and newsprint, and there was much finger wagging in the editorials. Specialist units had become an embarrassment and many of them were quietly wound down.

Some had publicly defended the work done by the units. But Flannery – a career cop through and through – was far too cute for that. He disappeared quietly into the backwaters of the Fines Office until the furore passed. He re-emerged a few years later with another promotion and now headed up the grandly entitled Internal Affairs and External Relations Division. A classic poacher turned gamekeeper, his role was to root out bad cops and ensure that the image of the force was always sunny-side-up.

He was a superintendent now. The talk was he'd make it all the way to Commissioner. In the old days Roche had been one of Flannery's golden boys. But the relationship had cooled once Flannery sensed that Roche had been less than supportive of his way of doing business.

Negotiations were going on in the background to end the hunger strike. There was no sign of any breakthrough. The men were determined to keep going. You had to admire their commitment. The mainstream coverage was hostile but the IRA was at a stage in its development where there was no such thing as bad publicity. Thatcher's hard-line approach was recruiting new members en masse and funds from the United States and elsewhere were pouring into the Sinn Féin coffers. The establishment was getting more nervous by the day. It was win-win for the men of violence. Top brass was obsessed, sending out circulars reminding members to be vigilant and to follow up all leads relating to the IRA no matter how apparently trivial they appeared.

At first he'd been sure that Daly had been exaggerating when he'd said that Christy Clarke was doing business with the Provos. But hadn't he seen it with his own eyes? A group of heavy-hitters stood around on the balcony, the bold Christy in the middle, everyone hanging on the words of the young priest. What was all that about? The priest was a cold fish to be sure. He was one to watch. There was a story there he had no doubt.

Clarke and the Provos was an intriguing, if unworkable, alliance. Clarke was far too headstrong for it to survive. It was beginning to look like Daly had got it wrong on the payroll heist at the tyre factory. There'd be some bean counter up in the garda HQ on the phone any day now complaining about the cost. He'd resist any pressure to stand down. The association with the Provos in the present climate would be enough to justify keeping things going. He'd see if Daly had anything more to say on why Christy Clarke wanted fast bikes. Something was going down and he wanted to be right on top of it when it happened.

nineteen

Wayne sat in the living room watching television while his Ma drank tea with the women in the kitchen. He heard Mrs Kelly complaining that the flats were being taken over by junkies and it was time to get the 'Ra to do a job on the people supplying them. They could start with a few kneecappings and if that didn't work a bullet to the back of the head would be too good for them. Another woman said they should put those drug dealers in a room with Christy for half an hour and that'd sort it out. He heard his Ma snort contemptuously.

There was a time when she'd basked in the fact that Christy had a reputation; the most she'd say was 'leave it out' whenever someone went on about him. But things hadn't quite been the same since she'd gone up to the priest to see if he could do anything for her. As if – he'd been a waste of space.

Wayne never thought his Ma would leave his Da. But the news that she didn't even have that option had brought out something in her that wasn't nice. She'd turned against him. Things had settled down since the attack on the birds, but she was poised, waiting for Christy to slip up. His Da was too far up his ass to even notice. But Wayne had. She was hardening towards him.

After the women had gone his Ma started in on him.

'Where's your Da?'

'I don't know, Ma – down the pub?'

His Da spent every Saturday drinking in Madigan's and backing horses in the bookies. She knew this better than he did.

'Well I've no money. Go down to your father and tell him I need housekeeping.'

'Ah Ma, I'm watching TV.'

'Get down there now. Do what you're told! Do you hear me?'

'And if he's not there?'

'Ask around, find out who he was with and where he was headed.'

She walked over to the TV and turned it off.

Wayne stood outside the mahogany doors of Madigan's bar looking in. The doors swung in and out as customers came and went. Each time he caught a glimpse of his Da supping pints at the counter with Jimmy Daly. That was good news. He'd be able to report back that he was drinking pints with him. He didn't like reporting to his Ma behind his Da's back. He felt like a spy. Still, it was much easier to do it when he knew he was telling her what she wanted to hear.

He didn't want to go up asking him for money. You'd never know what way Christy might react. He might stuff a wad of notes into his hand and buy him a Coke and a Tayto. Alternatively, he might scrunch his face up in rage and tell him to get the fuck out of here.

The bigger worry was that he'd just engage him in ordinary conversation. He liked to boast about his Kenny Dalglish shirt and might ask Wayne to go and get it or start asking him about the attack on his pigeons. He'd lie of course, if he were asked. But he was planking himself that his Da would see through it.

His Da was picking winners from the pages of the *Daily Mirror*. He'd often send Wayne down to Quigley's in the morning to get the paper. Wayne would then go through his dockets and calculate if there was any money due to him. His favourite bet was a £1 Yankee and on days when all four horses came up he'd have to work out the winnings on six doubles, four trebles and an accumulator. Once he'd got back £1279. He'd given Wayne £19 just for doing the sums.

Sometimes he mitched from school and got a job marking up the board in the bookies, writing up changes in the odds and marking out who finished first, second and third. The bookies was full of men smoking cigarettes, intently studying forms and reading the racing papers for information. Some followed jockeys, others stables, while others followed the nap selection in the *Sporting Chronicle.* They were a bunch of losers. Frank Brennan, a boy in his class, used to take his Da's bets and not put the money on, so confident was he that he wasn't going to win.

He waited until he saw that his Da was on his own. He'd be less likely to kick up a fuss without an audience. He walked in and stood before him. His Da patted the barstool and Wayne sat up on it.

'Gerry, stick us on a pint and a Coke for the young lad.'

'Well, what can I do you for?' he asked, turning his attention to Wayne.

'Ma wants a few quid for shopping.'

'Does she now?' Wayne nodded.

His Da produced a wad of notes from his pocket and peeled off a couple of tenners.

'So how is your mother? Is she nagging or what?'

'No, she's fine. She'll be grand when she sees the money.'

'I wonder what's going on with her these days. Is she goin' through the change or what?'

Wayne didn't answer. He knew the question wasn't directed at him. It was his Da just thinking aloud. It was about time too. If he didn't cop on he'd wake up one morning and she'd be gone.

'What time will I tell her you'll be home?'

'Jaysus, don't tell her anything. I've people to see, places to go, things to be doing. I'll be home when I'm home. Right? Do you get me?'

Wayne didn't really, but thought better of saying so. Jimmy Daly arrived back from the toilet or wherever he'd been, and Wayne stood up to surrender his seat. His Da handed him a betting slip and money and told him to put the bet on. He lowered what was left of his Coke in a single slug. He wasn't just being sent on a chore. He'd been given his cue to leave. And so he did.

twenty

Fr Brendan parked in the underground car park in the Setanta Centre. The air was putrid and the low ceiling made him feel claustrophobic. Cora Jameson was waiting for him on the ramp. She had cashed in every Brownie point with her party contacts to secure this meeting.

'Under no circumstances are you to shake hands with him,' Cora warned.

'Unclean, unclean!' Fr Brendan mimed shaking a bell.

'He's been shaking hands all his life and his tendons are always sore. And don't mention the Arms Trial.'

'You don't say. You'll be telling me next not to ask him how he came by his little spread out in Kinsealy.'

The mystery of how Haughey had moved from a common-or-garden four-bed semi-detached house in an estate in Artane to a Gandon-built mansion sitting on a couple of hundred acres in north County Dublin was an enduring one. Certain journalists were obsessed by it.

Cora hurried on. 'He is very punctual you know.'

Fr Brendan checked his watch. 'There's no point in arriving too early either. Haughey's the one who has to feel under a compliment if we're to make progress. We don't want to be too keen.'

They were ushered into his office at 3 p.m. precisely.

Haughey was dressed casually in a blue shirt, wine cravat and a fawn cardigan. A windcheater was draped over his chair. Cora's informants had said that he was sailing his yacht down to Dingle later that day. Works by Jack B. Yeats, Louis le Brocquy and Camille Souter adorned the walls. An enormous bust of himself stood on a plinth beside the window. It didn't work: the furnishings were all too big and grand for the cramped space around them.

Haughey rose imperiously from his desk to greet them. Fr Brendan noticed that he kept the palms of his hands pressed firmly down on the table. Cora, who was comfortable with ceremony, bowed respectfully. Haughey made eye contact with them, and gestured again with his eyes for them to sit down.

'You'll have to excuse my present surroundings, which, let me assure you, are purely temporary,' he said with a sweeping gesture of his hand. His challenging stare, masked by the laconic smile, gave off that legendary whiff of sulphur. Fr Brendan had heard all the stories about his lack of stature, the Savile Row suits, Charvet shirts, the gravelly gravitas, the socialite mistress who had flung an expensive crocodile handbag he had gifted her into the Liffey in a tantrum, but he was still impressed.

Haughey was well briefed and gratifyingly familiar with the experiences in other jurisdictions which had liberalised their abortion laws, initially in response to children who had been identified as Down syndrome, or where the mother's health was at risk if she carried to full term. These were the so-called hard cases, which it very quickly emerged were what the pro-abortionists used as a Trojan horse.

'Let me assure you,' he said when Cora had concluded her presentation, 'a former Taoiseach once said that he would not stand idly by when this country was in crisis and then did just that. That's not going to happen again.'

Jack Lynch had made that remark when Catholics were being burned out of their homes in sectarian attacks in Belfast. The words were taken to mean that he'd send the Irish army across the border to protect them, an interpretation which Lynch hadn't been anxious to dispel. The country had briefly gone onto a war footing. When it came down to it, Lynch didn't have the backbone for that sort of confrontation. It'd been left to a few real patriots to take up the cudgels. Subsequently, ministers Haughey, Neil Blayney and Kevin Boland had been prosecuted on charges of importing guns for the IRA. They'd claimed in their defence that the Cabinet had sanctioned anything they had done, which Lynch and some other senior figures had denied.

Lynch had only been engaging in rhetoric, making political capital. But his insistence that those who had taken his words literally be prosecuted cut to the core of the ambivalence towards physical force that lay at the heart of Fianna Fáil. Haughey might have been carried from the court on the shoulders of his supporters after his acquittal, but the powers that be in the party had ensured that he'd been cast into the political wilderness for years, and the affair had left deep divisions within the party which had still not healed.

It went some way towards explaining why Haughey was having a cut at Lynch today. But Fr Brendan was still dumbfounded by the indiscretion and pettiness of it. Haughey's own lack of leadership during the hunger strike had been a disaster. Many had expected him to use all those legendary Machiavellian powers to outmanoeuvre Thatcher and bring about some sort of an honourable compromise for the men. Instead he dithered and was ineffectual. It'd cost Fianna Fáil the election and the men their lives. In other circumstances he'd have been ousted as party leader but loyalty was the glue that kept this dysfunctional group together.

'So!' he said rubbing his hands together. 'The only real question is how are we going to do it?'

Cora produced a booklet and handed it to him.

'This is the comprehensive report that we have prepared, a blueprint for getting the amendment through. It features the combined contributions of big hitters in business and the finest minds in the Law Library. Once enshrined in the Constitution, not even the Oireachtas can override it.'

Haughey studied it closely, stress-testing it for flaws, looking for reassurance that it would do what Cora said it would do. After a few searching inquiries he asked, 'Would you mind if I adopted this report as my own working template to put before the parliamentary party?'

Five minutes later they left with a promise from the leader of the opposition, the man who would be Taoiseach (again), that he would support, and in government propose, a referendum to amend the constitution.

Outside Fr Brendan punched the air.

'My God, Cora, it was like meeting with the mafia!' He pronounced it 'maw-fee-a'. He began taking off Haughey talking to his press aide just before leaving his office: '"Cora Jackson and the Young Turk priest here want to protect the lives of the unborn. They want to know whether Fianna Fáil will be found wanting."'

Cora hugged him and screeched, 'I can't believe it!' They laughed giddily, high as kites at the improbability of it all.

Part Two

GBH

twenty-one

ACO Reynolds stood back and admired his new car. The spearmint green metallic finish gave it a certain élan. He pointed the remote at it and pressed the red button. He heard the satisfying click of the locks submerging into their silos. All that German technology had been a big selling point. But the remote control that activated the central locking had been the clincher.

There had to be some compensations for working in a shithole like Mountjoy prison. Doing endless overtime, surrounded by the flotsam and jetsam of delinquency. Fellas that'd ate yah for breakfast and shit you out by dinnertime with an ironic leer on their face. If they had brains they'd be dangerous.

It felt good to be finishing a week of nights. There wasn't a cloud in the sky; it was going to be another scorcher. Soon the estate would come to life. But for now, the only sound came from the surrounding gardens, which were alive with early-morning birdsong. Halfway up the driveway to his house, he became vaguely aware that a man was behind him. Next, he felt a glove covering his mouth. It was bright yellow, a Marigold. Eimear wore the same gloves for washing up. The smell of the rubber was right up his nose now and he felt the smooth texture of it on his tongue.

Almost instantaneously, he felt an excruciating pain in his testicles. He contorted in agony, twisting and turning like a corkscrew. There was no give. Yellow Glove had him in a vice grip. He looked down and saw that he was squeezing his balls with a nutcracker. There was one just like it in the cutlery drawer; it was used on Halloween night to open Brazil nuts and then put away again for a year. It must only have been a tiny fraction of a second, at most, before his body began to spasm, but it seemed much longer.

Next, he was bundled over onto the ground. Yellow Glove shoved a rag into his mouth. One man was back-heeling him right into his privates. Another was cutting orange nylon cord with a Stanley knife, while Yellow Glove ordered, 'Cut his fucking prick off.' Back Heel kicked him full-force in the face. Reynolds felt his head whiplashing.

Yellow Glove stamped his shoe down hard on his mouth. Immediately the white cloth jammed into his mouth turned red and Reynolds started to convulse. The rag was taken out and he leaned over, coughing and spluttering. He spat out fragments of teeth.

Orange Cord dragged him by the back of his shirt collar over to the edge of the road. He forced Reynolds to stand up, and then cable-tied his hands and ankles to a telegraph pole. Yellow Glove barked, 'Make sure to put 'em on good and tight.'

Back Heel then poured a sticky liquid on Reynolds' head which ran down his face. He jumped about as if being scalded before realising that it was only lukewarm. Some of it congealed on his lips. It tasted sickly sweet. Orange Cord took a plastic bucket out of his holdall. He jettissoned the contents into the air. Reynolds flinched. White stuff came flying out and then dispersed over him as if in slow motion. Hundreds of tiny white feathers stuck to the black liquid in his hair and on his face.

Yellow Glove held up a white piece of cardboard so that he could read the inscription. 'ACO REYNOLDS – PRISON ABUSER'.

Yellow Glove looped it around his neck and, for good measure, tacked it onto his jumper with a staple gun. Reynolds jerked in pain each time a staple went through his clothes and into the skin but the bloody gag that had been reinserted into his mouth prevented him from crying out.

Orange Cord produced a Polaroid camera, and Back Heel and Yellow Glove posed for a photograph with their arms around Reynolds. Yellow Glove shouted into his face, 'Darren deserved a little respect.' Yellow Glove rifled through Reynolds' pockets. He took the cash and scattered everything else on the ground. He stamped down hard on the remote control and it broke into smithereens. He poured the rest of the liquid over the roof of the car.

He walked over to Reynolds, pulled up his balaclava and shouted, 'Take a good look at that, fuckface. It's the last thing you'll never see.'

Orange Cord and Back Heel ran in behind bushes and re-emerged moments later on motorbikes. Yellow Glove got up on one of the bikes as a pillion passenger. Reynolds saw that he rested his shoes on the twin exhausts. The air was filled with the noise of the motorbikes going up in gear as they gathered speed before everything went very quiet.

Reynolds felt the tar congealing in his hair, and saw it hardening on the metallic surface of his new car. He'd been tarred and feathered. The Provos did it to informers or on girls that went off with British soldiers. He'd been made an example of because of the way he'd treated Darren Cassidy. The photograph would appear in the *Sunday World* under a headline ostensibly condemning the culprits as animals. But everybody would know the real reason that it'd been published was so that readers could get off on his private moment of hell. And there'd be plenty within the service, his own colleagues, who'd say he'd asked for it.

Reynolds looked up and down the street, hesitantly at first, as if unsure that his embarrassment outweighed the need to get help. His tongue moved into what felt like large crevices where his teeth had been. He tried to move forward and felt a stabbing pain in his testicles. There was something terribly wrong down there. He could tell that his face was all puffed up and that it would hurt a lot more as the day went on. He ran his tongue along the sharp, serrated edge of a broken tooth just to make sure he was not dreaming.

His attention was drawn to an upstairs bedroom of the house across the road. He didn't know the names of the people who lived there. They'd kept very much to themselves since they'd arrived. He saw a boy looking out at him. The expression on his face was a mixture of pity and curiosity. He opened the window and shouted down, 'Are you alright?'

Reynolds burst into tears.

twenty-two

Roche was putting the finishing touches to a fry-up when the phone rang. It was Superintendent Pat Flannery. It had to be something big to have Flannery on the blower on a Sunday morning. And it was: a prison officer named ACO Reynolds had been brutally assaulted. He'd been singled out, apparently, for the way he'd been allegedly ill-treating prisoners.

Flannery was apoplectic. It reached a crescendo when it got to the part of how a group calling itself the Prisoners' Revenge Force had released a statement to the media admitting responsibility for the attack and a Polaroid photograph of Reynolds tarred and feathered. 'The minister,' he concluded, 'has gone ballistic. I've been summoned to his house to personally brief him. What the fuck am I going to tell him?'

'Christy Clarke, sir,' Roche replied in response.

'What? I don't believe it. Not his style. He doesn't have a political bone in his body.'

He briefed Flannery on the row Reynolds had had with the Cassidys at the hospital, on the meeting between Clarke and the Provos on the balcony on the night of the wake. How he'd heard a whisper that Clarke was doing some bit of business with the Provos.

He neglected to tell him that Daly had as good as tipped him off that Clarke was going to do something with the Provos and that this was it on the basis that it wasn't going to improve the mood. He realised that he'd made a mistake in shooting the whole thing down without giving it proper consideration.

'Criminals know there is a line. Clarke has crossed it and you're to bring him to heel. Do it cleanly too.'

Roche smiled: he'd skip the ice-cold bath routine then.

'What's your take on this Prisoners' Revenge Force then?' Flannery asked.

'The Cassidys are a big Republican family. They weren't happy to let this pass. But the IRA knows it'll bring down a lot of heat the day they start attacking prison officers down here. Not only that – the action would take away attention from the hunger strikers. My guess is that the leadership have essentially subcontracted the job out to Clarke and a couple of his yobbos. They're using the PRF as a moniker.'

Flannery considered his analysis. It seemed to calm him.

'What have we got?' Roche asked.

'A statement from the PRF. A copy of a Polaroid shot of Reynolds in all his glory. The forensic boys are down there as we speak.'

'Reynolds?'

'A basket case. He's lost one testicle and they are doing emergency surgery on the remaining one. He saw nothing of any consequence. I wouldn't be counting on anything from him.'

'So, what's next?'

'Set up an incident room. Devise a method of reigning in Clarke. Handpick your own team. Anything you need for the investigation by way of resources or additional manpower, you've got it. And above all else go and get some convictions.' With that, he hung up.

Roche ate his breakfast and went into the box room that doubled as a study. He took out a pen and paper and made a few notes. Who had done this and why wasn't in issue. It was what he called a back to front case. You started at the end, the result, and worked backwards.

The aim now was to connect Clarke to the crime. He listed off the possible avenues of investigation – motorbikes (if and when found), a search of Clarke's flat (first light tomorrow when he'd have a better idea what he was looking for), witnesses who might have seen the bikes in transit and lastly a bit of lady luck.

He headed straight out to the crime scene. He moseyed around. The tar on the roof of Reynolds' car had set solid. There were still tiny feathers floating around in the air. The bits of the remote control were scattered along the ground. The orange cord lying on the ground where it had fallen after a neighbour had cut him free. There were spots of blood on the ground beside the telegraph pole to which he'd been tied.

On the face of it Roche had learned nothing that he wouldn't have adequately gleaned from the written forensic report or police photographs. But it gave him a feel for the scene that no report or photograph could ever get across.

Dr Jim Fahy, the head of the Forensic Laboratory, approached him and bowed in feigned respect. 'At your service, sergeant.'

Clearly, Flannery had phoned him too. He chatted away to him, small talk, for a few minutes. It was worthwhile establishing a rapport with the forensic boys. That way he became privy to small stuff that didn't make its way into the report but still added to his overall understanding of the case.

'We're going to do a raid on Clarke first thing tomorrow. I need a couple of you guys to come along.'

'Sure, not a problem.'

'Anything of interest so far?' Roche asked.

'We've synthetic fibres, probably from balaclavas, orange nylon from a rope, a bloody piece of cloth, a piece of tooth that apppears to contain streaks of shoe polish under magnification, a damaged remote control, goose feathers, tar that looks to be pretty bog-standard to be honest, and other bits and pieces.'

'Bugger-all, in other words.'

'Well, without suitable comparators to hand, it's hard to say what significance if any these things have. We'll know more when we get a better look at it back at the lab. But I'm not optimistic.'

A squad car pulled up alongside them and the observer alighted from the vehicle and handed him a piece of paper. He immediately recognised it by its serrated edges as an official garda telex. It read: 'Boy witnessed attack from vantage point of bedroom window and has information that may be of assistance. Please interview immediately.' It was signed Superintendent Pat Flannery.

twenty-three

The moment Christy walked in his Ma let a roar. 'And what time do you call this?'

Wayne wished she hadn't.

His Da ignored her. He sat down in his chair, the one by the window, and started to read the *Sunday World*. He went straight to the back pages to read the Liverpool match report. She moved over and stood in front of him, her right foot slightly bent and stroking it off the ground, a bit like a bull getting ready to charge. Except it was really more like a Jack Russell squaring up to a rhino.

All morning the tension had been silently building. Pots were banged. She flung the box of matches down on the table whenever she lit up a cigarette. She stood with her back against the kitchen sink, her smoking arm nestling by its elbow in her other hand which was folded across her midriff. She'd badgered Wayne over and over about what Christy had said to him in the pub the previous evening and whether Wayne had overheard him talking to anyone about his plans. Wayne had sneaked a look into her bedroom. His Da's side of the bed hadn't been slept on.

The last time he'd stayed out she'd thrown a kettle of boiling water at him and scalded his arm. Wayne was sure he'd kill her. He'd been amazed when his Da had put his arms around her and tried to calm her down. She told him to fuck off and scalded him a second time. There was punching and screaming then. Unsurprisingly, she'd come off worst. She'd a big black eye and heavy bruising all down her arm. Instead of going to ground, like she usually did, she had strutted around the block making sure everyone got a chance to see. The ground rules were being rewritten.

His Da hadn't liked that one bit. He went on a tear. He had looked really rough when he came back. But he'd promised, a hundred times over, that he wouldn't do it again, had begged for forgiveness. No one had ever seen Christy pleading for a second chance. He'd come home every night since then, no matter how drunk, or how late. Until this morning.

'Well?' Her hands were on her hips now.

'Ask no questions, tell no lies.'

'I'm asking.'

'What you don't know, can't tell.'

That was the code that his Da used when he was out on a job and it was usually enough to close down any further line of inquiry. Not anymore.

She reached down and pulled the newspaper out of his hands. Wayne winced. His Da used to say that when a dog is eating, there is an invisible arc around its mouth that, once breached, provokes an immediate involuntary snap. In an instant he'd grabbed her by the wrists, pulled her down towards him and began tapping her ankles with the instep of his feet until she lost her balance and fell onto her knees.

She bit hard into the calf of his leg. He pulled her hair so hard Wayne saw tufts on the ground. The pair of them were shouting and roaring.

'Fuck off, woman!'

'Where were yah?'

'What part of "fuck off" do you not understand?'

'The part that says I am entitled to know what floozy you're screwing.'

His Da stood up and walked across the living room, yanking her by her ankles. Her face was getting carpet burn.

'You don't fuckin' ask me anything. *Capisce?*'

Their breathing, for different reasons, was quick and loud.

'I'm going to let you up. If there's one word I'm going to do yah! Understand?' He was the one roaring now.

She went straight at him. Thankfully, she didn't land a single blow. To Wayne's relief Christy grabbed up his paper and took off. He slammed the door after him. Wayne noticed tiny white feathers blowing around on the floor. He must have been betting on a cockfight and lost bad.

Same old, same old – or was it? This wasn't the middle of the night. Da wasn't drunk. Ma was the attacker. Selling his stuff at the pawn was bringing the war to him. Putting the ferret into his pigeon loft was just the sort of thing his Da would have dreamt up to knock someone right off his stride. She was playing his Da at his own game. And getting results.

Wayne got her a glass of water and her tablets. She was sitting on the ground staring ahead, tears running down her face. After a while she opened the bottle and poured herself a handful. She gulped them down with the water.

Wayne sat down beside her. She turned her face in to the wall.

'Are yah alright, Ma?' He kept asking over and over but she ignored him. He put his fingers through hers. Eventually she stopped crying but her breath would quiver every now and again.

'He's gone, Ma. Maybe he won't come back this time. We're better off without him if you ask me.' She squeezed his hand.

twenty-four

The father of the boy showed Roche into the living room. The boy's name was Larry Cummins. The woman of the house brought in a pot of tea and a plate of milk chocolate Goldgrain. They exchanged a few short pleasantries and got down to business.

Roche pulled out a document and put it in front of the boy.

'Read it,' he advised. 'Do you see that bit there?' Roche pointed to the typed warning that appeared in bold. 'That means that if you don't tell the truth, you can be prosecuted.'

His Dad picked up the paper, read it and muttered something about being treated like criminals. Roche didn't respond. He wanted this done by the book. The father handed the paper back to him.

'We're only trying to help. Do we need a solicitor?'

'I am so sorry,' Roche replied.

What the hell had got into him? He'd close down good lines of enquiry if he weren't careful. But this was Christy Clarke. And how many times had he seen a good witness undermined by cross-examination picking up on minor mistakes? All stuff that was perfectly avoidable. Clarke would be using Denis Wise, and Wise could be relied upon to ruthlessly exploit any shortcoming in an account.

'I've been over the top. The truth is that we badly need every bit of help we can get. I'm only putting a bit of pressure on him to make sure he only tells us what he can stand over. It protects him in the end.'

The man thought about it for a few seconds, and then nodded.

'Now, son, in your own words, without any direction from me, tell me what you saw,' Roche said. There was no way he was going to direct the account of the witness, as such. On the other hand, he decided to let the boy have a dry run at setting out his recollection before he wrote anything down. If there were obvious creases he'd iron them out before putting pen to paper.

The level of detail he gave was impressive. But Roche's mouth practically dropped open when it got to the part where he described how the gang leader showed his face to Reynolds.

'Give me that again.'

'The man, the one who seemed to be in charge, he was going through his pockets taking his money, then he pulled up his balaclava and shouted, "Take a good look at that, fuckface. It's the last thing you'll never see."'

The local gardaí had briefed Roche upon arrival. Reynolds had been in shock and was being attended to by the ambulance crew at the scene when they'd arrived. Reynolds nonetheless had given an outline narrative of events. He'd been asked whether he had any clue as to who'd done it and he'd said no.

Roche had no doubt that Reynolds knew the reason he was being attacked was over Darren Cassidy. He also had no doubt that Reynolds knew Christy Clarke and that Clarke was thick with the Cassidys. Reynolds hadn't even mentioned the bit about the main man lifting up his balaclava. It was all very odd.

'His mate was revving the bike and shouting "hurry up". Your man ran to the bike and jumped on the back. He put his shoes down on the exhaust pipes and not the footrests. It sped off then.'

'Any idea what kind of bike it was?'

'Yeah. It was a big bike, a Kawasaki 350cc.'

'How come you know your bikes that well? This isn't a time to be showing off, you know? Your whole story will be undermined if this goes to court and you're wrong about something like that.'

'I couldn't tell one bike from another by looking if that's what you mean. But I saw the name written on the side of the petrol tank.'

'Really? Sure?'

'I'm sure.'

'Anything else?'

'The registration plate was yellow. It had an IRL sticker on it like it had been out of the country.'

Roche clarified a few more details before getting the boy to take it from the top again. He wrote it all down in longhand, pausing only to clarify minor bits. He read it back and asked the boy did he want to make any changes. He corrected the reference to the Audi car being new, he thought it looked new, and the tar being hot. Reynolds had jumped about when it was poured over him and he had just presumed that was the reason. The more it went on, the more Roche liked the boy.

Larry signed each page individually and initialled the changes. His Dad countersigned as the responsible adult. There was nothing in the statement that actually identified the attackers. But if the boy was correct, and Roche believed him, there was a good chance that Reynolds knew who had attacked him, or at a minimum ought to be in a position to give a very good description of him. The detail on the bike was a strong lead. The investigation was moving on at a pace. He felt a surge of excitement as he walked down the driveway.

twenty-five

The priest was to have been his next port of call. There was something about the way he'd reacted when he and Harrington had door-stepped him coming out of the flats on the night of Marie Cassidy's wake. He was happy enough that the priest hadn't done anything wrong. He was far too priggish to be a Provo hush puppy. He hadn't been the least bit fazed when they'd stopped him. But the cop in him had sensed Fr Brendan's discomfort when they'd mentioned that they had seen him chatting to the group of men on the balcony.

But that'd have to wait. He needed to put to Reynolds the boy's claim about the attacker showing his face. He'd phoned the hospital and spoken to the doctor who was treating him. He'd said that there was no way that Reynolds was up to being interviewed. Roche decided to call out anyway. This was too important to let it lie. It appeared that Reynolds was in denial. The longer he had to get comfortable with that, the less likely it would be that he'd talk.

Clarke was undoubtedly the leader of this bunch of malcontented psychopaths. The bit about him pulling up the balaclava seemed far-fetched. But yet it was a detail that he was sure the boy hadn't made up either. Clarke always took such elaborate steps to insulate himself from the crime. This was not in keeping with his profile.

But the fallout from the attack on his pigeons showed that maybe Christy had gone a bit soft. A few years ago he'd have bitten his tongue, bided his time, found out who'd done it and exacted some horribly spectacular revenge. Instead, he was openly going around beating people up. The reality was that being a career criminal was even harder than being a career cop. A guard had colleagues, supports and the law behind him. Most criminals imploded eventually.

At the hospital, the doctor stonily reiterated what he had already told him over the phone.

'Officer Reynolds is resting after surgery and is not up to being interviewed.'

'I'm not asking him to make a statement today or anything like it,' Roche said. 'It's more just to update him on the investigation. As the victim of such an appalling crime he's entitled to that.'

'It can wait till the morning.'

'Besides, Officer Reynolds may have important information. It's in everybody's interests that we get to hear about it.'

Roche could see the doctor was wavering.

'Let me go and talk to him,' he replied.

The doctor popped his head around the door.

'You've got five minutes.'

Reynolds was groggy, morphined out of it, but chatty.

'On my first day on the job I was afraid of my shadow. But I developed a swagger. Some officers took a live-and-let-live approach and then were surprised when the prisoners ending up running the jail. I set boundaries. In my experience everybody was happier when they knew where they were. I was the youngest Assistant Chief Officer ever and some said someone with my zeal would go all the way to Governor.'

He wasn't making a whole lot of sense and his speech was slurred. The loss of his front teeth meant that he couldn't pronounce words properly. A whistle noise came out of his mouth when he said the word 'shadow'. He couldn't pronounce the word 'the' or 'zeal' properly either. He sounded like a right pompous prick. Maybe it was the meds.

'I don't doubt that,' Roche said approvingly. 'Who is to say it's not still going to happen? Giving evidence against the perpetrator would be a big help to us – wouldn't do you any harm in the promotion stakes either.'

Reynolds looked at him with something approaching open contempt, but to Roche's relief he continued talking.

'I'd just finished a week of nights, and felt someone walking up behind me. A yellow-gloved hand shot over my shoulder and covered my mouth, and that was followed almost immediately by a searing pain rushing from my groin. The pain intensified so quickly that I'd have given anything to pass out. The gagging hand meant that I couldn't even get release by screaming.'

Roche nodded appreciatively, making no attempt to hide his disgust. Reynolds wanted to tell the story. This was encouraging.

'Bunch of bastards!' he threw in for good measure.

'I was gripped by fear and panic even. Fear as to what might happen next. Panic that I'd never have sex again. Yellow Glove was shouting: "Cut his prick off."'

Reynolds gestured down the bed towards his private parts, his pained and resigned expression conveying that he'd been at least partially successful.

'Their casual orderly viciousness left me in no doubt they were capable of actually doing it. The action would be performed in seconds, the cutter holding it up like a trophy, before throwing it onto my immaculately manicured front lawn.'

Roche marvelled at Reynolds' ability, even stoned out of his head, to describe the event like it had happened with such eloquence.

'Then one started back-heeling me in the balls. Do you know that was a relief? Yellow Glove was no longer holding my balls in a nutcracker. Someone stamped on my mouth. I started to swallow bits of teeth and I was sure I was going to die. They hung the placard around my neck and took photos. I knew then I was being punished for not allowing Darren Cassidy free rein in the hospital.' There'd be plenty of officers in the jail who'd say he'd been asking for it.

His voice was breaking now. Reynolds was brimming with resentment. Roche told him what the boy had told him about the leader of the gang lifting up his balaclava.

'Did that happen?'

Reynolds nodded.

'And?'

'And what?'

'Did you know who it was?'

'I won't be identifying him in court if that's what you mean.'

'You know who it is then?'

Reynolds didn't answer.

Roche was appalled. 'If you don't stand up to whoever did this, who's going to be next? Sure, we're all fucked if the perpetrator is allowed to get away with this.'

'I'm the one missing a testicle. I am in the newspaper. There is no "we".'

'Look. I've got a statement from one of your neighbours. He saw the whole thing, including the man in charge lifting up his balaclava and showing you his face. He'd back you up a hundred per cent. It wouldn't just be your word against his. You've got to do this. Got to give that evidence in court.'

He decided not to say for the moment that the statement was from a twelve-year-old boy.

'That won't be happening.'

'You'll feel differently when you get back to work. This is a big event. You'll be glad that you have faced up to it, met it head on. Prison officers are the same as guards when it comes down to it. You want to see this man locked up as much as we do.'

'Right now, I don't want to go back. I had pride in the job once. I couldn't face going back there right now.'

'Well,' said Roche, his frustration showing, 'what do you think it'll be like when you do go back and there's whispers that you didn't do your duty?'

'The Prison Officers' Association will look after my interests if it comes down to that.'

Reynolds was right of course. The POA would bring the prison to a standstill if there were even the slightest hint of victimisation.

'Look, you know exactly who it was that pulled up his balaclava. I know you know it. I know you know that I know it. By the time the case comes to court the whole world is gonna know it. Will you at least think about it?'

Reynolds shook his head and looked away.

'Are there any circumstances under which you'll make a statement?'

'Yes.'

Roche perked up. 'What are they?'

'When Christy Clarke is in a box.'

twenty-six

Fr Brendan watched the news with increasing incredulity. The attack on ACO Reynolds was the lead item. A reporter was doing his piece to camera in front of the entrance of an A&E. He said that Reynolds was in a ward under armed guard, adding that RTÉ had been requested by gardaí not to name the hospital. He'd spent the day in surgery and his position was described as serious but stable.

He then read from a statement issued on behalf of a previously unheard of organisation, the Prisoners' Revenge Force. It claimed that Reynolds had been punished for humiliating and degrading a prisoner who had been brought to hospital to visit his dying mother. The spokesperson added that the group reserved the right to take further action against other officers who did not treat prisoners with appropriate respect.

The minister for justice, Jim Mitchell, was interviewed standing in his front garden. 'Cowards!' he began. 'It's perverse to say that they carried out this vile and vindictive act in the name of protecting prisoners. It's an attack against common decency. I have already allocated additional resources to An Garda Síochána to ensure that these lowlife criminals will be met with the full rigours of the law, and in the end will be handed down a condign punishment.'

The thought that anything he had said on the balcony that night might have even been influential, if not actually decisive, in targeting Reynolds made him queasy. It was like waking up to find out that the handbrake on his car had slipped during the night and crippled someone crossing the road at the bottom of the hill. That was how directly he felt tied into what had happened.

The reporter quoted garda sources as saying that it was suspected that the Provisional IRA had sanctioned the attack and had worked with criminal elements to carry it out. 'Christy-bloody-Clarke!' he said aloud.

His first thought was that Detective Sergeant Roche had observed him conversing with Clarke and the so-called head of the IRA on the night of Marie Cassidy's removal. If Clarke was charged – clearly he had been hired by the IRA to do their dirty work – could Roche force Fr Brendan to give evidence against him?

There was nothing to indicate that Wayne had spoken to anybody about what had happened in the sacristy. But if he were a witness against his father, all of that could easily change. Christy's legal team would almost certainly put out an alert for any information about Fr Brendan that might be used to undermine his credibility. He had no doubt that touching up his boy would comfortably come under that heading.

The potential ramifications were truly awful. A garda investigation into such allegations would surely follow. He might very well end up on trial himself. And if he was convicted – it'd be Wayne's word against his, but with Wayne having the edge that went with telling the truth – he'd go to jail.

Fr Peter would no doubt tell everybody he'd instinctively known something was wrong. He felt the shame of it descend upon him as if it had already happened. He was also coming to the fore in the pro-life amendment campaign. He was doing interviews. His picture had appeared on the front page of the *Irish*

Times last week. He'd become the story. The press would have a field day.

How could he have been so stupid?

The Polaroid snap depicting Reynolds tarred and feathered flashed up on the screen. The reporter was saying something about how the viciousness of the attack had taken even hardened members of the criminal confraternity by surprise.

The embarrassment and humiliation on Reynolds' face spoke for itself. Strange, he thought, that even in that moment of terror the ego was still asserting itself, smarting at the prospect of being shown to the world in this way. Fr Brendan understood: the thought of being exposed as a child molester and his subsequent fall from grace frightened him more than actually going to jail.

Roche was bound to come knocking on his door. Telling him to take a hike wasn't practical. He knew the protocol for situations like this from the summer he'd spent working in the Diocesan office in the Archbishop's palace: a formal request for a statement through the Archbishop would be submitted. His superiors would expect him to co-operate and if necessary direct him to make a statement and appear as a witness. They wouldn't understand his reticence.

There were times when there was a fork in the road and it was easy to know which were the paths of right and wrong. He knew in his heart that the duty he owed to Reynolds ought to transcend his own personal difficulties. He was conflicted. Wasn't stepping up to the mark what principle and morality were about? Any priest worth his salt would get immediately onto Roche to help him with his enquiries, regardless of the consequences. And yet all he could think of was saving his own skin.

He could dither and prevaricate and feel bad about it. Beat himself up about not doing the right thing. Tantalise himself with guilt. Endlessly worry that he wasn't cut out to be a priest. But that wasn't going to change anything. He'd already decided that he wasn't going to do the right thing. There was theory and practice, academia and the world he actually lived in. Realistically, honesty wasn't always the best policy. Sometimes the price was just too high.

twenty-seven

Roche watched the item and sighed. He was all in favour of free speech. But the information here was of more interest to Christy Clarke than anyone else. The public might have a prurient interest in Reynolds fighting to save his testicle, but there was no public interest in feeding into what was voyeurism.

Reporters had been ringing the station all day, looking for a quote, on or off the record, and information about the crime that they assured him they'd only refer to as coming from a reliable source. There were plenty of colleagues who'd have been happy to facilitate. The fact that their names featured prominently in a laudatory way elsewhere in the reports was usually a giveaway.

He'd quickly tired of it and given a direction that all calls without exception were to be referred to the Garda Press Office. A reporter from the *Evening Herald* was parked outside his house when he got home. Roche had politely told him to fuck off.

The minister had lost no time in leaking his garda briefing on the case. Over the next week he'd be constantly on the airwaves vowing to crack down on subversives and crush the PRF out of existence. The usual windy rhetoric. In private, the minister would be busting the commissioner's fat ass. The commissioner busted ass downwards, in the first instance as far as Flannery, from where it continued its descent through the ranks until it reached someone who could actually do something about it, in this case him.

The minister's hysteria was only partially explained by the depravity of the attack. When it came right down to it, the Provos were politically motivated, and, although politicians would never publicly acknowledge it, that acted as its own restraint. The real worry was that this self-styled PRF might act as an umbrella under which the criminal dregs could unite in an organised structure, controlled by the Provos. Today, it was a prison officer or a member of An Garda Siochána. Tomorrow it could be a judge or, heaven forbid, even a politician. The powers that be had immediately recognised the attack for what it was – a direct challenge to the establishment – and that was what had given the story legs. It could take years of agitation to secure lifesaving equipment for a hospital operating theatre. But once a politician's unerring sense of self-preservation was threatened you'd invariably find that they'd move pretty damn fast.

He consoled himself with the thought that at least Clarke wasn't watching any of it. Clarke was getting pissed in his local, the sort of pub where TV was strictly rationed to sport. He was sitting up at the bar alone, drinking glasses of stout and half ones.

Why was Clarke on his own, he wondered? Was he reflecting? And if so, how effective would the whiskey be in numbing the experience of crushing Reynolds' balls in a nutcracker? Assuming Clarke had it in him to contemplate what it was like for the victims of his crimes.

That wasn't a safe assumption. Clarke was a thug. He used violence as a means to stamp his authority on those around him. If you weren't with him, you were against him. He'd snaffle an opponent's turf before they were cold. He just wasn't the sentimental type.

And yet, tempting as it was to think of Clarke as a psychopath devoid of feeling for any living thing that wasn't a good racing pigeon, he knew that wasn't the full story.

Word had it that in his day Clarke had been good at bringing on talent in the local boxing club. He was slow to take anyone into his firm. But if he did, he was generous with his knowledge, gave fellas their head and made sure their families were looked after if they did time. On one level he was only looking after his own interests, lessening the chances that one of his own would grass him up. But there were plenty in his position who wouldn't bother. It was one of the reasons that he was hero-worshipped within the confraternity.

He'd been sent to Daingean industrial school when he was twelve for stealing crisps from the Tayto factory. The Christian Brothers had treated the boys there with appalling brutality and some had used them for sexual gratification. Clarke had always maintained the treatment he'd received there had turned him into a criminal. Self-serving nonsense.

Roche didn't doubt that he'd been damaged. He'd been struck over the years by the number of vicious criminals who'd been physically and sexually abused as children. Lots of child abusers had themselves been touched up or worse as kids. It was a strange pattern. You'd have thought they'd be the last people to lay a hand on anyone.

Born into a different background, it might have been different. His ruthlessness and natural acumen for working out who was vulnerable and where the loose brick was would have served him well in business.

The papers would be full of it in the morning. He'd knock down Clarke's door long before he'd get a chance to read any of them. The publicity had upped the ante. That wasn't serving a useful purpose.

On the contrary: it'd only galvanise Reynolds into not cooperating. Still, maybe the saturation coverage might loosen the young priest's tongue. Picking up on him had been a good break. You made your own luck in this business, but in his experience the sort of coincidences that involved the priest and the boy were usually a good sign for the investigation as a whole.

twenty-eight

Roche walked into the incident room and took his place at the top table. Dr Fahy sat down beside him. It was unusual to have anyone from forensics sit in on a briefing. But forensics was at the heart of this case and he wanted to impress this upon his team from the outset.

Around the room fellas were sitting on chairs waiting expectantly. Wally Drennan was leaning against the wall smoking a fag, looking bored.

He'd spent a good part of yesterday handpicking his investigation team. He'd gone for a mixture of youth and experience. He needed a few young guards who'd wear out shoe leather chasing up all the leads that inevitably went nowhere but still had to be followed even for elimination purposes. It'd paid dividends already. One of the rookies had spotted a motorbike abandoned down by the canal half a mile from the flats where Clarke lived. It matched the bike described by the boy right down to the IRL sticker.

The chances of Clarke actually saying anything during interview were remote in the extreme. But Roche had still spent ages coming up with names of lads who were good listeners and who had the knack for knowing how and when someone might be in the mood to say something. He wasn't expecting a confession or anything. But who was to say that Clarke wouldn't say something, offer an explanation about some aspect of the case that they could prove was a lie? These were the things that gave a case an edge. You just never knew.

Everyone he'd canvassed had jumped at the chance to get on board. It was a measure of his own standing among the men that many had given up family holidays and then got out of bed for a six o'clock briefing. That wasn't the only reason, of course This was a great case – the sort that could make or break a career. His own especially. There'd be plenty of members with their noses out of joint. More senior colleagues who felt they should have got the call. Others who'd be surprised that Flannery had passed the case to him of all people and would decide that he'd only got it because it was a hospital pass.

He thought of the remark passed by ACO Reynolds that there'd be some in the job who would revel in his misery. Roche understood. There'd be some in the force who'd quietly cheer if he made a bollocks of it. And it'd all unfold under the glare of the spotlight. He wasn't fazed. The thoroughness of the investigation was the best way to manage a case. It insulated you against harm too.

'Morning, men!'

There was a grumpy murmur of acknowledgement from a couple of bodies.

'ACO Reynolds has been the subject of a brutal assault and will be scarred for life. The minister for justice has a bee in his bonnet about this group calling itself the Prisoners' Revenge Force. He wants us to nip this in the bud, to detect, prosecute and convict those responsible. He expects results. So do I for that matter. We're going to do this right.

'Christy Clarke and his gang are the suspects with a little help from the Provos. We're hoping that we can make a forensic connection between him and the crime scene.'

There were snorts of derision from around the room. Even though there was nothing these men wouldn't do for him, Roche prided himself on the fact there wasn't a yes man among them. That was the reason he'd picked them. Roche waited a few moments for the ripple of discontent to subside. His opening salvo would have an important influence on how subsequent events unfolded. He needed to keep morale up.

'We all know Clarke plans everything to the nth degree. But drink and his sense of self-importance are getting the better of him. He's fallen for his own publicity.'

Some of the men visibly perked up at the notion that Clarke was on the back foot.

'Clarke is losing it. He pulled up his balaclava and showed his face to Reynolds.'

'Well why are we here then? Charge him.' Wally Drennan wasn't a man to hold back.

'Even though ACO Reynolds has already lost one testicle it is too early to say that he has no balls. But for now, he is scared shitless. He has a wife and family. That's perfectly understandable. He isn't ready to ID Clarke in court. I don't think that's going to change any time soon. So we have to do this another way.'

He gestured to Dr Fahy with his thumb.

'What we have got Jim?'

'Two leads. A kid saw one of the attackers stamp on the remote control device for Reynolds' car. This man was driven away on a motorbike. The boy identified the bike as a wine-coloured twin exhaust Kawasaki 350cc, yellow coloured rear number plates and an IRL sticker on it. Yesterday a virtually identical bike – we're happy it's the same one – right down to the sticker was found abandoned down by the canal not far from where Clarke lives. The boy says that the pillion passenger rested his feet, not on the footrests, but on the twin exhausts. We found rubber residues on both exhausts of the abandoned bike.'

'Thanks, Jim.' Roche said. He let the men think about Dr Fahy's words for a few moments before moving on. He stood up and held out a search warrant directed at the home of Christy Clarke.

'In short, we're looking for a pair of shoes on which the soles are melted and that is a match for the residues on the exhaust.'

There was another murmur now, this time in perfect unison, and it was one of approval. There was a buzz. You could feel it. The ball was in play. Clarke was vulnerable and the time had come to go after him. Roche headed for the yard where the unmarked patrol cars were parked and in no time three cars left in convoy to travel the short distance to the flats.

twenty-nine

Fr Brendan stood at the door of the Georgian offices in front of the law firm's brass plate.

He'd spent the night tossing and turning, running the permutations of what might follow from his talk with Christy and the Provos. It was obvious now that the conversation was an important step along a journey that had culminated in the attack on Reynolds. Seamus Cassidy had escorted him down to the group, made the introductions and skedaddled. What happened after that was on a need-to-know basis. He was as sure as he could be that everyone on the balcony was fully aware why he was being interrogated.

He wasn't a lawyer but he was happy enough in his own mind that he was in the clear. He hadn't done anything wrong, much less committed an offence. There was no way he could have been expected to anticipate that they'd been planning to launch an attack upon Reynolds. He'd assumed that they were asking out of concern for the family.

But that wasn't the end of it. He was also fairly sure that the conversation was evidence of a conspiracy between the men to cause grievous bodily harm to Reynolds even if he wasn't part of it. This had all sorts of ramifications and Roche might descend on him at any moment.

Roche would be well capable of putting the frighteners on him by suggesting that he ought to have known that they were up to no good. And that while he didn't want to unnecessarily alarm a man of the cloth it was always so much better to be a witness than a suspect. His next move would be to demand that he tell the gardaí exactly what the man who was on the IRA Army Council had been saying to him, and just how much attention Christy Clarke had been paying to the discussion. That wasn't going to happen.

He'd phoned Harry McGovern, the Diocesan solicitor, at around midnight and told him there was a matter on which he needed a steer. He'd had lots of dealings with Harry during the time he'd worked in the Archbishop's secretariat. In addition to being discreet, McGovern was highly intuitive in his dealings and that's what marked him out as someone to talk to in a matter as delicate as this. Nor was he someone who told you what you wanted to hear. McGovern was assiduous in ensuring that he could stand over his advice. He'd readily agreed to see Fr Brendan first thing. When Fr Brendan said that it was pressing, McGovern obligingly moved the meeting forward to 7.30 a.m., no questions asked.

McGovern ushered him into his office without ceremony. The floor to ceiling shelves of leather-bound law reports, the tidy expanse of the partners' desk and the Turkish rugs on the stained mahogany parquet flooring were all reassuring in an understated way. Harry fussed around, shuffling some papers on his desk before getting down to business.

'So, Father, give me the lowdown and we'll take it from there.'

Fr Brendan had said nothing to him about the purpose of the meeting, but it was clear McGovern had already worked that it wasn't about a stolen church poor box, that he might be in some kind of personal trouble.

Fr Brendan had thought a lot about what he could say. This was a damage limitation exercise. But he had to be careful. He didn't want the advice to blow up in his face, or compromise his relationship with an admission that would embarrass the firm providing representation. At the same time he needed to give enough information for the lawyer to formulate his advice. How often had Harry told him, when he'd sought advice on behalf of the Archbishop about some recalcitrant cleric that was rapidly becoming an embarrassment, that he needed the bare bones before he'd be in a position to deal with it? 'Garbage in, garbage out' was his constant refrain.

Fr Brendan began, 'While ministering to a dying patient, I interceded on behalf of the family in an argument that broke out. Later I was asked for my views on the conduct of one of the individuals involved. This, in turn, has unfortunately led to another dispute. It has escalated quite seriously now. It's being investigated by the gardaí. I apprehend that I may be asked to make a statement.'

He paused for a moment to let the solicitor complete his attendance note and then added, 'Where do I stand?'

'Is making a statement a problem?' McGovern asked.

'Well I'd prefer not to, if you know what I mean,' Fr Brendan replied. 'I will if I have to, I suppose. The whole thing has got out of hand. It's all a bit, how can I put it . . .'

He hesitated, searching for the right word.

McGovern had put down his pen now, as if to reassure him that he could speak frankly.

'Sordid' seemed the appropriate word to describe the latest turn of events, but he was afraid such a description might only whet McGovern's appetite further than was necessary. McGovern was full of empathy but part of him seemed to relish the discomfort Fr Brendan was feeling, as if he was an errant little boy who had got up to mischief and needed to be rescued. He'd be poking and prodding for detail that Fr Brendan didn't want to give in no time.

'The whole thing is a bit, ahem, embarrassing, actually.'

'You say that a family row broke out when you were administering to a parishioner who was dying, is that right?'

He hadn't said anything about the row being confined to the family, but decided not to draw this to McGovern's attention. He merely nodded.

'So you were acting in your capacity as priest?'

Again, Fr Brendan nodded. 'There's no doubt that my interceding was in my role as a priest. None.'

'And the subsequent conversation in which you were asked for your opinion? Were you acting in your capacity as a priest then?'

It was clear to Fr Brendan that the wrong answer would seriously inhibit the advice that McGovern could give. Equally, there was no point in framing his instructions in such a way just to get the correct response. That would be a purely short-term gain. This was no time to be coy. McGovern might be called upon to stand over the advice down the line. It'd be useless if the factual plinth upon which the advice was furnished couldn't stand up to scrutiny.

'Well, no, not exactly. That came after the event. I was at the removal. And I was taken aside and asked about what had happened during the row.'

'I see. Were the persons who approached you talking to you in confidence?'

'Well it was certainly all done very discreetly.'

'Did you think that you were free to discuss what had been said with others?'

'No, not at all. I'd have regarded it as a breach of trust.'

He reckoned that if he'd disclosed the conversation to anyone, the only thing that would have saved him from being kneecapped was his clerical collar. But he didn't believe that McGovern needed to know this to determine the issue.

'How strong is the connection between this discussion at the removal and the argument that had occurred earlier? Can they be separated out do you think?'

'Well that's very much in the eye of beholder, you know. You could argue it either way, I suppose. They're closely connected in time and context.'

'Did both discussions arise out of the same incident?'

'Yes, I believe so.' He could just about answer yes to that – it was certainly true in a literal sense.

'Well, in those circumstances, you would be entitled to claim that the conversation took place on an occasion of sacerdotal privilege and you are barred from discussing it.'

Fr Brendan was relieved but taken aback.

'Really? I mean it wasn't like it was confession or anything.'

'It doesn't matter,' the solicitor replied. 'The leading case is *Cook v Carroll*. It emphasises that the privilege goes way beyond the confessional. It covers any discussions between priests and their flock which are of a pastoral nature and which are confidential in nature.'

It seemed too good to be true.

'And the gardaí will accept that? This guard, Sergeant Roche, he's a very persistent fellow.'

'The gardaí have no choice. If Roche or any of his superiors have a problem, refer them on to me and I'll deal with him on your behalf. It's as simple as that.'

thirty

Wayne awoke to the sound of pounding on the front door and men shouting, 'Armed gardaí! Open up!' He got up and looked out the window. On the balcony below, a man was smashing the front door with a sledgehammer. He was wearing a yellow tabard with 'GARDA' emblazoned across it. Sergeant Roche was standing beside him. His Da must have been very full last night to be sleeping through it.

Others around the guard were similarly attired. Two stood on either side of the door, both hands around pistols, pointing skyward, ready to pivot around when the door opened to take aim at anyone in their line of sight. One made eye contact with him but said nothing. Wayne saw another toting a submachine gun. They were all bulked out by bulletproof vests.

Whatever it was that his Da had not done this time must have been pretty serious. His Da said the cocking of weapons was to psych themselves up. Everyone knew the idea that his Da would ever have any kind of a weapon here was daft. No, this posse was strictly for show.

Behind them stood two others who were wearing what looked like paper spacesuits. They didn't have any guns. Instead, they carried small black attaché cases. His Da hated forensic fellas. A mate of his was put away for murder on fibre evidence found on the clothes in which he'd been arrested that connected him to the carpet in the home of the deceased. It couldn't have happened, according to his Da, as Charlie had burnt all his clothes immediately after the job. He was fairly sure that it was the cops who'd rubbed his clothes off the carpet after they had confiscated them on his arrest.

He heard his Ma running down the stairs shouting, 'Give over! I'm coming.' The guard with the sledgehammer grinned and swung harder. The lock gave way and the door flew open.

The sound of several heavy sets of footsteps pounding up the stairs echoed around the flat. He could hear change rattling around the pockets of one of them. He got out of bed and pulled his door back just enough to be able to peep through.

On the landing it was the same drill. A man stood on either side of the door with his gun pointing upward. A third kicked the door open and ran in with his firearm drawn. The two others pivoted around, giving him cover. This was always the most dangerous moment. Would his Da lose it and charge them? Would some cop full of adrenalin use it as a chance to plug him?

'Get up yah lazy bastard.' Wayne saw bedclothes through his' Da's half-open door.

'Where's your warrant?' he heard his Da shouting.

Wayne heard the sound of scrunching paper. 'Blow your fuckin' snot in that,' the copper shouted back.

There was a loud thud and a grunt as Christy hit the ground.

'Me fuckin' head, yah cunt yah!' Christy roared.

They dragged him across the landing. An ashtray was caught under his back. Wayne dashed out of his room, bent down and pulled it free. A pair of them roared at him to get the fuck away.

They each held one of his Da's legs up high to make sure that his head impacted off each step with maximum force. By now, his Da had regained his composure. Not one sound or word was emitted through his gritted teeth.

At the bottom of the stairs, the two guards held his legs aloft like fishermen with a trophy catch. His Da was puffing and panting trying to get his breath back. Roche put his foot on his chest and speaking in his thick lilting Kerry accent said, 'You're an evil man, Christy Clarke.'

Funnily enough, Wayne thought, that was just what his Da always said about Roche whenever he told the story about Flannery and Roche ducking him in the ice bath.

'Take a good look around. The next time you see this room you're going to be walking with a stick.'

His Granddad was the only person Wayne knew who'd used a stick, and he was eighty-one when he died. Da was forty-two.

'Fuck off, cunt,' Christy replied and then shouted at Lillian, 'Ring Myles. Get a doctor to the station.'

'Solicitors and doctors, is it? Them are for civilised people. It's a fucking vet you need, and if he was here now, I'd have him do us all a favour and put you down.'

'I've done nothin'!'

Wayne marvelled how whenever Da said the word 'nothing', he always crammed the sound with such righteous indignation.

One of the spacesuits appeared on the landing. He held up a transparent plastic exhibit bag containing shoes. Roche tapped his foot down on Christy's chest and gestured with his eyes for him to look upstairs. Spacesuit shook the bag and gave Roche the thumbs up.

'The melted remnants on the exhaust of the abandoned bike? I'm betting that it came from the soles of those shoes all right. And we've found minute fragments of plastic which look to me like a very good match for Reynolds' remote control.'

Roche pressed his foot down on his Da's chest, harder this time, causing Christy to involuntarily grunt.

'Book him!'

thirty-one

Christy Clarke strutted down the corridor from his cell to the interview room, flanked on each side by a couple of uniformed guards.

The investigation to establish that Clarke had inflicted grievous bodily harm on ACO Reynolds was in full swing. He'd been arrested under section 30 of the Offences Against the State Act on suspicion of committing malicious damage to the remote control of Reynolds' vehicle. It wasn't as ridiculous as it sounded. There was no basis upon which a person could be detained for questioning for offences like rape, murder and assault. Instead the gardaí had to rely on an act passed in 1939 to suppress the IRA and which allowed for suspects to be questioned about certain types of offences – IRA membership, possession of firearms, withholding information about such offences and, for reasons no one could quite fathom, malicious damage.

Roche had once detained a suspect in a murder investigation on the basis that pages from a book that he'd clocked his victim over the head with had scattered around the floor and amounted to an act of malicious damage. You had to work with the law as best as you could, was his experience.

Clarke sat down on the seat provided and crossed his arms and legs.

'Did you get a bit of grub, Christy?' Detective Garda Harrington asked. 'Is there anything else you want? A cup of tea?'

Wally Drennan stared at Clarke and muttered something about Clarke being the devil's spawn, the bit that'd run down his mammy's leg. Clarke didn't acknowledge any of them.

'Alright, Christy,' Roche began. 'I will formally reintroduce us for the record. I am Detective Sergeant Roche, and these are my colleagues Detective Sergeant Drennan and Detective Garda Harrington. It's 16.38 and we're in interview room number two. I am now going to give you the legal caution. You are not obliged to say anything, but anything you do say, will be taken down and may be given in evidence. Do you understand that?'

Clarke yawned.

'Do you know why you've been arrested?'

Clarke fidgeted with his nails and looked out the window.

Roche asked the questions. Harrington kept a record. The necessity to write everything down in longhand slowed everything up.

'ACO Reynolds was brutally attacked by three men outside his home. We believe that you were the leader of this gang. Do you have anything to say to us?'

Clarke didn't answer.

'It looks bad, Christy. The bikes used by the attackers were stolen. We found a Kawasaki 350cc abandoned down the road from your flat. And we have a positive ID that it was the one used on the job. Is there anything you can tell us which would explain how the bike got there?'

Clarke didn't answer.

'Do you think that it's just a coincidence that a bike used in the attack was found so close to where you live?'

Clarke didn't answer.

'Christy, there were rubber residues found on the twin exhausts of the motorbike. Have you any idea how they got there?'

Clarke didn't answer.

'Would you agree with me that the rubber on the exhausts is consistent with someone resting their shoes on them while the bike is moving?'

Clarke didn't answer.

'I have to inform you that both the residues on the exhaust and the soles of your shoes which we took from your bedroom while searching your house earlier this morning have now been examined at the forensic science laboratory. Would you like me to outline their findings?'

Clarke didn't answer.

'The rubber on the soles of your shoes was compared with the rubber residues found on the exhaust. Their chemical composition matched in every material respect. Is that another coincidence, do you think? Can you explain it?'

Clarke didn't answer.

'If there is an innocent explanation for any of this, will you volunteer it now so that you can be eliminated from our inquiries?'

Clarke didn't answer.

'We also found minute fragments of plastic in the heel of your left shoe. These match the remote control belonging to the victim of this crime, ACO Reynolds. Can you explain this please?'

Clarke didn't answer.

'There is a witness who'll say that one of the attackers, a pillion passenger, stamped on the remote control and rested his feet on the twin exhausts. What do you think of that?'

Clarke didn't answer.

'Where were you at seven o'clock last Sunday morning? If you can prove your whereabouts it may be the end of the matter.'

Clarke didn't answer.

'A forensic scientist has also found tiny strands of goose feathers encased in sticky tar deposits on the soles of your shoes. What do you say to that?'

Clarke didn't answer.

'Christy, the prison officer was tarred and feathered during the attack. This doesn't look good. Is there anything you want to say?'

Clarke didn't answer.

'The forensic laboratory has also found head hairs probably belonging to a gang member who attacked ACO Reynolds. We have taken a hair sample from you. Do you think the hairs will match?'

Clarke hummed softly to himself.

And on it went. Roche put the questions. Harrington noted after each one: 'Nothing to say.'

At the commencement of the first interview, Clarke had produced a sheet of paper that had been prepared by Myles Sweeney, his solicitor, which read *I am innocent. I have committed no crime. I have no information that can assist your investigation. On the advice of my solicitor I am exercising my right not to answer any questions.*

This was day two, interview seven. Not one question had produced a single response. Clarke had so far stuck doggedly to the script.

thirty-two

Roche chaired a conference with the detectives in the incident room. As the meeting reached its conclusion, he noticed that the atmosphere was gloomy. The custody part of the investigation wasn't going very well. Interviewing was always going to be a gamble. It wasn't that no-comment interviews were a draw; Clarke was getting information about the investigation in the questions. He'd parse, analyse and react accordingly.

Ultimately, if Clarke were charged he'd be served with a book of evidence that would set out the whole case against him well in advance of the trial. But the worry was that they were disclosing too much too early. It increased the opportunities for Clarke to get at people. That meant the boy. He'd instructed the interviewers not to identify the boy under any circumstances and instead to concentrate on the forensics, on the basis that test results couldn't be got at the same way as an eyewitness.

More interviews were scheduled but it was not anticipated that they'd go any differently. He sensed that some of the men had no faith in the strategy and were critical of him for having pursued it in the first place. He wound up the conference with a direction to continue on in the same way.

Time was marching on. He made his way on foot to the presbytery. He'd decided to take a break from the station and see what he could shake out of the priest.

Mrs Hendricks opened the presbytery door and greeted him effusively.

'You've come at a bad time, Sergeant. Fr Griffin is out on a message.'

'Actually it's the curate, Fr Brendan Walsh, I was looking to see.'

'Well come in and I'll fetch him up for you.'

She left him in the study saying that that she'd wet a pot of tea.

He craned his neck to see what was on the desk. He saw a letter of recommendation the priest had written to a school of music on behalf of Wayne Clarke, putting him forward for a scholarship. He referred to the boy having a prodigious talent. The image of Wayne dashing out from his bedroom in his jocks to pull the ashtray from under his father while the guards had been effing and blinding him was an unsettling one. It was funny to think of him playing the piano, or the priest advocating entry into an exclusive college for him. Was he getting long in the tooth, only able to see people as caricatures? He hoped not.

Roche immediately stood up when Fr Brendan entered. He didn't want to be talking up to the priest. The two of them shook hands. He noted that the priest had a firm handshake. There was still something stilted in his posture. The offer of tea had evaporated. Something wasn't right. He was sure of it. He decided to take the initiative and go in with the studs up.

'Good afternoon, Father. You've no doubt heard about the very brutal attack on Officer Reynolds. His assailants castrated him. I understand that you can help us with our inquiries.'

'You are misinformed, Sergeant. I know nothing about this unfortunate incident, other than what I've heard on the radio or read in the papers.'

Roche heard the antagonism in his voice and decided to match it.

'Come now. Wasn't there a scene at the hospital when Darren was brought down by ACO Reynolds from the prison to say goodbye to Marie?'

'I wouldn't describe it as a scene, no. The prison service has to ensure that prisoners are properly chaperoned even on an occasion like that. There was a bit of tension, but it was resolved quickly enough when Officer Reynolds agreed to remove the handcuffs for the duration of the visit.'

'Really?' Roche asked, making no effort to mask his incredulity. 'Our information is that the cuffs were taken off and reattached in the presence of his dying mother and both she and the family were very upset about that. And understandably so, if I may say.'

'Well, it wasn't ideal. I'll give you that. Marie was dying and that's where people's thoughts lay. That was the priority.'

'And what about your little chat at the removal? What did the IRA say to you?'

'Isn't that a bit like asking when I stopped beating my wife?'

'I'd like to know what was discussed, please. I've no doubt that it has an important bearing on my investigation. I take it you have no objection to telling me, or should I put in a formal request higher up the line?'

'That won't be necessary. I perfectly understand why you're here. I even anticipated it and got advice on the matter.'

'Advice? You got advice? Why? Surely you haven't committed a crime.'

'You must understand, Sergeant, a priest cannot disclose every conversation he has with his parishioners.'

'They were at confession, were they?' Roche replied, unable to keep the sarcasm out of his voice. Every time he opened his mouth he knew he was playing into the priest's hands, driving whatever chance he had of salvaging the situation further out of his grasp.

145

But his anger was getting the better of him and he couldn't stop himself.

'Look, you may not know this. Sacerdotal privilege extends much further than the confession box. I'm bound to respect things said to me in a wide range of circumstances. I'm simply prohibited from discussing them with anybody, no matter what the circumstances. But let me assure you, Sergeant, for your own peace of mind, no one asked me to do anything illegal. No one so much as hinted that they were going to commit any crime.'

Roche could barely contain himself. It was one thing for a scumbag like Clarke to exercise his right to silence – he was a suspect – but quite another for a respectable person, a priest at that, who ought to be assisting him in every possible way.

'Father, I've no doubt that you are telling me the literal truth. Tell me what was said and by whom. Christy Clarke is down in the station as we speak. I am imploring you to help. If we don't have enough evidence he'll walk. Do you follow me?'

'I do. But I wonder, have you listened at all to what I've said?'

Roche realised now why he'd got so angry, why he'd handled it so badly. He'd underestimated him. This priest was as cute as two pet foxes, no two ways about it. He was smarting because he'd been out-thought. He'd made a grievous error in allowing Fr Brendan time to get organised.

Roche raised his hand in an entreating manner, the anger climbing back up his throat.

'Oh, I hear you alright – loud and clear. You're invoking some dubious privilege to avoid personal embarrassment. That's what my gut is telling me.'

The priest said nothing. Roche sought to press home his silence.

'Is it Clarke? Are you afraid of him? Have you been got at? We can provide protection, look after your security. Is that it?'

'Good day to you, Sergeant. I've nothing further to say. If you have any further queries I suggest that you take them up with Harry McGovern, the Diocesan solicitor. Now, I have some other important matters to which I must attend. Please excuse me.'

The priest held the the living room door open to indicate that the meeting was over. He saw the sergeant out. The front door had already been quietly closed over by the time Roche had reached the bottom step.

thirty-three

Back at the station there was at least some positive development. The Director of Public Prosecutions had directed that Christy Clarke be charged with causing grievous bodily harm to ACO Reynolds. A cheer reverberated around the station when Roche announced the news. The younger detectives punched the air and exchanged high-fives.

Roche brought Clarke down from his cell and had him stand in the middle of the incident room. He got Detective Garda Harrington to read out the charge to Clarke in front of his team of detectives and then asked Clarke did he have anything to say.

'Not guilty, stitched up, I know nothing about it,' Clarke emphatically replied. There were loud derisory jeers from the guards and shouts of 'yah boyah'. Some booed him. Nothing was going to upset the bonhomie. Here was a bit of history in the making. Roche wrote down what Clarke had said beside the charge. It would be read out in court at his trial. He offered him the chance to sign it but he declined.

'OK, Christy, that's the formalities completed. We're off to a special sitting of the District Court. Myles Sweeney, your solicitor, has been notified. We'll be opposing bail. And tomorrow, you, the hitherto anonymous thug, will be on the front page of every newspaper in the country.'

Roche then leaned over and spoke softly into his ear. 'Of course, our attitude to bail might soften if you wanted to help me out with a few things. It's hard for a man of your age to be going to jail tonight knowing that you won't see the inside of a pub again until the next millennium.'

Clarke hated the police. But he was at a point when he might hate jail more. Jail was a young man's game. It was like drinking. At a certain point most men eased up. It was too much hassle. It took a lot of discipline to be a criminal in for the long haul. Most of them didn't have it. That was why they'd become criminals in the first place. There really wasn't much honour among thieves. Jimmy Daly was a classic example. When it came right down to it, people looked after number one.

Roche didn't really think that Clarke was for turning but sure what of it? Winding Christy up was its own entertainment.

Clarke cleared his throat, looked downward to the floor and hocked onto Roche's shoe. Sticky green saliva landed squarely on his toecap. Roche calmly rubbed his shoe on the back of Clarke's leg. It was a moment. Every guard looked on grinning. This too, in another way, was a moment to savour. There'd be stories told down the line how the boss and Christy Clarke had squared off to each other with Dick Roche flicking him away like a minor irritation.

Clarke spat again, this time into Roche's face. Roche hit him a dig in the stomach.

Clarke doubled over, fell down and rolled around theatrically roaring, 'I've been assaulted! I want to make a complaint against this man!' over and over. The detectives and uniformed gardaí who had gathered to witness a spectacle started to mill around doing tasks as if the pair of them were invisible

Roche pulled Clarke up off the ground by the back of his shirt. He could feel the dead weight of him as he clutched his stomach, writhing in mock agony. He frogmarched him out to the yard where there was a convoy of cars waiting.

He spoke to the two young guards assigned to drive him and the prisoner to court.

'There's a change of plan. We'll travel separately. Bring him in the back entrance.' He saw the disappointment on their faces. But he wasn't going to gift Clarke the opportunity to appear on the nine o'clock news shouting that he was a victim of garda brutality.

The Bridewell Courthouse was a venerable court building. Chiselled into the masonry were the words '*Fiat justitia ruat caelum*', which every guard knew meant 'Let justice be done though the heavens fall' by the time they passed out of Templemore.

Roche felt a knot in his stomach. The one thing his time had taught him in the force was that justice was a very subjective thing. It was often in short supply in a courtroom, particularly one presided over by Judge Mahony. He was always just on the edge of being tetchy and liked to stir the shit.

Guards from stations around the city had gathered to watch a man they universally despised get his medicine. The press benches were crammed. As head of the investigation, it ought to have fallen to Roche to give evidence of arrest, charge and caution before the judge. It was only formal evidence, but as it would be the only thing the media could report about the case it would have guaranteed his name in lights. At the very last moment Roche handed the mantle over to Detective Garda Harrington. Harrington rattled off the evidence low-key, knowing what was coming. They all did.

Myles Sweeney, Clarke's solicitor, rose to cross-examine.

'Were you present when Christopher Clarke was charged?'

'Yes, I was.'

'I'm told that he was charged in the incident room before the full complement of the investigation team. Is that right?'

'I'm not sure that everybody was there, but yes.'

'Did you see Sergeant Roche speak to Christopher Clarke?'

'No, other than just prior to the reading over of the charge.'

'Did you see or hear him speak to my client immediately after that was done?'

'No.'

'Did you see anything happen?'

'No.'

'Heard nothing, saw nothing, said nothing, is that it?'

Harrington stared straight ahead. Sweeney paused for effect, swivelling around the courtroom before his gaze settled back onto the witness.

'Is there any reason why Sergeant Roche, who is the man in charge of this investigation, is not giving this evidence?'

'No. None that I know of.'

Roche winced. The quite unnecessary tail on his answer made the whole answer sound dodgy.

'Hmm,' Sweeney replied. 'Would it be anything to do with the fact that Sergeant Roche assaulted Christopher Clarke?'

'Certainly not,' Harrington replied.

Several questions followed about the size of the incident room, the view and the number of people present.

'You were there, for the whole thing, and a number of your colleagues were too. But it comes down to this. No one saw Sergeant Roche punch Christopher Clarke in the stomach, is that it?'

'I didn't see anyone punch him,' Harrington replied.

'My impression is that if I called everybody present, guard after guard would say they saw nothing. Am I right do you think?'

'I can only answer for myself,' Harrington said.

The cross-examination only lasted a few minutes but Sweeney made the most of it. How could it happen, he kept asking rhetorically, that a man could be clocked in a station full of gardaí and no one noticed? Sweeney then addressed the court in his most funereal voice:

'Judge, my client is alleging that he has been beaten up by Sergeant Dick Roche. This type of allegation is regrettably all too common, and difficult to either prove or disprove. However, Mr Clarke informs me that the attack took place in the incident room that was full of gardaí. If he was assaulted, it is therefore impossible that they all could have missed it. I am asking the Court to direct an inquiry.'

'You know very well, Mr Sweeney, that I have no such power. That's a matter for your client to take up with the Garda Complaints Commission. That's what they are there for.'

The judge looked out over his glasses and stared ostentatiously at the press bench.

'However, I will order that your client be physically examined upon admission into Mountjoy and that his own doctor is to be admitted into the jail tomorrow morning to examine your client if he so wishes. I will also direct that any medical reports be placed on the court file.'

The atmosphere back in the station was muted. Everyone gathered around the battered old portable TV in the incident room that someone had rigged up to watch news and sport. RTÉ led with the charging of Christy Clarke. But any euphoria was quickly dampened by the prominence given to Clarke's allegations of ill treatment.

Roche watched in silent mortification.

Had he snatched defeat from the jaws of victory?

Roche knew the men – his men – were disgusted that he'd allowed Clarke to manipulate him. His delay in approaching the priest had allowed him to come up with the sacerdotal privilege bullshit. He'd rushed his fences with Reynolds. His surefootedness appeared to have deserted him – he was more like a bull in a china shop. He ought to have seen these things coming, but he'd been too busy counting his chickens.

It'd been a long day and he felt a wave of tiredness sweep over him.

Part Three

The Trial of Christy Clarke

thirty-four

The Portakabin was packed as usual, teeming with snotty-nosed kids and pasty-faced women smoking fags. The usual suspects week in, week out. Until the sentence was served. More often than not, they'd be back a few months later, acknowledging the other familiar faces with a cheery but weary nod.

The Portakabin was supposed to have been temporary. The first time Wayne had come here he'd been in a buggy. Back then, his Da used to tell him that he was working as a brickie on a top-secret project, and that he wasn't allowed leave until the building was completed. Wayne worked out the real story, the same way he had worked out so many other things, by listening to his Ma in the kitchen talking to the women from the block while they drank tea and smoked.

The floors were pockmarked with thousands of neat round burns from people stamping out their cigarettes. Random black scuff lines running in haphazard directions broke up the grey of the walls. In winter, convection heaters sucked out every drop of moisture in the air. Twin fluorescent lights recessed behind metal grilles gave off a bright light, but it was artificial and cheerless.

Above the door someone had written: 'PRF 1 Screws 0'. 'Reynolds is a bollocks'. Someone had then scribbled out the 's' on account of him having only one testicle.

His Da hadn't actually done too many sentences. Six months here and there. Stupid rows, mostly with cops, after closing time. Some men could do time standing on their heads. Not Christy Clarke. He was too much of an anarchic free spirit to accommodate the routine of rote.

His trial was starting next week. It'd been eighteen months since his arrest. Not being convicted meant there was hope. But it was doing his head in not knowing his fate.

Harry and Liam had been caught red-handed robbing the payroll at the tyre factory the week after his Da was arrested. There'd been a huge falling out. They'd practically accused his Da of grassing them up. His Da had been very hurt. They'd pleaded guilty and were serving fourteen years each. On the outside the three of them had been inseparable, and now, confined by the prison walls, they didn't even talk.

He came here with his Ma every Wednesday and Saturday, barring the time after the shouting match over Sharon Wilson's fortieth birthday party.

'Party?' his Da had shouted at her, the veins on his neck protruding like drain pipes. 'Are you having a laugh?'

The idea of his Ma having a night out, enjoying the craic, when other men might be sniffing around, was too much for him. She didn't hold his outburst against him. She understood the way certain men got jealous about their women when they were locked up. She'd quite happily not have gone to the party if it meant peace and quiet.

It was the shouting and roaring that she was a tart and a slag, making a show of her in front of everyone, that was the problem. She stopped visiting him as punishment.

After three weeks, the Governor had called in person down to the flat and begged her to give him a visit. Christy, he said, was making everyone's life a misery. The only reason that she'd relented had been because she appreciated how big an ask it was for the Governor, taking into account the crime his Da was supposed to have committed.

A screw came in with their docket pinned to his board and called out their names. They joined a queue outside the big riveted arched door of the jail itself. Visits always involved plenty of waiting and getting in line. Nobody complained – nobody dared: that was sure to slow the whole process down even more.

It was more like the entrance to a medieval castle than a prison. Another screw opened a small door within the big door and admitted them into a large porch area. Wayne watched their reflection set into the dull sheen of a large aluminium sheet that was affixed to the roof. It was the screws' way of checking that prisoners weren't escaping on top of a supply truck leaving the jail.

Directly in front of them was a second gate, made from thick steel bars that ran from ceiling to floor. The brass lock was as big as a paperback book. Its surface was smooth and shiny, worn by over a century of daily polishing. They had to wait until the front door through which they had entered was locked before the screw was allowed open the inner gate. It was a strict rule that you couldn't have two gates in a prison unlocked at the same time.

They walked a few steps across the yard to the visiting area. They sat down at one of several long tables and waited. A six-inch piece of wood ran lengthways up the middle and acted as a barrier between prisoner and visitor. A sign warned that passing contraband was an offence and would be prosecuted. Screws sat at each end as monitors.

Christy came in, sat down, folded his arms and immediately began talking. 'Denis Wise can't do my case. He's double-booked. Defending a Provo in the bomb factory case.'

'Jaysus, who else is gonna do it?' his Ma gasped.

'No one – or at least no one that's any good.'

'There must be someone else free. What about Hugh Hartigan, Willie Russell, Ger Canning?' she asked.

'They're all tied up. Solicitor says he's briefing some young fella, Paul Rooney.'

Wayne knew all the leading defence counsel in the same way other boys knew the names of all the well-known soccer players. He'd never heard of Rooney.

'Who?' Lillian asked.

'Exactly. Some chinless fuckin' wonder. The only fuckin' thing standing between me and twenty years.'

He went very quiet on them. Wayne was taken aback. His Da wasn't a man to countenance defeat on a setback. Normally he'd greet Lillian with a list the length of your arm of things that Lillian had to get Myles, the solicitor, to do. Myles would take the list and read it before putting it down on the desk and asking his Ma how she was getting on. There'd never be any mention of the things on the list again by him or his Da.

It always raised their spirits even though they knew it was mostly bollocks. But there was no fighting talk today. Instead, his Da sat in front of them, keeping his arms folded, barely answering yes and no to everything. The closer he'd got to this trial, the more his Da seemed resigned to just take whatever was coming. That was new. In his experience his Da fought everybody every inch of the way. Giving up wasn't in his repertoire.

As the visit came to a close his Ma leaned over and kissed his Da on the lips. He knew from listening to Nuala Kelly and Gracie Lawlor gabbing over tea in the kitchen that his Ma was passing him over a bit of hash with her tongue. The prison was awash with gear – heroin, speed and benzos were popular, but his Da hated all that stuff. He drew the line at a bit of hash. His Ma always joked with the women that she got more affection out of him when he was in jail.

Wayne looked down at the floor. He didn't like to see her giving him a wear. It wasn't just because he found it creepy. He didn't understand how she could do it after everything he'd done to her.

There was always a risk that a prisoner could be strip-searched after a visit but in his Da's case that was purely theoretical. It wasn't just down to the attack on Reynolds or fear of retribution from the PRF. After the row over Sharon Wilson's party, his Da had wrecked his cell and took out the three prison officers sent in to restrain him.

When they got up to go, his Da ran his hand lightly through Wayne's hair and hugged him over the barrier in a boisterous way. 'Look after her, Wayne, right?' And he was gone. Never even acknowledged his Ma. Wayne watched him exit the visiting room without looking back. He could never understand, for a man that was supposed to be so bright, how incredibly stupid and selfish his Da could be. It'd cost him nothing to make a bit of a fuss over her. But he never did. And then he wondered why she was so cranky with him all the time.

thirty-five

Tonight was Tuesday, which meant that it must be Ballinasloe. The community hall was full, the audience sitting expectantly in row upon row of red plastic seats with skinny metal legs. It was run down, like so many other venues they'd used on their incredible journey. The damp had caused the plaster to peel in places right down to the wooden lattices. The light from bare bulbs was too bright to create an ambience. But Fr Brendan still drew them in. His reputation was preceding him.

Mornings, there were walkabouts in the shopping centres in the major towns; afternoons they canvassed the bigger housing estates. At night they attended rallies. This was Fr Brendan's favourite part of the day – hustings old style; they were truly interactive and punctuated by the odd worthwhile piece of rhetoric.

Cora ran an extension lead round the dais so that she could plug in the three-bar fire. Fr Brendan had laughed the first time she'd produced it. He wasn't laughing now. He'd discovered that he could put up with just about anything the campaign could throw at him except the cold.

Pictures drawn by local school kids adorned the walls. The one he liked most was of two men loading up a lorry owned by a well-known cosmetic company, with bags marked 'Handle with care – baby product'. The vehicle was parked outside a building called

'Quik N Easy Termination Clinic'. In the corner a man was handing over a big bag of cash to the clinic's owner. The clean simple lines of the drawings, and the matt finishes of the acrylic crayons, were far more effective than the expensive glossy posters of the pro-choice campaign.

Cora assumed her position in the chair flanked by the local Fianna Fáil TD and councillors. A red 8' x 6' banner proclaiming 'Choice is Murder – Vote Yes!' hung from the rafters. She had spent hours stitching the words in black lettering. At the back of the hall, pro-choice supporters had unfurled a banner: 'Keep your rosaries off our ovaries'.

Cora warmed up the crowd, pumping up the volume, with pointed references to the liberal intelligentsia in Dublin 4. Fr Brendan walked up to the podium and straightaway began speaking.

'A woman gives birth after a long and difficult labour. Over the previous nine months she had worried that her baby would be healthy. Her sister, a midwife, told her some women cried at the first hint of discomfort. She worried that she might let herself down. Needlessly! The enormity of the task had acted as its own pain barrier.'

The couple in the front row were writing copious notes. They were Shinners. He remembered them from Aughrim, Ballybay and Dundalk, where they had made rambling political speeches dressed up as questions.

Post hunger strike, Danny Morrison, the Sinn Féin Director of Publicity, had asked, 'Who will object if the IRA take power with an armalite in one hand and the ballot box in the other?' The phrase had resonated and, along with Liam Cosgrave's reference to 'mongrel foxes' and Garret FitzGerald's description of Haughey's 'flawed pedigree', had immediately entered the political lexicon. Now the Shinners were everywhere!

'Once, she didn't do little people. Not even nephews and nieces. But something happens. The cord has been cut, the bloody torso of her infant son cleaned down. A nurse has wrapped the newborn in swaddling clothes and placed him in her arms. At that precise moment she is overcome, not by exhaustion, but by love. In her relationship with her husband, she quite naturally expects to be treated as an equal and with respect. That's a given. But this love is unconditional. Until the day she dies. And, through thick and thin, that love will be effortless. How do I know this?'

The Sinn Féin woman shot him a demonic look. She clearly questions his entitlement, as a man, as a celibate, as someone with his own agenda, to speak with any authority on this subject.

'Because I met her last week and she told me this. She also told me how her son Stephen had brought her more happiness than she could have ever believed possible. He died last year, aged twenty-four. He was Down syndrome. She told me that the family's grief was offset a thousand times by the huge joy that he brought into all their lives. She made me promise to spread the word and I intend to honour that promise.'

The Shinners had downed pens.

'She also told me that she knew, and always had known, that her own parents loved her. But knowing and understanding, she said, is not the same thing. And it was only at Stephen's birth that she had properly understood it.'

Fr Brendan pointed to the child's drawing of the abortion clinic.

'When will the pro-choice stalwarts understand? Not any time soon I think. Last year, more than 3,900 women made the lonely journey to England to abort their babies. Pro-choice wants to increase the numbers. But only, they say, because they want babies to grow up in the right atmosphere. They bleat about a society which produces only wanted babies. Try telling that to the couples who are waiting years to adopt!

'Stephen's mother worries, as I do, as you must also, that if this amendment is not carried, others like Stephen may never see the light of day. Instead they will be hoovered out of the womb into plastic bags and sold to some cosmetics company.'

'Of course, some babies will be born into broken homes and reared in an atmosphere of dysfunctionality. And it is very likely that some of these children as adults will perpetuate that cycle; it will manifest in alcohol or drug abuse, violence, serious crime and other anti-social behaviour. Others, admittedly a tiny number, will grow up to be the next George Best, or Gay Byrne. The majority will grow up to be parents, doing what comes naturally, striving to make the life of the next generation that much easier than it was for them. And who would begrudge them?

'*The Irish Times* excoriates us daily for insisting on a referendum that it describes as unnecessary and divisive. But it's the men from D'Olier St – and despite what the *sisters* in the feminist movement say, they are nearly all men – who are out of touch. Even those who don't support the amendment, or are unsure, want to talk about it.

'I am pro-choice. I believe in the right to grow up and to make a hames of your life. That itself is a choice, one that is personal to the individual. The entitlement and opportunity to make that choice does not belong to a mother or father, social services or even government.

'I recognise, of course, the society which those pro-abortionists want. All the babies have blond hair and blue eyes. It's very liberal but only up to the point that you agree with them. Thereafter it is totalitarian, and ironically has at its heart the very intolerance they accuse my Church of practising.

'Change the Constitution. Protect our unborn. God bless.'

People stood up to applaud. It was always hard to say if the tipping point would be reached where the urge to stand among the remaining people seated would become almost involuntary. Fr Brendan gathered up his notes and saluted them. More and more people rose, clapping loudly. The photographers below the rostrum clicked furiously. He was in the zone, on song, tonight.

thirty-six

Roche picked up the bible and held it aloft. 'I swear by almighty God that the evidence I give shall be the truth, the whole truth and nothing but the truth.' He reamed it off with all the assurance of someone performing a well-practised ritual. Swearing the oath was the formulaic precursor to giving evidence against the accused. Usually it never failed to give him a lift.

But this was different: today, he was giving evidence before the Garda Complaints Commission into an allegation that he'd assaulted Christy Clarke. Today he was going to dishonour the oath. He was going to lie and lie. It felt bad already. What would it feel like later?

With impeccable timing, the case had been listed a couple of days before Clarke's trial. Coincidence? He detected the hand of Superintendent Flannery at work; he wanted the decks cleared before the criminal case came on for hearing.

Flannery had come to see him soon after Clarke's allegations of being beaten up had featured on the RTÉ news report. Dropped into his office like it was a casual chat. He was there, he said, as a courtesy given how long they went back, to let him know that he was appointing an inspector to investigate matters. 'I want to let you know, Dick,' he had said, 'if any mud sticks to your shoe you're on your own.'

There was any number of inspectors who could have been relied upon to conduct a perfectly adequate investigation that wouldn't ruffle a single feather. But Flannery hadn't appointed one of them. Instead he had nominated Liddy. Dour and exacting, he seemed to take an almost special pleasure in putting a colleague on the rack. The thinking behind his appointment was clear: top brass was insulating itself against fallout. Flannery actually harboured ambitions of getting to the Park. Any fool could see that he wasn't Commissioner material. But he was reformed now and applied himself with all the vigour of the true zealot.

Earlier in his evidence, Clarke had doggedly insisted that he'd been punched in the stomach. He hadn't helped his case by omitting the fact that he'd spat on Roche's shoe and then in his face. Roche's counsel had done a good job discrediting Clarke and highlighting him for the reptile that he was.

The doctor who had examined Clarke on admission into Mountjoy found lots of bruises. But several gardaí had given evidence as to how Clarke had been unruly on arrest, kicking and screaming, and had to be restrained. There had been seventeen members and one officer who had been looking on when the incident occurred. Dickie Harrison and Charlie Boyd were the only turncoats. Harrison had the grace to concede under cross-examination that he might've misinterpreted Roche's defensive action against further spitting as a punch. Boyd wouldn't budge. Previously, Roche had vetoed his application to transfer to the detective division. Twice. He'd thought Boyd lacked bottle. He'd got that part wrong. Maybe he'd have to take a different view on his next application, assuming, that is, he was still a member then himself.

'I had just charged him and we were getting ready to go to court,' Roche began. 'Clarke spat on my shoe, and then in my face. I stepped back, but at the same time I pushed him away. It was just a reflex action. I thought he was going to spit again or worse. The next thing he was rolling around the ground claiming that he'd been assaulted.'

Liddy, whose job it was to prosecute the case, stuck it into him but Roche held the line. Being unpleasant didn't make him an effective advocate. The chairman of the panel asked him to comment on Clarke's claim that he had punched him into the stomach ('absolutely not') and the suggestions made by his colleague Garda Harrison that he'd lashed out ('he's mistaken').

The chairman then asked him to withdraw while they considered the evidence.

He waited in the consultation room. Normally half a dozen colleagues and a senior officer there to give moral support would have flanked a man of his standing but he'd insisted on facing this hearing alone. A bad result and he'd be tainted, and he didn't want it projected onto others. He also couldn't bear the humiliation of having an adverse finding handed down to him in their presence.

What had happened with Clarke had occurred in the combat zone.

Clarke had been asking for it. And Roche had obliged. Man to man. Any guard or gouger worth his salt knew the rules. He'd known guards who had come off the worst with criminals, and got more than a bloody nose in some cases, but the unwritten rule was that what happened on the street stayed on the street.

In a perfect world he'd have put his hands up and taken his medicine. It wasn't easy to tell lies even when it was neceessary. It wasn't only his career and reputation at stake. Clarke's trial was about forensics, and to a lesser degree what the boy had to say. But putting the gardaí on trial was always a useful distraction. Clarke's legal team would use it to undermine the prosecution's case. Clarke might even end up walking. Who would thank him for that?

And yet, there was still no getting away from the fact that a hoodlum like Clarke had turned the lot of them into a bunch of liars. His experience working under Flannery had taught him that a little part of you died in the process.

An hour passed, then two, and then two and three-quarters.

This was far longer than was needed to find in his favour. He'd spent his entire working life doing cases. He was programmed to believe that the system was fair, or at least that it worked. What the hell was keeping them? It was an open and shut case. It was Clarke's word against his. The evidence was piss poor. Clarke was a scumbag, after all. How could someone like Clarke ever be believed over someone like him?

He readily saw the irony in expecting the commission to back him even when Clarke had given a true account of being assaulted. It sounded like he was being arrogant. He wasn't. You simply couldn't have the likes of Clarke trumping a policeman in the witness box in the absence of any independent confirmation of his story. That wasn't the way the real world worked.

Eventually the door opened and the clerk nodded to him, meaning that the board had reached its decision.

Judgment, as pronounced, was peremptory. 'The panel has closely examined the claim made by Christopher Clarke that he was punched in the stomach by Detective Sergeant Dick Roche. The allegation, it must be said, was firmly denied by Sergeant Roche. This conflict is at the heart of this complaint. We heard from over a dozen members who were on duty. Only one, Garda Boyd, offered any real support for the allegation. But it emerged on cross-examination that he did not have a clear line of sight, and the Commission was of the view that he had been mistaken in his assertion that he had seen Sergeant Roche punching Clarke.

'Christopher Clarke, on admission into Mountjoy, was examined by a doctor who noted a number of injuries on his person, including bruising and tenderness in his stomach. We find that this and other injuries are attributable to his arrest. We preferred the evidence of Sergeant Roche over that of Christopher Clarke on any point that is in conflict. The complaint is dismissed.'

Having the allegation hanging over him had been a huge strain. It was good to have this particular monkey off his back. But there was little or no sense of jubilation. Certain people seemed to be able to buck the system without fear of recrimination. The experience of lesser mortals, of which he was one, was that there were no free lunches. He just hoped that he wouldn't pay too high a price for it down the line.

thirty-seven

Wayne played the piece through. It was by some bleedin' Russian composer called Shostakovich. Ordinarily, Wayne didn't get classical music. But he had to admit that this clanging, brooding piece, otherwise known as Piano Concerto No. 2, was great to play. There was a bit in the middle that could pass for the Stranglers on a good day.

The pervert priest didn't dig pop music, and didn't play very well himself. He'd no talent for that end of things. But he understood very well how melody and harmony made a song work. It was one of the reasons why he was such a good teacher. He'd introduced Wayne to Bach, Brahms, Beethoven and a host of others.

Wayne was blossoming under his tutelage, and he'd flown through his Grade III pianoforte examination. The priest combined an ability to communicate ideas simply in terms Wayne could understand while encouraging, cajoling and even bullying him to play out of his comfort zone. He found himself responding no matter that he hated him.

The pervert priest never stopped going on to his Ma about the high hopes he had for Wayne. It sounded well and good. She certainly got off on it. But Wayne wasn't convinced that he didn't have an ulterior motive in making these reports, that it wasn't his way of keeping him prisoner.

Within a month of his Da going into prison and almost to the day after the court had refused him bail, the pervert priest had been at him again. Touching, groping, cuddling (the sickly sweet smell of the Polo mint he was sucking wafting under his nose), wanking (forcing his hand onto the priest's penis) in the first few months. After that he'd started buggering him. The fact that he was committing sin like this with a priest made it feel worse.

Child molesters were the lowest form of life. One day during a visit to his Da a prisoner had come into the visiting area to meet his wife. His Da spat out words of contempt for him and said he'd geld him if he got his hands on him. His Da would kill the pervert priest if he knew. He'd make sure it was a slow, painful death. Strangle the life out of him with his bare hands maybe, watching the tiny capillary veins in his face burst as the blood supply between neck and brain was trapped by the compression of his hands. That'd be too good for him. It made Wayne feel better just thinking about it.

The pervert priest leaned over Wayne's shoulder and pressed the rewind button on the tape machine. Lately, he had taken to recording the lesson, and then playing it back. At the end of the lesson Wayne took it home and played it on the Walkman that the priest had bought him for that purpose. Wayne saw the Walkman for what it was – a cool device designed to buy his silence. He'd no qualms taking full advantage of it. Meantime, anyone passing the music room hearing the music would assume that the lesson was in full swing. But what did they know?

The pervert priest placed his arm around Wayne's shoulder, ostensibly to guide his hands across the proper keys whenever he spotted an error. He stroked the top of his hand while talking, managing to make the action both absentminded and intimate.

With the speed which practice brings, the pervert then dropped his hand under Wayne's jumper and rubbed his tummy before moving down to open the top button of his jeans. Snakelike, his hand slithered into his underpants.

'No, please stop. Stop,' Wayne pleaded.

'Stop!' the priest said in a little girl's voice, mint wafting the air from his breath. 'Stop? I have something else in my hand right now that says different.'

It was true: no matter how hard he tried Wayne couldn't stop himself going hard. Even the thought of how disgusted he'd feel after the event wasn't enough.

Some days the pervert priest only wanted to pull him off. That was disgusting but still way better than the having to touch the wiry hair around the priest's prick. Wayne's hand always smelled sour afterwards. He'd put it up to his nose and start retching. He'd hurry the whole way home to wash his hands. Shostakovich, according to the pervert priest, had been obsessed with cleanliness his whole life. How come he felt so dirty then? Maybe they should take a good look at who his teachers were, was all Wayne could think.

The pervert priest tapped Wayne on the shoulder. Wayne stood up. The pervert pulled down his pants and knickers and bent him over the desk. The priest spread the cold cream between the cheeks of his bum.

Afterwards, Wayne wriggled free from underneath him and made himself decent. A load of coins fell out onto the floor as the pervert priest pulled up his pants. A fifty pence piece rolled lazily across the floor. Wayne followed its progress until it hit the wall and capsized, the noise echoing around them as it wobbled to a standstill.

He could feel the pervert priest's awkwardness now that he'd got his relief. It was the one moment in the whole process when Wayne had a bit of power and he always made a point of exploiting it. He stared the pervert priest down, daring him to make eye contact, but he was too chicken. It was another reason to hate him. But try as he might, he could not make himself hate the pervert priest as much as he hated himself.

thirty-eight

The moment Roche reached for his hat and coat, Mitzie, a terrier of indeterminate breed, ran to the front door and danced around ecstatically. She'd happily lie around all day and not venture further than the front gate. But she'd go to the end of the earth on a walk with him. It was the pack instinct, he surmised. For his part, he'd never have gotten off the couch if he didn't have her to walk. It was a perfect coalition of self-interest.

There'd been twenty-eight houses in the estate when he'd bought here and cows in the field at the end of the road. Back then he'd known every child in every household by name. There were plenty of houses where he could walk in and make himself a coffee and have a read of the paper if there was no one about. Several hundred houses had been built in the intervening years. He hardly knew a soul now.

He let Mitzie off the lead when he reached the soccer pitches. The rain was coming down heavy. Roche had never known a dog that got such value out of a walk. She was hardy too, seeking out the dirtiest puddle of water. She seemed to run aimlessly, nose to the ground, and then bark as if singing and dancing in the rain. Roche didn't mind: you were as wet as you were ever going to be after a few minutes. You just got absorbed in your thoughts after that.

Clarke's trial had been assigned to Mr Justice Frank Corless. A diminutive, portly figure with a small-man complex, he modelled himself on a predecessor, nicknamed the Rottweiler, but because he was an inferior specimen in so many ways he was universally known as the Shitzu, phonetic spelling deliberate and for reasons that were self-evident.

Clarke wasn't going to go quietly. Why would he plead guilty? What was in it for him except a small discount on his sentence? A guy like him would only become bitter and eventually institutionalised in jail. It was like locking up a tiger in a zoo.

Clarke would throw the kitchen sink at them. But they had a strong case built on circumstantial evidence and unimpeachable forensic evidence.

As he'd predicted, Clarke's gorillas had got busy once the book of evidence had been served. The boy had been targeted. Silent late-night phone calls, the intermittent slashing of his dad's car tyres and excrement through the letter box all combined to drive home their insidious message.

The mother was windy as fuck. In the end he'd told the father to grow a pair of balls and direct her to stop whinging. He hadn't liked coming the heavy. But there was no choice. If the Christy Clarkes of this world could set a court at nought, they all might as well give up and hand over the reins to him and his ilk.

Besides, he was pretty sure that once the evidence was given there'd be no recriminations. Clarke wasn't a complete fool. He bucked the system wherever he could, but he was smart enough to lie down once it had bested him and concentrate on other pressure points.

Good cases reduced themselves to very simple propositions in the end. The boy was a small but essential cog in the case. The only thing they really needed him to say was that the attacker who had pulled up his balaclava had rested his shoes on the twin exhausts of the Kawasaki motorbike as he was driven away from the scene. Once the boy put Clarke on the motorbike, the science kicked in.

He'd tried several times to bring Reynolds around. He'd been banging his head off a wall. The more he'd tried to nudge him into doing the right thing, the more entrenched he'd become. Reynolds had got quite thick about it in the end and began making noises about harassment.

Roche's victory at the Garda Complaints Commission now effectively closed off the avenue of garda brutality. There were far fewer places for Clarke to hide. He'd quickly run into a cul-de-sac trotting out that line. The hearing still left a bad taste in his mouth. But all in all he was happy he hadn't handed Clarke a stick to do down the case.

Harry Brown and Liam Kinsella had wanted to show their mettle, that they'd an existence separate from Christy. He'd busted both of them at the tyre factory ten days after Clarke was remanded into custody. They'd gone down like lambs, effing and blinding that Clarke had set them up. Roche had just smiled broadly at them, being careful not to disabuse them of the notion. Causing trouble behind enemy lines was good police work.

He'd gone from hero to zero after he'd given Clarke a dig in the station. But putting Brown and Kinsella away, and the Complaints Commission throwing out the complaint, meant he was well back into the fray. Putting Clarke away would put him right back on the pinnacle of his career.

Just what was it that Clarke going to say about all the stuff the lab had found on his shoes? That the guards had planted it? That was pretty implausible. And high risk too. If the jury didn't buy it they'd decide very quickly the reason that he was running that line was because he was guilty.

Roche had checked and re-checked with the exhibits officer that all their ducks were in a line. There was to be no foostering around. The twin exhausts, shoes, the remote control and the wisps of goose feathers were to be handed up in sequence and without fuss to the witness giving evidence and then immediately passed onto the jury for them to inspect. The presentation had to be crisp.

They had the right judge for the job. The Shitzu had what Roche regarded as an 'attention deficit disorder' – if he wasn't getting attention there was a deficit, which he made good by descending on whatever hapless individual was close to hand. Gardaí, counsel, witnesses, a member of the public – anyone but a juror (the only people who could afford to go against him) – were all equally likely to be vaporised for the most minor transgression.

But he also had the dirty nose – the name Roche gave to people who were good at intuitively sniffing out badness. That and a razor-sharp intellect that contextualised information at speed. Christy Clarke would get his fair trial alright, but if he were convicted, he'd get hammered and might well need that walking stick by the time he got out.

thirty-nine

Paul Rooney descended the stairs to the holding cells in the company of his instructing solicitor, Myles Sweeney. The case had been a late handover from Denis Wise, the moiley doyen of the criminal bar. 'Have fun,' Wise had said, flashing a mouthful of expensive dental work that included two perfectly straight gold lines symmetrically positioned on either side of his front teeth. 'No pressure!'

Indeed.

All he'd ever wanted to be was a criminal lawyer. A chip on his shoulder, a college flirtation with left-wing politics and a good smattering of clichéd courtroom dramas (in particular Al Pacino in *And Justice for All*) had combined to make him a man on a mission.

Hollywood always cast the DA prosecuting the child molester, or the defence attorney as the only thing standing between his innocent client and the gas chamber. The plot lines were clean and simple. In real life most accused were committed recidivists and judges followed their prejudices over the law. Solicitors very often didn't take proper instructions and good leads weren't followed up. The quality of investigation was poor and gardaí didn't really know how cases worked in court, and this would continue indefinitely for so long as nine out of ten accused continued to plead guilty.

There were incompetent cops but few bent ones. More often than not, guards were telling 'good' lies, like telling a judge at a sentence hearing that the accused had no previous convictions. It was the quid pro quo for getting a file closed, or for information received, or as a down payment against information that might become available later. Even the 'bad' lies, the manufactured verbal that amounted to a collateral admission (as in 'I was only down there to meet a friend' to bolster a weak ID), were usually told in the firm belief that the accused was guilty. And usually they were.

He'd got a sinking feeling when he'd read the papers. It was a circumstantial case, one where a jury would decide that the bits added up to conviction or they didn't. There was no long grass in which to hide. This was more like a putting green. Counsel's sphere of influence on how the case would play out would be negligible.

He'd spent most of Saturday up in the jail making sure that there wasn't anything he was missing. It had been hard to keep Clarke focused. Clarke had been whinging about how the Garda Complaints Commission had stitched him up. Rooney had patiently explained to Clarke that it didn't really matter. Eventually, after enough repetition, Clarke had reluctantly accepted that even if he'd been able to damage Roche's credibility in the trial, that wasn't going to impact on the forensic evidence, which, after all, was what the case was about.

Another lengthy debate had then ensued in which Rooney had explained to Clarke over and over how the omission of the letter 'e' in the spelling of his name on the court document sending him forward for trial didn't have any effect on the the court's right to try him.

It never ceased to amaze Rooney how a prisoner would triumphantly point to a single word misspelled in an official document, and indignantly demand as a matter of law *and* justice that all charges be dropped against him forthwith.

Towards the end of the consultation, when it was becoming apparent even to Clarke that his options were limited, he said something about how if it came down to the wire he'd have to rely on his secret weapon. The secret weapon was probably some dodgy alibi, but Clarke had steadfastly refused to disclose what it was. Clarke didn't trust anyone, least of all barristers, whom he regarded as being right up the establishment's arse.

He'd expected Myles Sweeney to wade in and tell him to cop on. Later, Myles had simply shrugged when Rooney asked him what Clarke had been on about.

The whole thing had generated more heat than light. But it was an essential ritual for a barrister of his lowly standing. You couldn't leave yourself open to complaint from a client like Clarke that his case didn't get the attention it deserved. It was bad PR within the prison and he'd have to undergo the humiliating formality of answering a complaint to the Bar Council.

They waited in the holding area below the courts for a prison officer to fetch Clarke from the cells. He emerged all smiles.

'Morning, Mr Rooney!'

'Morning, Mr Clarke. All set?'

'I'm ready. I've always been ready. Question is are you ready?'

Rooney smiled weakly in response.

'Now,' Clarke said, sounding more like the lawyer than Rooney did. 'We've covered all the points. If you don't get the case thrown out at the end of the prosecution case we'll still have my secret weapon.'

Rooney shifted uneasily on his feet and began flicking through his papers. You'd have thought that on the morning of the case he might stop speaking in riddles. The case seemed unanswerable but there wasn't a bother on him.

'Now, Mr Clarke, you don't need me to warn you again about the dangers of calling alibi evidence. It'd better stack up or it will sink the case even deeper into the muck.'

Clarke just stood there with an insipid grin on his face. They exchanged a few platitudes until Rooney looked at his watch and said he'd see him in court for the swearing in of the jury.

On the way up the stairs Myles had impressed upon Rooney the need to follow Clarke's instructions to the letter.

'His type squeal like pigs when convicted.'

He was blessed to get instructions in a case like this. It was ahead of his time. But he found the reference to *when* dispiriting. Myles probably hadn't meant anything by it, but he could feel the confidence draining out of him. He was already on an adrenalin overload. The flight mode was rushing into ascendancy.

He said something to Myles about going to look up some law. But he headed for the toilet instead. He pulled the bolt across the cubicle door and leaned against the wall.

In half an hour the trial would begin. His mouth was dry, his hands clammy and he could feel his heart palpitating. He stared hard at the toilet boil to stave off the vertiginous feeling that was gathering momentum. He closed his eyes, drew in a breath through his nose all the way down to his diaphragm and slowly exhaled, a relaxation technique he had seen opera singers do on a TV documentary.

This was good old-fashioned stage fright or its nearest court equivalent. Before his biggest case. Acting for the most obnoxious client. Being prosecuted by Des Curran, a man who could give even the most sanguine of judges an inferiority complex. And tried by the Shitzu, a judge who instinctively knew which barrister had not yet developed a thick skin. A few gentle souls who'd been lashed out of it had never seen the inside of a courtroom again. Some said his approach only accelerated the Darwinian selection process that was already underway. Others, like Rooney, simply saw a tyrant.

Clarke would in all probability get convicted and there'd be an appeal, and no doubt a reserved judgment in which some tendentious point of law raised by Rooney would be gently derided in the polished language and mellifluous tones so beloved of their lordships. Something really lame along the lines that the document recording Clarke's return for trial to the Circuit Criminal Court on the court file was inadequate as it was a photocopy and the original ought to have been produced.

Ultimately the judgment would make its way into the law reports and merit a minor footnote in the textbooks. The future generations of students who actually got around to reading it might wonder at Christy Clarke's brass neck. That'd be the closest that college would ever come to preparing a lawyer for a case like this.

He breathed in deeply again and exhaled through his puffed cheeks.

forty

Roche looked around the State consultation room and tried to see it through the eyes of the boy. A sign on the wall written in the old Irish script with the dot for the *séimhiú* said: *Ná cait tobac*. It never failed to remind Roche of the Máistir in national school, the one who beat the boys with a leg of a chair when they didn't know the *tuiseal ginideach*. He'd hated Irish with a passion ever since. He hoped it wasn't having the same effect on Larry Cummins.

A small fat man wearing a tattered wig, a long braided coat like a footman's under a black silk gown and a white starched wing collar was thumbing his way through a sheaf of papers. The tips of the collar were stained yellow from contact with his neck. His shoulders were liberally doused with dandruff. Crumpled elasticised tabs around his neck completed his attire. In his decrepit wig (which looked like it might disintegrate at any moment) and court garb he must have cut an intimidating figure to the boy. It was hard to believe that the man behind this crumbling façade was one of the most brilliant advocates of his day.

Roche introduced him to the boy as Mr Curran, the barrister for the State. Larry told him in his own words what he had seen. The account was deficient in many respects. And Roche knew that this was no mere oversight. He felt his hands getting sweaty. Clarke's bullyboys' tactics were paying off. The mother's perpetual whinging meant that the boy was no longer prepared to swear up. When he had finished, Curran addressed him sternly.

'You say that you saw the man go over to the grass area and rub his shoes on the grass, is that right?'

The boy said nothing.

'It says here,' the barrister said pointing to his statement, 'that he went over beside the grass and stamped on something.'

'Yeah, he did that too.'

'Well that's important.' It was said gently enough, but the tone left the boy in no doubt that he was being ticked off. 'And you say that you *think* he might have put his shoes up on the exhaust pipes? In your statement you seemed more certain.'

'Will I get anyone into trouble?'

'Look, son' – the voice was hard and cold now – 'you are here to tell us what you saw. To tell the truth. If you don't I can have you treated as a hostile witness. Do you understand?'

The boy nodded even though it was clear that he didn't, but he was smart enough to know this wasn't the right time to say so.

'Good,' said Curran, 'I don't want any misunderstanding. Do I take it you will be giving evidence in accordance with your statement?'

Larry nodded again.

'Alright, go and sit in the courtroom for now like a good man and we'll call you to give evidence later in the day.'

Roche went in with him to keep an eye on him. Thank God, he thought, that the Director had briefed Curran to do the State's case. He was a class act who knew how to work a jury and how to react to things appropriately. He'd been deft in his handling of the boy; firm enough to turn him but not so much that he frightened him away.

They sat on the bench reserved for witnesses. Court 14 was cramped and windowless. The judge sat on a bench on a raised dais. Below him sat the registrar and the stenographer. The jury box was to the left. The barristers spread out their papers on a big table and their instructing solicitors sat opposite them. Prosecution counsel sat immediately below the jury. The accused sat on a bench on the opposite side of the room close by the defence team. There were four benches behind the table to accommodate witnesses and members of the public.

The side door of the courtroom opened and the tipstaff emerged calling, 'Silence in court!' The Shitzu trailed in his wake and everybody stood up. The judge sat down and, lynx-eyed, scrutinised the court to see where the main *dramatis personae* were located. To Roche he seemed to linger on Rooney, appraising him quizzically, his mental Rolodex turning furiously to see what he knew about him.

Mick, the court registrar, rose with the indictment in his hand and arraigned Christy Clarke on counts of causing grievous bodily harm to ACO Reynolds, stealing the motorbike used in the attack and causing malicious damage to Reynolds' Audi car. Clarke replied 'not guilty' to each charge, cramming as much steely resentment into the two words as he could manage.

The jury was then selected. Names were pulled out of a box in batches and read out aloud. They then made their way up to the top of the court. The solicitors looked at the list of names, which recorded their addresses and occupations. They'd a few seconds to read them and raise an objection before they commenced swearing the oath. They all solemnly swore to try the case and a true verdict give in accordance with the evidence.

After the third defence objection, the Shitzu couldn't contain himself.

'That's another perfectly good juror,' he said glaring down at Myles Sweeney. 'It's nothing personal,' he said to the well-coiffured woman who was making her way back down to the well of the court. 'Each side can object to seven prospective jurors without giving any explanation. It's the law, unfortunately.

'Sometimes it's because you are too well turned out, other times it's because you're not well turned out enough. It might be because you're wearing an earring or a bomber jacket, or maybe it's because you're wearing a suit. It could be because you work in a bank or equally because you're unemployed.

'It might be because you look right wing, or a liberal. There's no science in it. The only hard information each side has on you is your name, address and occupation. So it tells us more about the prejudices of the solicitors acting in this case than it ever will about you! Please bear that in mind.'

His lips parted into an acid smile again directed at Myles Sweeny.

Eventually twelve persons were selected. 'Please go to your room now and elect a foreman,' the Shitzu instructed them. 'It can of course be a woman if you wish.' They returned after a few minutes. A man by the name of Tom O'Dowd announced he had been picked.

The registrar stood up and read the charges out for a second time. He read aloud into the record the names of solicitor and counsel appearing for each side and then put the jury in charge of the accused, indicating that it was now for them to decide whether he was guilty or not guilty of the charges before them. Roche liked the formality of the process. It underlined the seriousness of what the charges were about and was a necessary incantation to give a courtroom the solemnity of a chapel.

Mr Curran then opened the case for the State. He faced the jury. His first words were: 'Mr O'Dowd, ladies and gentleman of the jury.' Tom grew a few inches on the spot.

Curran told them the story of how ACO Reynolds had been assaulted. He made no mention in the opening of Reynolds' visit to the hospital and the row over Darren Cassidy getting in to see his mother. Roche approved of the strategy: there was no point in antagonising the jury towards Reynolds unnecessarily. Curran reminded the jury that it was for the Director of Public Prosecutions to prove the case – the accused didn't have to prove anything, least of all his innocence.

A mapper and photographer were the first witnesses. One booklet was a picture of the housing estate where the attack took place. The second was photos of the bike, the twin exhausts and the shoes with the melted soles.

It was Larry's turn then. Roche already liked the stride of him on his way up to the stand. The Shitzu asked a few simple questions to see if Larry understood what an oath was and the importance of telling the truth. 'Swear him,' the judge said at the end of his little interrogation.

Larry was a bit nervous at first but soon settled down. He gave a clear account of the man pilfering Reynolds' pockets and stamping on the car's remote control before lifting up his balaclava and shouting, 'Take a good look at that, fuckface. It's the last thing you'll never see.'''

Clarke's barrister rose to his feet. Denis Wise must not have been available. There were plenty of other experienced alternatives. Rooney still plied his trade mostly in the District Court where the offences were only summary. Roche had asked around at the station. The young guards had said that he was one of the up and comings but, critically, that he'd not yet earned his stripes.

Myles Sweeney had a knack for spotting and then nurturing talent. What had he seen in Rooney that had impressed him enough to brief him in this case? he wondered.

Looking directly at Larry and then swinging slowly over to the jury, Rooney said in a crisp clear voice, 'I have no questions for this witness, my lord,' and sat right down.

Roche clenched his hand into a fist: game on.

forty-one

Rooney reviewed the case with Clarke over the luncheon adjournment.

The boy had made a connection between the shoes and the motorbike. There had been a temptation to cross-examine, and put it to him that he had got the identity of the bike wrong, breaking the one tangible link in the case, but Rooney had figured by the determined way the boy gave his account that asking questions would only reinforce his testimony. He thought it better to hold back until the summing up, when he could comment without fear of contradiction on his tender age and the fleeting opportunity for identification.

It had been an executive decision that he'd had to take on the hoof.

He'd expected Clarke to go ballistic. He was in no mood for a tantrum. Rooney had geared himself up to tell Clarke that if he wasn't happy to let counsel make a call on what questions to ask, he could do his own bloody case.

But to his surprise, Clarke, who had not hitherto shown a capacity for subtlety, had agreed with this approach.

'What about Reynolds?'

'Reynolds isn't actually implicating you. I suggested to Mr Curran that his statement could simply be read out to the jury so as to spare him the trauma of giving evidence.'

'What'd he say to that?'

Curran hadn't actually replied. He'd simply smiled.

'There's no way, Mr Clarke, that the prosecutor is going to pass up the chance to parade a victim who had a testicle squeezed out of existence in a nutcracker. The curiosity factor alone is high, but the empathy factor might even be higher.'

'So what are you going to ask him then?'

'I'm not going to ask him anything. It's never a good idea to allow the jury to see too much of the injured party. It only reminds them that the case is about a real person. In a murder trial, it's usually a boon to the defence that the victim never appears in person.'

Clarke grunted, which Rooney interpreted as reluctant acquiescence to the strategy.

Curran took Reynolds through his evidence after lunch. Reynolds spoke in a clear, matter-of-fact voice that was almost devoid of emotion. The jury's eyes were still on sticks by the time he got to the point where one of his attackers was shouting to cut his prick off. You could have heard a pin drop. He agreed that one of the raiders had pulled up his mask and said something. However, he had been in shock and couldn't make out what he'd said or what he looked like.

Dr Fahy, the forensic scientist, was next.

His experience made him a witness who was at home in a court. Fahy went through the book of crime scene photographs, honing in on how bits of the remote control on the ground, tar and goose feathers had all been detected on the shoes taken during the search of Christy Clarke's bedroom.

Curran then had Dr Fahy carefully hold up the various exhibits, explaining what they were, and where exactly they fit in the case. Curran had Fahy pay particular attention to the black rubber residues on the twin exhausts, and the corresponding damage to the soles of the shoes.

'And so, Dr Fahy, speaking as a scientist, can you tell us what your conclusions are?'

Curran glanced over at the jury, with a phony air of suspense, as if he was just about to hear it for the first time. It was tacky but effective, Rooney conceded.

'The chemical composition of the rubber residues we found on the twin exhausts of the Kawasaki bike matches the rubber on the soles of the shoes which we found in the bedroom of the accused.'

Fahy held the shoes up again. 'You can see that bits of the sole have melted, which is as a result of contact with a hot surface.'

Fahy then held up the exhaust pipe and ran his fingers along the visible black residue. 'It is my opinion those deposits on the metal here came from these shoes.'

Curran held his hands aloft to pause the testimony and allow the jury a moment to digest what they had just heard.

'And all of that means?'

'It provides very strong support for the suggestion that the shoes were in contact with the twin exhausts.'

'Carry on!'

'The minute fragments of plastic embedded in the sole of the right shoe were identical to the plastic used in the remote control unit.'

Curran had him produce the remnants of the remote control.

'And the feather? What can you tell us about that?'

'We found it embedded in a bit of tar that was on the sole. It is in fact a goose feather similar to many others found at the crime scene.'

'Tell me – are there many geese around the inner city these days?'

A few cackles echoed around the courtroom.

'Not that I know of,' Fahy replied, deadpan.

'What does this tell us?'

'Well, I suppose it certainly suggests that the tar must have been fresh when the feather stuck to the shoe.'

'And just remind us, the motorbike was found where?'

'In a laneway just behind the flats where the accused lives.'

'Is it the same bike that was identified by the boy, Larry Cummins?'

'Well I can't say that for sure. It's the same model. The part of the bike registration that the boy gave to gardaí matches with this bike. In addition, one of the footrests was broken off, which might explain why a pillion passenger might rest his shoes on the exhaust. And there can't be too many bikes going round with a yellow registration plate and an IRL sticker on the back. It's a lot of coincidences if it isn't the bike he saw.'

Rooney could see that the jury was loving all of this. And it wasn't only what Fahy had to say. The urbane and detached delivery gave it a stamp of authority. Curran folded his arms across his chest, smiled beatifically into the middle distance, and sat down.

forty-two

'Are you familiar with the Summerhill area of Dublin, Dr Fahy?'

'Reasonably, yes.'

'Do you know that on the day the gardaí raided Christy Clarke's flat the Corporation was carrying out roadworks outside the complex?'

'I don't remember that, but I will take your word for it.'

Rooney held up a pair of shoes in the air.

'My instructing solicitor, Mr Sweeney, walked half a dozen times from Christopher Clarke's flat to the local newsagent. These are the shoes that he wore. They have picked up tarry deposits on the soles. Does that surprise you?'

'Not at all, no.'

'If it's a hot day, and the tar is not fully set, it will quite easily stick to the sole of the shoe?'

'That's quite right.'

'The police raid was two days after the attack on Officer Reynolds.'

'Yes, that's right.'

Gaining in confidence, Rooney produced a pillow from a bag.

Dr Fahy was only sitting three feet away. He threw the pillow up to him in the box. Just as he had hoped, a couple of feathers came out of it and floated gently to the ground. The Shitzu glared at him, and motioned by holding out his hand to the witness that he wished to see it. There was only one ringmaster in this court.

'That pillow is filled with goose feathers.'

'Apparently, yes.'

'Do you use gooose feather pillows yourself?' Rooney asked Fahy.

'Well not anymore, but we have done, yes.'

'Yes, they're out of fashion now. The Clarke household may still be playing catch up,' Rooney suggested.

Curran rose to his feet. 'Really, my Lord, there is no evidence where this pillow came from. My friend is not on firm ground here.'

The Shitzu barely heard Curran. He was too engrossed in minutely examining the break in the seam, looking for a tell-tale sign that might suggest the gap which had allowed the feather to escape was manmade. The snob in him didn't think it likely that goose feather pillows were all the rage down the flats. And even if the Clarkes did have such a pillow it was far too convenient that it had made its way into this case.

The Shitzu looked up and glared at Rooney.

'I will be calling that evidence if it is required, my Lord,' Rooney quickly replied. The Shitzu nodded his assent and Rooney continued with his cross-examination.

'I take it you checked the pillows in the flat on the day of the search.'

'No, my Lord.'

'Ah you're not serious?'

Fahy didn't answer. He anticipated that Rooney would launch into a diatribe. Instead he stood there waiting for Fahy to speak. Rooney felt the long silence that followed was more effective than anything he could have said. Rooney spoke gently.

'Sure wasn't it an obvious potential contact point for the trace on the shoe?'

'Well, the bits of feather were very small – we only found them later in the lab under microscopic examination. They couldn't be seen with the naked eye,' Fahy replied.

'Fair enough. But did you go back to examine the pillows?'

'No.'

'Why on earth not?'

'No reason.'

'Tell me, did you find that loose feathers would pop up around the house when you did use goose feather pillows?'

'Yes, I did.'

'It's very hard to keep the pillow sealed, isn't it?'

'It can be difficult alright.'

'Especially when you have a few boys using them to knock the lights out of each other.'

'I suppose so,' he replied.

Rooney had now raised the possibility that the feather could have come from Clarke's flat, and that the tarry deposits could have come from the roadworks. But the hardest bit was yet to come.

'When was the bike stolen?'

'A week before the attack.'

'Assuming you can make a connection – and I don't, by the way – between the shoes and the exhaust on the bike, you can't say when the marks on the exhaust were made, can you?'

'No. I can't.'

'I mean, for all you know Christy Clarke was on that bike every day for a week before the attack, resting his shoes on the twin exhausts.'

'Well now!' The Shitzu hadn't spoken for at least fifteen minutes and no doubt felt the jury had been deprived. 'I think that theory can safely be discounted unless he owns shares in a shoe company.'

There were guffaws around the court, including some titters from the jury box. Rooney was still scrambling for his next question when two men broke the impasse by screaming, 'You scumbag, Clarke! Fuckin' drug dealer! Fuckin' kids on the street dying coz of you.'

The men continued shouting abuse until a couple of burly gardaí got them in a headlock and brought them down to the cells. The Shitzu immediately ordered the jury to go to their room.

The court was momentarily stunned into silence. Rooney was taken aback by the sheer audacity of what he'd just witnessed. It was crass. It was an extremely blunt instrument designed to create a mistrial that had Clarke's grubby hallmark all over it.

Nonetheless, he rose to his feet to protest that the outburst was bound to irredeemably prejudice some, if not all, members of the jury against the accused and that the court had no choice but to discharge the jury. He made the case forcefully and with as much enthusiasm as he could muster. But he, and everyone else who knew what was going on, knew that he was making the argument purely for the transcript. For the inevitable appeal which would now surely follow conviction.

The Shitzu did not pause for breath.

'The application which Mr Rooney has made would be unanswerable if the eruption that we have just witnessed was spontaneous. That possibility can safely be excluded. This was a crude stunt orchestrated by the accused to have a mistrial declared, impeccably timed, it must be said, to coincide with the demise of the defence case. Application refused. Bring the jury back down please.'

Rooney stole a glance at Clarke. The faintest shake of his head indicated that this was not the secret weapon. It was dawning on him that he might have underestimated his client. Rooney was beginning to understand just why it was that Christy Clarke was regarded as a player.

forty-three

Wayne climbed the stairs up onto the roof of the block and made his way into his Da's pigeon loft, or what was left of it. The door was hanging off its hinges. The wire mesh was sunken in places by people putting their boot through it. A dirty mattress was on the floor. There was a map of the universe in spunk stains on it.

Bits of blackened tinfoil were scattered around. Wayne had come up here early one morning last summer and found Sharon Walsh strung out – a works hanging lopsided out of her arm. The barrel was full of blood. The medical attendant had resuscitated her; she'd puked her ring up and her eyes had been rolling in her head. But then she'd arrested in the ambulance on the way to the hospital and flat-lined. Wayne had liked Sharon a lot, fancied her even though she was seventeen. But he hadn't mourned her passing. She'd been a fuckin' fool for getting turned on. No matter how bad things got that wasn't going to happen to him.

He lifted up a pile of papers in the corner and took out a flagon of cider. It tasted cold and sweet. Herself was drinking herself silly. Not going mad and getting mad drunk like his Da. Just tippling away constant. She was still going around all the surgeries getting multiple scripts for tablets. She was away with the fairies.

He smoked one of the fags he'd robbed from her. It went down well with the cider. He smoked every day now. Sometimes he'd rob money from his Ma's handbag, buy a ten-packet and hide them down his socks. The shop on the corner sold loose fags for 9p each. Once when he was little he'd picked up a butt that his Ma had thrown into the fire but had fallen short. Afterwards he'd put his fingers under his nose and the smell had made him retch. The first time he'd taken a drag he'd felt sick and light-headed. But he'd persevered. He liked it a lot now. He worried that it'd slow him up playing football was all.

His Da was much happier within himself now that the case had actually started. The fighting talk was back. He was full of it. He'd got a couple of lads from the flats to create a diversion during the case trying to get the jury discharged but the judge had seen right through it. He still referred to his barrister Rooney as a 'chinless fuckin' wonder' but Wayne could tell by the way he spoke about him, how he kept saying he needed to discuss this or that with him, that he was gaining confidence in him.

He'd horsed them off the visit early so he could talk to Wayne's brother Maurice about the case. Maurice was the only one of the family allowed to attend the hearing and was downstairs in the kitchen right now holding court with the neighbours. It annoyed Wayne the way Maurice went around with his head up his arse like he was someone important, rabbiting on how his Da would win the case and how great it'd be, that he'd be home very soon.

Wayne wasn't so sure. He loved his Da. There was never any doubt about that. He didn't want his Da to be locked up for twenty years. But the worst of it was that he didn't want him home either. He felt bad about that. It was up there with the sex with the pervert priest. It was something else unnatural, and it ate him up.

He'd missed him at first. But then he noticed how people weren't going around on tiptoe, afraid of the next eruption. His Ma wasn't missing him either. If anything she was enjoying her independence, not to mention the peace and quiet. He'd heard her explain to the women in the kitchen that she'd reached the point where her only option was to harden her heart towards Christy.

He'd seen too many beatings of his Ma. It hadn't been enough for him to pummel her with his fists. He'd made sure to try his level best to crush her spirit in the process.

And then he'd started dipping his wick elsewhere. She'd played him at his own game then, fucking up his head. You didn't want to cross his Ma. She was punishing him now.

Wayne had tried every excuse not to go to any more lessons with the pervert priest. His Ma was pushing him into his waiting arms. In a strange way her coercing him to go had strengthened his resolve not to say what was going on. The thought that she'd feel bad, if and when she found out what the priest had been doing to him, always made him feel better. He didn't know how or why, just that it did.

Being touched up wasn't the worst of it. He worried more that he'd turn queer.

Could that happen? Would it, fuck? He'd kill himself for sure. But not before he killed the pervert priest. He'd hang him off the roof of the block by his ankles for several hours and then watch the fear in his eyes as he cut through the rope with a knife.

He took a pull from his cigarette and washed it down with a slug out of the flagon. It was funny how the smoke could pass through the liquid. 'Sweet smokin' amber,' he said to himself.

There were melodies and harmonies buzzing around his head and some days he couldn't get them down on paper quick enough. The pervert priest's lessons on how to read and write sheet music had their uses. Then he'd write the words that'd expresss it. Other times, a phrase came first, and he'd fiddle around on the guitar until he got something that worked.

The pervert priest talked a good game. He said that songs, even pop songs, were layered. There was a natural tension between bass, rhythm and lead guitar. There was in turn a different interaction between percussion and vocals. The seeds of creativity lay embedded in the spaces between these components, he said.

According to the pervert priest, it was only through constant immersion in the act of playing chords and notes that he could get into these gaps and realise his creativity to its full extent. Wayne wasn't sure about all this, but it sounded about right.

The cider was hitting him up good now. He imagined places he'd like to go to while he was tanked up with a flagon of cider. He did a lot of living in his head these days. A disco? He'd have no problem getting a shift! Croke Park? He'd get in with a few heads and kick the shite out of a few culchies. The presbytery? He'd sort out your man quick enough. Cider didn't taste sour like other drinks. In fact, he was sure that people tasting blind couldn't tell cider and Cidona apart. The difference wasn't in the taste though. It was how he felt on the inside that mattered. He'd come up here feeling shitty, and go back down feeling he'd flick life's troubles away with his fingertips. He was in control.

forty-four

Cornfields Farm, where Cora lived, was named after the fields in which grain crops had been grown for as long as anyone could remember. The land sloped gently down to the plains of the Curragh, and in summertime their golden hue could be seen for miles around. Being here reminded Fr Brendan of home. Mam and Dad were getting on and he felt a twinge of regret that no one in the family wanted to farm their land.

It had been rather wonderful to deliver an open-air homily in which he'd spoken about the innate goodness of God as a giver of life in an environment that was so richly productive. He'd stressed the virtue of living close to the land and not off the fat of it. There was a faint autumnal nip in the air. They'd been lucky with the weather, a crisp cobalt blue sky broken up by white cumulus clouds. He'd liked the springy feel from the grass under his feet as he gave out Holy Communion. The pungent smell of manure had added to the ambience.

It was also a wonderful way to mark the end of the campaign and to thank all the volunteers for their hard work and dedication. Cora's nephew Donal had been his altar boy. He'd followed him down the line, the communion plate shaking in his hand, so anxious was he a host would fall to the ground. The bespoke congregation had been large enough to generate an atmosphere but still retain an intimacy.

There was a holy water font positioned on the wall immediately inside the door of Cora's house, and there was an old-fashioned picture of the Sacred Heart in a plain frame beside it, lit up by its distinctive votive light. He passed a wall of photographs on the stairwell taken by her husband Jack of various missionary priests from Africa studying at universities in Ireland and England and who had come to Cornfields for a holiday. The monochrome images underlined their blackness. Scattered around were wooden elephants, crocodiles carved from ivory and other knick-knacks that the visitors had bought as gifts. Fr Brendan picked up a white oval object wrapped in a coloured braid. It was quite heavy and firm and he recognised it as an ostrich's egg.

Fr Brendan went to the guest bedroom and hung his vestments in his suit carrier. Cora was an avid fan of furniture and fine art auctions and the whole house was a monument to good taste. A large Markey Robinson painting, showing women in shawls gathering firewood, hung over the fireplace. Its distinctive blues and yellows were thrown into sharp relief by dividing black lines. An exquisite nineteenth-century French clock with beautifully hand-painted Roman numerals in turquoise and gold stood on the mantelpiece. There were ornate cabinets and tallboys dotted around the house in mahogany, teak and walnut veneer.

He'd counted on the hall stairs and landing what seemed to be close to a full set of the *Cries of London* surrounded by ornate gilt-edged frames.

A William IV table (and a fine specimen it was) was creaking under the weight of freshly baked fairy cakes, shortbread, fruit flans, cheesecake, scones, sponge cake, Bakewells, banana bread and chocolate rice crispy buns. There was a large bowl of whipped cream and jars of homemade berry and rhubarb jams with greaseproof covers held in place by elastic bands.

Cora approached him carrying a plate with smoked salmon on freshly baked brown bread with wedges of lemon. It was a staple delicacy when entertaining a priest, but he wasn't really a fish man. He took it cheerfully so as not to cause offence. Cora paraded him around the room, and neighbours and supporters thanked him for all his work on the campaign and for saying such a lovely Mass. The polls showed that the yes vote was comfortably ahead. In his final address to a crowd of several thousand gathered in the Diamond in Donegal he'd hammered home the message that there was only one poll that counted and exhorted everyone to get to a polling station and cast their vote.

Cora re-approached him, this time with her nephew who appeared to be reluctantly in tow.

'Donal, why don't you show Father what you've been doing with Bó?'

They walked down the yard together. Donal prattled away the whole time about his Uncle Jack, Aunt Cora and his precious and much-loved Bó. It was nice to meet a boy who was so spontaneously friendly.

Bó, it turned out, was a calf that had been born bowlegged. Donal had christened him Bó on the spot, on the basis that it was the Irish for cow. He'd taken him under his wing and was teaching him to walk so that he could become a fully paid up member of the herd. Donal opened the door of the shed in the corner of the yard and Bó obligingly hobbled out, clanking around the yard under the boy's direction. He'd spent all summer designing and building callipers so that Bó could walk. Fr Brendan had to admit the manner in which the boy had taught the calf to negotiate tight corners was very impressive.

Donal talked about his plans to have Bó grazing in the fields soon. Fr Brendan knew enough about animal husbandry from growing up on a farm to know that the plan was doomed. Once the calf grew to full size you'd need industrial strength supports for his legs. And what'd happen in the heavy rain when the ground turned to mud? He said nothing, what was the point in upsetting the boy?

After the demonstration Donal settled Bó back into his straw bed and cuddled up to him. The calf revelled in it, licking the boy's hand and face to show his approval. The calf's eyes, he noticed, anxiously followed Donal's every movement. Did the calf sense that he was going to be used as veal when the boy went back to school? he wondered.

'Come closer,' Donal said to Fr Brendan.

Fr Brendan knelt down on the straw. Donal took his hand and guided it along the pelt of the animal. He massaged Fr Brendan's hand across the calf's stomach. Bó arched his back in appreciation. Donal then took his hand and placed it under the animal's head and moved Fr Brendan's hand across his chest. The animal moved his head in the opposite direction to get full traction from the contact. The feel of his pelt was pleasant.

'Feel how silky his coat is?'

Fr Brendan had wanted to reply that the texture and softness of Donal's hand in his own far exceeded anything Bó had to offer. Instead, he'd managed to sit on the floor still holding the boy's hand in his own without the boy even noticing.

He'd stopped abusing Wayne in the run up to the trial. The prospect – however remote – that Christy Clarke might be acquitted and back living in the flat was also a very effective restraint. Wayne was full of resentment now. Some days he'd turn up late, or announce he was leaving early. His demeanour was cocky and he was challenging him all the time, trying to push boundaries. Fr Brendan missed Wayne. He missed the sexual gratification too.

Donal told him excitedly about everything that he had done with Bó. The energy and love he'd put into being the calf's surrogate mother was total.

Fr Brendan had wanted to run his hands down along the inside of the boy's thighs and into his nether region; the bricktappers stirred into action and stepped into the breach, encouraging him to be bold. He saw that Donal was, like Wayne had been when he'd touched him up for the first time, right on the cusp of puberty and this excited him.

The thought unsettled him. He'd hoped that the attraction he felt for Wayne had been a one-off. The idea of touching up a child had sneaked up on him. Was it something that was going to become part of the bricktappers' repertoire, goading him into touching up boys?

He took stock. This was not some anonymous encounter in the Phoenix Park where two people sought mutual release. This was a boy. Not just any boy. He was surrounded on all sides by heavy-hitters. The consequences of having to deal with a complaint in an environment such as this didn't bear thinking about.

Even a person like himself who was susceptible to the bricktappers could see it would be mad. You needed a cast-iron sense of survival to do what he did and avoid coming on the radar. But there were limits. Once again, fear was an effective restraint. Donal rabbited on, oblivious. Fr Brendan offered up his self-denial as a sacrifice in the hope that someone else's suffering might be alleviated.

forty-five

In Roche's experience it was rarely good news when the phone rang late. It was Inspector Barry Kirby from Special Branch. He rubbed his eyes. It was ten past three in the morning. He'd have trouble getting back to sleep.

'Morning, Dick. We arrested Jimmy Daly earlier this evening for possession of a Thompson submachine gun. Daly says that he was working for you and that you had sanctioned him carrying the firearm as part of an ongoing operation. Any thoughts?'

He'd warned Daly umpteen times that their relationship didn't offer any immunity in respect of his own actions. But he'd known that when it came down to it Daly would use whatever he could to protect himself. What could you expect from a pig but a grunt?

Now, though, wasn't a good time. He'd survived the recent outing at the Garda Complaints Commission. Flannery had let it be known that he'd regarded the result as a lucky one. The lads didn't blame him for the Clarke case going south. But there was a perception growing that his best work was behind him. He could feel himself being moved towards the periphery of things. Right now he wasn't the sort of cop that another cop – even a decent skin like Kirby – would go out on a limb for. He had to be careful in his responses.

'I can confirm that Daly is a registered informer. He has provided valuable information on a number of occasions. Others not. But I'd have to say that, all in all, he's one of the best touts I've ever had.'

'You have any knowledge that he was carrying tonight?'

'Not a chance.'

There was a silence on the other end of the line.

'Look,' Roche began, 'Daly's trying to wrap himself with the cloak of respectability that his relationship with me provides. He's looking at plenty of jail time if he goes down on this. He'd say anything to improve his position. You know it, I know it, Daly knows it.'

'Cheers. That's how I read it myself.'

'He knows the ground rules. He's on his own.'

'Well thanks for being upfront. These cases can get messy.'

'Are you going to charge him tonight?'

'Probably not. The gun was found under the seat. He's not saying anything in interview. We have no evidence right now to show that he knew it was there. We may release him and send a file to the DPP. Will I tell him that you'll be over to see him?'

'No thanks, Barry, I'll pass on that. Jimmy is toxic right now. I wouldn't go within an ass's roar of him. Like I say, he is registered: I've kept records. He's nothing on me and that's the way I intend to keep it.'

'How's the Christy Clarke case going?'

'Sitting pretty. The evidence makes the case look a certain way, like he is very guilty. Absent an explanation from Clarke it'll stay looking that way.'

'Will he take the stand?'

'Doubt it. Too many hard questions for which he's no answer. He'd certainly be worse off by the time Curran cross-examined him.'

'Well best of luck with it. I'll keep you posted on the Daly thing.'

The call rang off. He made a cup of coffee. Dunked a few biscuits in it. He liked Daly. They'd soldiered together for a right number of years now. It'd be a shame if they'd come to the end of the line. He was as straight as any tout was ever going to be.

But touts had been known to turn on handlers, make allegations to embarrass them, if things weren't going their way. It was down and dirty stuff that never looked pretty under the microscope. Usually he wasn't great on paperwork, but he'd written up a journal of all his meetings with Daly. He hoped that he had his back adequately protected.

Meantime he had to concentrate on the task in hand and not get distracted. The consensus was Clarke wouldn't give evidence, that tomorrow it'd be closing speeches and then the judge's charge to the jury and they'd retire to reach a verdict. Hopefully it'd be quick.

Having reached this hallowed point in the case, he was willing to acknowledge that he might have been a bit too hard on Reynolds. Was it so surprising that he hadn't been willing to spend the rest of his life looking over his shoulder?

The priest seemed to be everywhere on the radio and TV as a spokesperson for the Yes crowd. He was well groomed, articulate and quite the celebrity.

He'd asked around to get a fix on him. He'd been surprised by what he'd learnt. Sure, Fr Brendan was regarded as being full of himself, irritating and a snob. But he regularly called in to see elderly people living alone, went out doing meals on wheels and worked as a volunteer with the Simon Community helping people sleeping on the street get a bed for the night. Fr Peter, the parish priest, apparently disliked him intensely, but some of the old daws were saying that was only because Fr Peter was lazy and his young curate was showing him up. No deed was too small if it involved doing a turn for a parishioner.

But his failure to cooperate still rankled. It was unfinished business. Roche didn't buy the line about breaking confidences. The cop in him said there was something else to it. Wayne Clarke was apparently one of his many good causes. Was it that he hadn't wanted to shop Christy on the basis that it'd upset Wayne? He'd get to the bottom of it sooner rather than later.

forty-six

'Counsel for the defence, Mr Rooney, has made an application that I withdraw this case from the jury on the basis there is insufficient evidence to ground a conviction. The prosecution case is closed. He says that his client has no case to answer. He points to the fact that the only evidence is of a circumstantial nature – that there is nothing to directly connect his client to the crime scene.

'He concedes that the damage to the shoes, the presence of tar and goose feather on the sole and the minute plastic fragments similar to the broken remote control are suspicious, but he argues that it would be perverse to conclude that the only explanation for this state of affairs is that Christy Clarke is guilty of the offences charged. If he is correct in his argument then I have no choice but to stop the case.

'I must take the State case at its highest in deciding whether his submission has any merit. In my view, it has not. The accused does not have to prove or explain anything. That is for the prosecution. But a strong inference of guilt that can be drawn from a particular set of facts may become an inevitable one absent some other credible alternative possibility.

'I don't lose sight of the fact that Mr Rooney has advanced certain hypotheses relating to pillows and roadworks carried out in the neighbourhood where Christy Clarke lives. But the weight, if any, to be given to these theories is a matter for a jury to decide.

'If I were a member of this jury, which of course I am not, I would have no hesitation in reaching a conclusion that the only sensible inference from the evidence on the shoes is one overwhelmingly consistent with involvement in the attack on ACO Reynolds. Indeed, I wonder whether I would even have to leave the courtroom to render such a verdict. The application is dismissed.'

The jury keeper brought the jury back to court.

'Mr Rooney?' the trial judge asked.

'My Lord, the accused will not be going into evidence.'

The Shitzu looked down smugly. The sheep was in the pen.

'Mr Curran, are you ready?'

Rooney had drawn out the pause for as long as he dared. Timing was everything. Curran was rising to his feet on the basis that he was to commence his closing speech.

'The defence calls Maurice Clarke,' Rooney said. Curran sat down again looking slightly perplexed. Maurice walked to the stand and held the bible in his right hand, staring at the jury just as Rooney had suggested, and spoke loud and clearly: 'I swear by almighty God that the evidence I shall give will be the truth, the whole truth and nothing but the truth.'

'State your name, please.'

'Maurice Clarke.'

The registrar then turned to the judge and repeated quite unnecessarily: 'Maurice Clarke, my Lord.' Rooney didn't mind. He loved the ritual of trial court.

'Mr Clarke, I'm going to ask you some questions. And in due course, Mr Curran, no doubt, will too. The acoustics here are very poor. Speak out. The natural reaction is to look at the questioner. Try and remember that you are giving your answers to the ladies and gentlemen of the jury and that woman furthest away in the back row must be able to hear you.'

Maurice Clarke nodded.

'What is your relationship with the accused?'

'He's my Da.'

'Could I have Exhibit 3 produced to the witness, please?' The exhibits officer produced the shoes. They were the beginning, middle and end of the case. Rooney held them aloft.

'Do you recognise these?'

'Yes.'

'Who owns them?'

'Me.'

'Are you sure?'

'Sure I'm sure.'

'How can you tell?'

'There's a little smiley on the sole of the right shoe drawn in blue marker. I got locked down by the canal and fell asleep. One of the kids from the flats drew it, messing like.'

Maurice said the word 'locked' like it was a merit badge. Rooney displayed the shoe, sole out, to the jury so that they could see the face. A couple even smiled.

'What size are you?'

'Eight.'

'Perhaps you would like to try them on.'

Curran shifted uneasily in his seat, but a look from the bench said that while Rooney should proceed cautiously, he was, for the moment at least, within limits.

Maurice walked up and down the courtroom wearing the shoes that had been taken from his Da's bedroom on the morning of the raid. He paraded like he was on a catwalk. They were a perfect fit.

'Perhaps we could compare your father's shoe with the ones you're wearing?'

Myles moved with the speed and stealth of a hungry alligator sliding off the riverbank to get his supper. He had collected the shoe (which Christy held out baton-like) and was halfway across to the witness box before Curran could get to his feet and muster an objection.

'My Lord, this is highly irregular. The accused isn't giving evidence and I can't cross-examine him.'

'My sentiments entirely. Mr Rooney, explain your conduct please!'

'My Lord, the prosecution have introduced the shoes into the case by showing they came from the Clarke household. That is so the jury can be satisfied as to the antecedents of the shoes.'

'Not just found at his flat, Mr Rooney, found in the accused's bedroom,' the Shitzu cut in.

'That's the evidence. It's the defence case that these shoes do not belong to him. I'm entitled to compare my client's shoe, which is the one the jury can see he is wearing now, with the shoe the prosecution allege belongs to him. Taking his shoe off his foot in the presence of the jury is evidence that it is his shoe.'

'But you see he is not giving evidence.'

'That's true, my Lord. But you see everything done in the jury's presence by my client is capable of being evidence. If a particular piece of evidence is being led and his demeanour is that of a guilty person, that is something the jury can and will take into account.'

'I'm old-fashioned. I still believe that the only way your client can give evidence is under oath from the witness box, where he can be cross-examined.'

'In my submission, my Lord, that is not correct. The only reason he would need to give evidence, at least on this issue, is to prove the provenance of the shoe. But the jury have seen for themselves where I have got it from.'

The Shitzu thought about it for a moment. For all his faults he liked a point of law, particularly if it was a novel one.

'You're close to the wind, Mr Rooney. Carry on.'

'You have told us you are an eight. What size is on your father's shoe?'

'Eleven.'

'Could I see them for a moment?'

Rooney put the shoes sole to sole to emphasise the difference in size. Maurice stepped into the shoes Christy was wearing. They were hanging off him.

The shoe was handed back to the accused. Before he slipped them on Clarke theatrically measured it against the length of his foot. All saw it was a good match.

'Would you answer Mr Curran's questions, please?'

In as deprecating a tone as possible, Curran commenced: 'So let me understand. It wasn't your father who carried out this vicious attack. It was you, and the stupid gardaí inadvertently got the shoes mixed up?'

Rooney jumped to his feet. 'Don't answer that! My Lord, there is a duty to warn the witness that he is not obliged to answer any question which would incriminate him.' The Shitzu shot Curran a withering look.

'Mr Curran, the question was ham-fisted. I have no choice in the circumstances.' The judge turned to the witness.

'Mr Clarke, you are usually obliged to answer all questions. You are, however, entitled to refuse to answer a question if it would tend to show that you might have committed an offence.'

The formula was legalistic but Rooney was in no doubt that Maurice had been well schooled by his Da in the nuances of how it worked.

'All right so. Thank you, Judge. Well then, I am refusing to answer that question on the grounds that I would incriminate myself.'

The jury were agog. Curran tried a few variations but Maurice repeated over and over that he was refusing to answer. When Curran testily asked what offence he was referring to Maurice replied mantra-like that he was refusing to answer even that question on the grounds that answering might incriminate him in a crime. The effect was to put him beyond cross-examination. Curran was stranded. As secret weapons went, Rooney had to admit that Maurice wasn't half bad. He hadn't seen it coming.

'Tell me, do you sleep in your parents' bedroom at night?' Curran asked, changing tack.

'Of course not, except when they are away.'

'What, so you move out of your bedroom and into theirs, is that it?'

'Not really. I don't have my own room. I sleep on the couch in the living room. But whenever they go on holidays I sleep in that bedroom.'

Rooney asked one question in re-examination.

'When did your parents go away together last?'

'The weekend before the house was raided.'

forty-seven

Fr Brendan listened to the six o'clock news report on the Christy Clarke case with mounting anxiety. The publicity had brought him right back to the night on the balcony when the head of the IRA Army Council had interviewed him in Clarke's presence, and Roche's subsequent attempts to have him give evidence. There hadn't actually been too many times in his life that he'd been really afraid but that'd been one of them. Thank God for Harry McGovern. It had been clever, but within the rules. He'd changed his view of lawyers after that experience.

He'd followed the evidence closely, and taken comfort from the fact that the case was obviously open and shut. The suggestion made by Maurice that the shoes – the ones undoubtedly worn by the assailant – belonged to him was patently absurd. The account was so obviously a ready-up it'd surely only end up bolstering an already overwhelming prosecution case.

And yet the jury had failed to reach a verdict and had been sent to a hotel for the night. Deliberations had been suspended and they'd resume in the morning. What could be keeping them? Was it down to some maverick, the sort who wouldn't convict Hitler of cycling a bike without a light? Or was there more to it than that?

His imagination was beginning to run away with him. What if the unthinkable happened? The longer the case had dragged on, the more stressed he'd become. Every now and again he'd tell himself that he was working himself into a lather over nothing. It had a soothing effect but not for long.

Fr Brendan knew about prison visits from talking to women whose husbands were doing time. A visit was purely for chitchat, for reassurance. The men especially avoided intimate discussions about home matters. The women, for their part, avoided unnecessarily burdening their husbands with the difficulties arising in the household due to their absence. Their men were vulnerable enough as it was without adding to their sense of impotence by getting into matters over which they had little or no control.

He'd always been confident that Wayne wouldn't talk. He was too ashamed for one thing. And he was probably troubled in the same way Fr Brendan had been at that age about his ambivalence towards the sex. And he'd be afraid that he'd be in trouble if he told. All of this went a long way to ensure that their little secret would remain buried.

But all that could change if Christy were acquitted. He didn't think Clarke was much of a family man, at least in the way that role was traditionally understood. Lillian's visit to him in the presbytery evidenced that. But he was also fairly sure that Clarke was the sort of person who took stock of what'd been happening in his absence. He'd be anxious to ascertain who had been loyal to him and who had drifted away. In other words, he'd be asking lots of questions.

There were bound to be some inquiries within the family about how things were. Things that might have been kept from him while he was in jail but which they could all now speak about. Wayne's unwillingness to talk about what they'd done might evaporate if he was put on the spot by his Da about whether there'd been anything going on that he needed to know about.

He'd already imagined the scene several times. Each time it got more graphic. He'd see Wayne, saying nothing, and looking down on the floor. Christy would press him for information, gently enough at first, but that'd soon give way to impatience and he'd leave Wayne in no doubt that he wanted full answers to his questions.

And what then?

The story would come first, followed by the rage, after that he didn't like to envisage.

He'd heard the stories about boys that were terribly abused in reformatory school. It was one of the reasons Christy Clarke hated the Church as much as he did. Christy would see his touching up Wayne as the ultimate insult.

Clarke had just seen the wrath that he had brought down on himself for attacking one member of the establishment. That might thwart him initially. But for how long would that last? There was no way he'd be prepared to let this pass.

The psychology underlying the attack on Reynolds was the product of a mind that was sick but creative. That suggested that punishment would be swift, violent and public. And that was a benign scenario. Christy was also capable of kidnapping him and performing unspeakable acts of terror upon him before maybe visibly marking him for life. Ever the man for the big statement Clarke would want him to bear his punishment as an emblem. He might physically brand him a child molester with a red-hot poker or something. His humiliation would be complete. The thought of it all made him sick. He'd rather be dead.

He didn't think God would help in bringing in the right verdict. Justice not only had to be done, it had to be seen to be done. It hadn't stopping him praying fervently that the jury would convict him. He'd promised to do Lough Derg if the jury delivered the right result.

forty-eight

The Tilted Wig pub across the road from the Four Courts was jammers. It had been another long day and no sign of white smoke. The majority view was that even though Rooney had done a great job, Christy Clarke's goose was cooked. The tension was mounting and a lot of people were saying they'd have to come back tomorrow for a verdict.

Roche beckoned to the barman to set up another round of drinks. Clarke was in the charge of the jury. He couldn't leave the courtroom. His supporters were working in relays to keep him company and his spirits buoyed. Waiting on the jury was always the hardest part of the case but it was hardest for Clarke. The time Roche had spent waiting for the Commission to determine Clarke's complaint had dragged. It wasn't nice.

Rooney had pointed out in his closing address that if the jury believed that the shoes belonged to Maurice, that was the end of the case. If they thought that they were *possibly* his, that was enough. And even if they didn't believe his account but still thought the shoes might belong to him, that was enough. That meant the jury had a doubt and were bound to acquit.

Common sense dictated that Clarke ought to have told them in interview that the shoes weren't his. The law prevented the prosecution informing the jury that he hadn't on the grounds that it would infringe his right to silence. The law, in Roche's view, was an ass. He hadn't quite yet worked out how but it was obvious that the defence case was manifestly false and opportunistic.

The prosecution had to tell the defence everything about their case before the off. The defence sat on their hands and didn't disclose anything until the very last moment. Normally the accused bounced a last-minute alibi into the case which the State had to try and disprove while some perjurer was setting it out for the first time in the witness box. Using Maurice as a switch had been smarter. But where was the fairness in that? He was sure if they'd been on notice of this case the guards would have shown his story up for the lie that it was.

Instead, it was a hook, articulated in terms that the jury could readily understand. Last week the scientific evidence had seemed unassailable. The whole emphasis of the case had now moved away from the forensics and onto Maurice's claim that the shoes were his. And there had been times in the last twenty-four hours when he'd got a feeling that claim was gathering momentum in the jury room.

Rooney had come out of nowhere. There was a naivety and freshness about Rooney that he was sure some of the jury had found attractive. There were a couple of middle-aged women who had sons the same age as Rooney. They might be happy to give Rooney (as opposed to his client) a break at such an early stage in his career.

And Curran, despite all his experience, had walked headlong into it, unwittingly bolstering Clarke's case by blundering it into evidence that Maurice had allegedly been sleeping in the bedroom shortly before the raid.

Roche did his best to discount his prior knowledge of Maurice and the family, of which the jury would know nothing. But juries weren't stupid. Anyone could see that Maurice Clarke was a gouger like his father and was revelling in his fifteen minutes of fame.

More often than not a jury did convict when presented with strong forensic evidence. But there had been plenty of times Roche had been sure he would get a conviction only to be flummoxed when the verdict was read out. And there had been other times – admittedly not as frequent – when he had thought the evidence fell way short of what was required but nonetheless a conviction was secured. You just never knew with a jury.

The inability to effectively cross-examine Maurice was a worry. As was the fact that the defence had been able to close on a neat forensic argument – if the shoe didn't fit, and the evidence suggested it didn't – that had gone largely unanswered by the prosecution.

Christy Clarke's supporters had swelled as the case came to a close. A motley bunch of skangers, scumbags and hoods huddled around tables, talking in hushed tones. They wanted to be part of it too, in for the kill, even if it was to see one of their own falling down. The fact that the jury had overnighted had raised their expectations. Clarke had the name for being able to walk on water. If he pulled this off he'd be guaranteed legendary status.

The two camps spoke about each other quietly and with mutual loathing but the sense of occasion had brought about an uneasy détente.

Roche had spotted Jimmy Daly sitting at one of the tables. Daly had followed him to the toilet and told him that he expected Roche to sort him on the gun charge. Roche had been appalled at the risk he'd taken. He told him they'd have a chat later. Meantime, from now on he was to keep his ears pinned to the ground for anything that was being said about Christy Clarke. He'd also directed him that in the event – what he still regarded as an unlikely event – that Clarke was acquitted, Daly was to ingratiate himself with him and find out everything that was to be known about him. Then, and only then, the two of them might talk about his recent problem with a Thompson submachine gun in a meaningful way.

On the surface everyone was skulling pints and having a laugh. People chatted away but their minds were across the road in the jury room. Wondering how they were approaching the task in hand, concentrating on the important parts of the evidence and fretting about what way it'd turn out.

Roche recognised guards from all over the city. Fellas he hadn't seen since he had trained with them in Templemore. The great and the good were here and a few senior men as well. There were plenty of younger guards too, who only knew of Clarke by reputation.

The pints were coming thick and fast. But tonight was much more than about trading gossip and war stories. The reason so many people, guards especially, had turned out went beyond the case itself. They wanted to avail of a chance to see the look on the face of an evil man when the jury found him guilty. It wasn't just schadenfreude. This was part of the ritual of being a policeman. This was part of their reason for being.

forty-nine

At ten minutes to nine Frank, the Shitzu's tipstaff, popped his head around the door of the pub and announced there was a verdict. The pub emptied in a moment, as gardaí, lawyers, supporters and hangers-on abandoned their half-finished drinks and ran to the courthouse.

Rooney sat in counsel's bench as the nine men and three women filed into court and sat in their jury box. Curran leaned over to him, put his hand gently on his shoulder and whispered that whatever the outcome he had done a good case. Coming from Curran, that meant a lot.

The Barristers' Tearoom convention said that if jurors did not look at the accused it was a conviction. Rooney saw Tom O'Dowd, the foreman, lead the group back into court. He could not actually bear to look at the expression on any of their faces. Instead, he glanced over at his client. Clarke was fidgeting with his hands, doing his best to look composed, but you could see the fear in his eyes. There hadn't been too many times in Clarke's life when he had been afraid, Rooney was sure. The next time would be on his deathbed, he thought.

Mick, the registrar, stood up and spoke to the foreman.

'Mr Foreman. Just answer this question yes or no. Is there any count on which you have reached a verdict?'

'Yes.'

The foreman then handed the registrar the issue paper. He silently scrutinised it. The slightest grimace usually meant guilty. Again, Rooney couldn't bear to look up at him. There was so much tension in his body he thought he would explode. He knew that he'd not trade this moment for a million pounds. The first charge on the indictment was grievous bodily harm on Reynolds.

'You say the accused is not guilty on Count Number One,' the registrar announced, looking at the issue paper. The foreman nodded. It was all duck or no dinner. The acquittals on the subsidiary charges of taking the motorbike and malicious damage to Reynolds' car followed as a matter of course.

This was not the first time a big and bad criminal had got a result in a difficult case. But such occasions were, in truth, few and far between. The system, for all its safeguards, was weighted against the criminal. That was probably what accounted for the moment, a nanosecond, of mute silence before Christy's supporters cheered and punched the air, shouting indignantly about bent coppers and justice being done.

Then the atmosphere turned nasty. The taking of the verdict after two days of heavy drinking added to the sense of menace and the crowd was now close to becoming a rabble. The Shitzu banged his gavel down several times on his bench.

'I will put every last one of you in jail forthwith if this doesn't immediately stop!' he shouted. 'Guards, arrest those people!' But the noise had magically abated before any member could get near to anybody. The group sat down with their arms folded, their faces set in expressions of triumphant defiance directed against an authority they despised.

The Shitzu thanked the jury politely for their deliberations, which anyone could see had been conducted with great care, the witnesses who had given up their time to give evidence and the respective solicitors and counsel. He discharged Christy Clarke from the indictment and glared down at his supporters, daring them to react. He needn't have worried. The mood had quickly given way to a giddy arrogance and they were determined to make the most of it.

Frank the tipstaff then announced, 'All rise.'

The Shitzu stood up last. He gave Rooney a discreet appreciative nod before exiting stage left, walking behind Frank who led him to the door leaving the courtroom.

Christy Clarke very briefly – perfunctorily even – thanked Rooney for all his hard work on the case. Myles solemnly told Clarke that his handling of the case – his footwork was as sure as a goat on a nasty escarpment – meant that he had got his life back, and that there was an onus on him to use it well. Clarke nodded but you could see that his attention had already fallen on the group of men waiting behind them.

Rooney looked over his shoulder. Maurice was to the fore. They were in celebration mode, jostling among themselves and anxious to get going. Clarke shook hands with both Rooney and Myles and then headed off into the midst of his retinue.

Myles congratulated Rooney again and told him to enjoy and savour the moment. Rooney was feeling a huge surge in his own emotions – relief had given way to a mixture of elation and exhaustion.

Outside, the detectives were huddled together in a corner, sucking on their cigarettes and stamping their feet on the floor. They were all experienced and seasoned members of the force. Their expressions were still forlorn. They'd believed that they'd done enough to see Clarke locked up for years to come. Now he was going back out there cock-a-hoop. Their view of the world was in tatters. Even in the short time he had been at the bar, Rooney understood: you could almost get used to winning cases but losing always left the same uncomfortable knot in the pit of your stomach. It was what made criminal cases different, for heaven's sake.

Clarke, who was ahead of him now, stopped at the door to the street and his first taste of freedom in two years.

'Roche!' he shouted. Roche looked up, the shock of the verdict visible all over his face.

'Get up the yard, yah cunt yah.' Clarke gave Roche the two fingers. Clarke was surrounded by his entourage and grinning maliciously. Roche went ashen. The crowd pushed through the door, which swung in and out on its hinges after the last man went through.

Clarke's tone had been so full of hatred that Rooney swore he could actually, physically feel it wafting through the air.

Had he, by virtue of his robust defence, aided and abetted the acquittal of a guilty man? His colleagues, the ones like Denis Wise who regarded these cases as 'fun', would have laughed contemptuously at this notion. He'd been retained to do a job, to thwart the prosecution case to the point where a jury listening to the evidence entertained a doubt. He felt momentarily queasy but it passed, swept away by the euphoria that went with bringing home a big case against the head.

fifty

Wayne was standing in an empty bath playing the opening chord sequence from 'Smoke on the Water' by Deep Purple when he heard the sound of raised voices. He played on. The notes from the lead guitar sequences bounced off the cold tiles and up into the air. The sound had a clarity that he couldn't get in any other room in the house.

The noise from the people outside got louder as it came closer. He heard cheering and laughter. He went into his bedroom and looked down into the courtyard. Four men were carrying his Da shoulder high. Jimmy Daly was leading the charge, his hands moving around like he was conducting an orchestra. A large following fell in line behind them.

His Da was waving all around him like he was a lord or something. The group stopped directly below the balcony. Lillian was standing there breaking her heart laughing. Christy blew her a kiss on the fingertips of each hand and stretched his arms out all regal.

He was carried up the stairs to the flat right onto the balcony. 'Let the celebrations begin!' his Da proclaimed, before signalling that he should be put down on the ground. His Ma was still creased over laughing. He picked her up and carried her bridal-style over the threshold. Wayne watched the pair of them smiling and laughing together the way people who haven't been carefree for ages did. He felt a surge of resentment shoot through him.

His Da spoke again to his assembled group of supporters.

'Welcome to my humble abode. Come in and make yourself at home. My wife and myself will be your perfect hosts. But first, I have a little bit of business to deal with. Eighteen fuckin' months is an awful long time in jail.'

To cheers and jeers he carried Lillian upstairs.

Wayne felt his stomach tightening. This was a ritual with which he was familiar. Christy would come in on a Sunday afternoon after the few pints. 'Woman!' he'd say and point upstairs. She'd tell Maurice, Orla and himself to watch TV and head upstairs after him. He'd picture his Da jamming the door handle with the back of the chair and then getting undressed. And there'd be grunting and creaking of bedsprings and his Ma doing a bad job of trying to stifle herself.

Today, he felt disgusted. And disappointed that his Da was home. He didn't want him back now or ever. He'd clearly been acquitted. He should be up in the Joy until he was ready for that walking stick. But young Rooney had done the business for him.

How could she do this after all he'd put her through? Smiling and laughing and having sex with him. He felt something else too. Was it jealous? What was there to be jealous about? It wasn't that they were competitors for her affection. It was more that it just shouldn't have been so easy for him. Where was his Ma's hardened heart when it mattered?

They were back downstairs in a few minutes. He looked at their faces to see could you tell what they'd done. But apart from a few sheepish grins it was like nothing had happened.

The flat had already filled up. People brought carry-outs of beer with them. Gerry Wilson, the manager of Madigan's bar, sent up a keg of Guinness and one of his barmen to set it up. There were bottles of vodka, Malibu and Bacardi too. In no time there was a party going.

Wayne moved around the room nicking vodka and mixing it in with his Coke, listening to Maurice telling and retelling how one of the prisoners had made a cast to put on his Da's foot so that the size elevens he was wearing in court looked a snug fit, and how he had got into the witness box and said the shoes found in the bedroom were his. Maurice had already got too big for his boots since his Da had gone into jail. He'd be insufferable now.

There was one awkward moment when his Ma told his Da that she had pawned his Liverpool stuff. She made out that she'd done it when he was in jail and stuck for cash. He looked at her incredulously, his eyes bulging. Wayne thought for a moment that he was going to clatter her. But even his Da knew better given the night that was in it. It was a clever move telling him on the night he got out, when even his Da could see going mental wasn't an option.

Late into the night Wayne slipped a naggin of vodka down his pants. He went into his bedroom and drank it neat. His thoughts drifted back to earlier, to the happy and excited look on her face as he carried her up to their bedroom.

It contradicted everything she'd said to the women in the kitchen. It made no sense. How many beatings did it take? He knew that his parents' relationship must be more complicated than he knew, fused with love and hatred. But there had been something between them tonight which had effortlessly trumped all the badness and united them as one.

When would she ever learn? His Da was never going to change. The leopard had scored a big kill today, but was still a leopard. It'd be business as usual soon. There'd be a few digs, black eyes and gnashing of teeth. She'd come looking to Wayne for support. She'd be waiting as far as he was concerned.

Everyone partied till it was bright. There were a lot of faces Wayne didn't recognise. Hangers-on most of them, he'd say. Jimmy Daly was one of the few that he did know. But in all the years he'd known him from drinking pints with his Da in Madigan's, he'd never come here. His Da ran a tight outfit and Daly was never going to make the cut. But since Harry Brown and Liam Kinsella had been banged up and with everyone not talking to each other his Da was very isolated. He'd no real close friends left.

Wayne was out of it by then but everyone was too drunk to notice.

Part Four

Fallout

fifty-one

'Well?'

It was noon outside the Hunter's Lodge. The morning after the night before. Daly looked like shit. It'd been six in the morning when he'd left Christy's flat. But Roche had no interest in hearing about how Christy Clarke had celebrated being free.

He was feeling plenty of pain himself without going there. He'd spoken out to several colleagues last night, telling them that Clarke had pulled a fast one, and that he'd get to the bottom of it. He'd been more vocal as the night wore on. Nobody had been particularly interested. Moreover, they'd spoken down to him. Gently, but he knew when he was being condescended to. There'd be another day, was the prevailing attitude. What goes around comes around. It was time to let go and move on, they said. Wally Drennan had been more to the point. He'd told him to cop the fuck on.

It was a bit like losing a match to an offside goal or a penalty that shouldn't have been. Logically, there was no point moaning about it. He sensed that the lads thought it was sour grapes on his part. The whole thing was a fucking nightmare.

'It was a bogey foot,' Daly said.

'You what?'

'He'd one of the prisoners make up casts so that it looked like he was a size eleven. That's how he scammed the jury.'

'Listen, you've a new brief, do you hear me? I want you sticking to Clarke like glue. I want to know everything about him, do you understand?'

'That's not the way Clarke works and you know it. The moment I'd show the slightest interest in knocking around with Clarke is the day I'd sign my own death warrant.'

'I hear what you're saying. But you're not listening to me. I'm prepared to give you a bit of time to work yourself in, but getting in on him is what you're goin' to do. Have you got me?'

Daly looked away and didn't answer.

'And when you're bedded in come and talk to me about that firearms arrest, see if I can do anything for you.'

Daly got out of the car muttering that he'd see him next week and that he wanted danger money on top of his usual stipend.

Roche drove back to Dublin mulling over the news that Clarke had put a cast on his foot.

He rang Flannery's office and made an appointment for later. He went back to his office and wrote up a detailed report setting out how Christy Clarke might be prosecuted for perverting the course of justice. He advised that statements be taken from members who were in court when Maurice had given evidence, describing how they'd seen Christy Clark measure the shoe found in his bedroom against his stocking foot to show how the shoe came up short.

Christy Clarke himself, he suggested, might then be arrested and a measurement of his foot taken, which would establish beyond aye or nay that he was a size eight. Other alternatives such as taking a statement from an assistant in a shoe shop where he had bought shoes before might usefully be explored. It wasn't beyond the bounds of possibility, he suggested, that they could enlist the help of a sympathetic shoe store owner to encourage Clarke to buy shoes by reference to some bogus special offer.

He couriered a copy of the report over to Flannery so he'd have it read before their meet. He hoped that was the reason Flannery kept him waiting over forty minutes before he was ushered in.

'What's this?' Flannery asked, holding the report up at an angle between his thumb and forefinger and swinging it gently from side to side.

'It sets out a workable strategy for bringing Clarke back before the courts. A blueprint if you like. The law books say that the correct sentence for perverting the course of justice is on par for the offence that has been thwarted. He'd do a big sentence alright.'

Flannery looked at him, quizzically.

'It's not a wind-up then?'

'No, sir, certainly not.' Roche could feel his cheeks colouring.

Flannery then unceremoniously tossed Roche's report back across the desk at him.

'Bin it. Shred any copies. Make it so that it never officially existed. And I'll keep your dignity by never alluding to it again.'

'You don't want to see whether it's even viable?' Roche had asked incredulously.

'I don't,' Flannery replied. 'I don't want Christy Clarke to make a laughing stock of us again.'

And with that Flannery dismissed him with a wave of his hand.

Had Flannery intended to be so cutting? There was no love lost between them. Flannery was a man known to pursue vendettas. Flannery was out for himself. There were plenty of others who thought the same way, like in any big organisation. He'd have coat-tailed the conviction to enhance his promotion prospects if the case had come home.

Some of the top brass were despised by the ranks. They were no more than glorified bean counters. But Flannery, for all his faults, had been a working policeman. He knew how cases worked. He knew what would play out in a court. Roche knew, deep down, that if Flannery had thought there was any mileage in his scheme he'd have backed it. That's the sort of cop he was. The dismissal of his plan by someone of his calibre hurt him.

fifty-two

The ball came in hard and low. It ran out of play. The Joey's keeper kicked the ball back into play. The ref blew up for full time. Coláiste Caoimhain players punched the air and hugged each other. Wayne elbowed the chap called Ryaner, the lad he'd been marking, hard in the back. The lanky streak of misery let out a yelp and creased over into an arch.

Wayne had played on this Joey's team for the last five years. And until today they'd never been beaten. Most matches were won before the throw-in, such was their reputation. They'd always known that they'd get beat someday, but they'd never envisaged that it'd be by some school with a poncy Irish name.

When Joey's had gone behind they had started giving the Caoimhain lads digs and all, and had used their innate roughness to intimidate them. That tactic had worked before. But today the opposition hadn't rolled over. It was hard to swallow: a better team had actually beaten them.

Wayne saw Ryaner walking off the field rubbing the small of his back. He'd been quicker off the mark and scored five points from open play. Wayne had run greater distances and did more press-ups in training than anyone else to try and make up for the fags but today he was just too slow. Maybe he needed to stop the smokes now.

In the dressing room the manager Padraig Duffy racked up the misery. 'How could yah let yourselves be beaten by a team of ballerinas like that?' he'd asked. They knew what he was saying. At heart, the Caoimhain lads were soft. They'd beaten so many other teams like them. Snobby accents and well-nourished physiques that had never really been tested were the tell-tale signs.

'Youse didn't give the commitment that was needed. Too fuckin' sure of yourselves, that was your problem,' he added.

Again, Padraig was right, but now wasn't the time to say it. Not when resentment was giving way to rage. Not when the sour taste of defeat was so strong and already had all of their focus and attention. But Padraig kept going, winding them up. 'Youse were fuckin' useless,' he went on, 'a sad day when people wearing this jersey are beat by the likes of them.'

That was when the talk started going around the dressing room about getting them, and a few indignant shouts about killin' the streaky lanky cunt Ryaner that had scored the winning goal from inside the square. Wayne knew they were being serious when he saw the speed with which they got changed. He hurried along to keep up.

The Caoimhain lads were on board their minibus when he got out. A crowd had already strategically placed itself between the bus and the gate. Wayne ran over to take up his place. The engine of the minibus started up, was put into gear and moved forward.

The crowd hemmed in together to form a strong nucleus. It was like an unseen hand was guiding it. The driver beeped his horn and inched forward.

'Fuckin' cunts!' someone shouted. Wayne ran forward and kicked the chrome grill on the front of the minibus hard. It buckled in the centre. 'Pity you couldn't kick straight like that during the match,' someone shouted. There was giddy laughter. 'Fuckin bastards!' someone else roared. Others joined in. Wayne recognised the voices; some were teammates, others were older lads from the area. Mickey Brady, the team captain, threw a big stone at the front window. It cracked and then quickly frosted over.

The driver stood up and forced the glass out onto the ground. Inside, the Caoimhain lads looked scared. The crowd cheered and heckled. Emboldened, the ranks, now swollen and top heavy, rolled towards the bus. A bloke armed with a corner flag attacked the vehicle from the side, lashing out at the windows. The sound of more smashing glass and panicked voices could be heard from within.

Then the side door opened. It was the Coláiste Caomhain manager, Brother O'Sullivan, a Christian Brother, whom his players called Sully to his face. He was five foot tall, if even, and had roared from the sideline without any let up. He'd kept his side on the tip of their toes for every ball. Wayne had been impressed by that.

Sully alighted. He moved quickly around to the front of the bus, breaking into a determined stride, his black soutane swinging around his hips as he faced into the crowd. He marched forward, a black umbrella with a pale yellow handle held aloft in his right hand.

'Get back! Now!' he roared.

'Wanker!' someone shouted from the back of the crowd. Sully poked the air with the brolly for emphasis. 'Now! You'll pay for this in ways you can't imagine. Mark my words.' There was something about the way he said it that made them listen and then think about what it was they were all doing there.

'You'll pay for this in ways you can't imagine,' Wayne shouted out impersonating him in as haughty a voice as he could muster. There was laughter, but this time it was nervous. The collective self-assurance was waning.

'Move back! Get that gate open! I'll have the guards down here in no time and we'll see who's so brave then.'

Sully stepped forward using the brolly as a buffering projectile, his expression uncompromising. They could easily have taken him out. But the exuberance and sincerity with which he'd spoken had broken the spell. In that moment, doubt crept in and the cohesiveness of the mob was undone. Once the stragglers on the periphery started to move off, the centre dissolved into a formless bulk of persons who had to think for themselves.

The crowd involuntarily lurched backwards a few inches. Sully, sensing that the advantage was his, advanced through them and drew back the bolt on the gate. He opened it out and beckoned the bus forward.

Sully had lifted his team by his sheer force of personality in the match. And he'd done it again. Wayne picked up a stone. He knew that it was going to hit its target with pinpoint precision just by the way it felt in his hand.

Sully didn't take his eye off the crowd until the minibus had safely passed through the gates. He walked briskly after it. He'd just reached the door when the stone cracked him on the side of his face just above his right eye. He turned around, scanning faces for the perpetrator. Blood trickled down his face in several directions at once. Several pairs of hands reached out and pulled Sully on board and the minibus accelerated away at speed. Wayne felt exhilarated. In a perverse way what he'd done was justified. It was power of the black cloth that had made everybody back down. Just like it worked for the pervert priest.

fifty-three

Kennedy's was filling up with people who worked in offices coming in for a drink after work having the craic. It was one of the few times that Roche regretted being a policeman working long anti-social hours. How great it would be to knock off at five o'clock every day and head to the pub.

Daly was being a real prick, constantly whinging about whether or not he'd be charged, making noises that he'd have to highlight all aspects of their relationship if he was. In ordinary course, Roche wouldn't have given a damn. He'd managed Daly in accordance with all the protocols. He'd nothing to worry about.

But he'd seen guards compromised by their relationships with touts. It wasn't a natural state of affairs, working on the margins where lines were blurred, and there was lots of adrenalin coursing through the system. Running touts meant sending and receiving curve balls to get things done. It sometimes paid spactacular dividends. But like any exercise that involved cutting corners it came at a price, was habit forming and compromised standards. Some cops succumbed to the effects of working in an environment which often went with the least line of resistance and just found it too much effort to play a straight hand thereafter.

Touts were devious. They knew better than anyone how to spread misinformation. They could wrap up a big lie around layers of truth. And it would take years of investigation to break it down. Sometimes that wasn't possible. A person's integrity was called into question. Promotions never materialised. People's careers were stalled. They got posted to backwaters as a damage limitation exercise.

Flannery had his beady eyes all over him. It wouldn't take much – one more moderate fuck-up maybe – to activate a policy of marginalising him. He sensed that some colleagues were already wary of him. He'd seen it happen so many times. A member got a name for cutting a few corners, or being a bit sloppy, and had management looking over his shoulder. People stayed away from him. They didn't want to find that association tainted them too.

He waved over to Barry Kirby up at the bar, who raised his empty glass in the air. He ordered two pints of stout and Tayto crisps, and they adjourned into the snug. The two men watched the drink settle into a dark black without talking.

'*Sláinte*,' Roche said lifting his glass.

'*Sláinte*,' Kirby replied. He took a long swig of stout and put it down on the table with a contented sigh. The head was still a creamy white and unevenly peaked up the glass. Kirby opened the crisps and started tucking into them.

'The word is that the case against Jimmy Daly for possession of the submachine gun isn't strong enough for a prosecution,' Roche said to get the conversation moving.

'The gun was under the seat. Daly denies knowledge. The case is stalled.'

'Daly has, at my insistence, ingratiated himself into the company of Christy Clarke. He's his new best friend.'

'And how much bang is Daly giving for your buck?'

'Nothing really tangible so far. Titbits. Apparently prison was much harder for Clarke than he'd expected. He was upset by the thought that he'd miss out on Wayne growing up. It made him realise how badly he'd treated Lillian and he's now anxious to make amends.'

'Jaysus, you're breaking my heart. Christy Clarke, the little lamb.'

'I know. I know. Daly will come good, I just know it.'

'Do you really? How come he's feeding you chicken shit then?'

Guards up to the rank of sergeant were classed as members of the force. Inspectors and above were officers and Kirby revelled just that little bit too much in being a member of the officer class. How many touts had Kirby run in his time? Not many, Roche guessed. But this was not the time to fall out with him over it.

'Barry, I need Daly at the coalface. Without him it could take years to nail Clarke. He's all I've got. I am as anxious as anyone to move things up a gear. That's not going to happen unless Daly still has an in with him.'

Kirby drained the remaining stout from his glass. It was personal with Clarke now. Roche hoped that he hadn't sounded too needy.

'And the reason you're telling me all this is?'

'Right now, Daly believes that I can stop the DPP prosecuting him. I haven't exactly said I couldn't, to be honest. It'd help me if you sat on the file for a while. My influence over him will end the moment he finds out that he isn't being done for it.'

'How long are you looking for?'

'As long as you can give me.'

Kirby weighed it up.

'Well, on the basis that the case isn't going anywhere, the file can fall behind a radiator and, within reason, can stay there as long as you need.'

'Thanks, I really appreciate it. It gives me a bit of space to do my work.'

fifty-four

The Simmonscourt Pavilion in the RDS was thronged with anoraks all there to savour the result at close quarters. The multiple counts in a general election that went on until the final candidate reached the quota, or rivals were eliminated, under the complicated proportionate representation weren't a feature today. The last person elected in a five seat constituency might be decided by a couple of votes in the small hours of the morning, only for a recount to be called by the unsuccessful candidate. Such counts had been known to last for several days.

Today the result was on a first-past-the-post basis. It'd been clear within an hour how the referendum on the eighth amendment to the Constitution was going to pan out. The people had voted nearly two-to-one to protect the life of the unborn. Dun Laoghaire was the only place in Dublin to reject the amendment. What else could you expect from west Brits? It wasn't for nothing that it had been called Kingstown. They'd disgraced themselves.

Cora was stood beside him, her deportment and aura the living embodiment of happiness. The result meant that all the hours going around never-ending housing estates, and attending meetings in parish halls, hotels and town squares, constantly flannelling the egos of the local politicos, had been worth it.

He'd marvelled at her ability to reduce complex issues into bite-size pieces that could be served up in ways that were capable of being understood and were relevant to people's lives. Cora was constantly persuading and cajoling, admonishing those who didn't respond in harsh terms, but she was nonetheless a firm believer that you caught more flies with honey than vinegar.

It'd been a useful but steep learning curve. He'd found Fr Peter's implacable opposition to every idea he proposed very wearing. He'd taken a leaf out of her book and now outlined any new proposal in a memo, and then solicited his advice before going any further. Fr Peter had stopped seeing him as a threat and had even come up with a few modest improvements of his own.

As a regular commentator on radio and television debates, Fr Brendan's profile had soared. Several people in the pavilion gave him the thumbs up. He'd spotted some of his adversaries too, fellas that he'd had a right cut off during exchanges. Most of them had nodded sagely at him with a cheery smile, keen to acknowledge that he'd earned the right to enjoy today.

But for now it was a moment to savour: the liberal media and Dublin 4 intelligentsia had been routed. Fr Brendan had spent a good part of the morning on the radio sticking it into them. God, it felt good.

For all that, there was a niggling discontent. The moment was ephemeral. He used to think that he experienced this feeling on the basis that victories like this were devoid of any spirituality. But there was more to it than that.

Just then there was a flurry of activity to their right. Charlie Haughey strode imperiously across the floor towards the makeshift RTÉ studio, a clatter of camera crews in his wake.

Haughey had been successfully, albeit briefly, re-elected as Taoiseach since that fateful day that they had visited him in his office. But his government was dependent upon the raggle-taggle support of independents. Tony Gregory, the atheist socialist, held the balance of power.

The pundits had a field day contrasting Haughey, the supplicant gangster, with Garret FitzGerald, the principled naïve white knight who had refused to enter into auction politics for Gregory's support. It was light and darkness.

Haughey had been forced to commit tens of millions of pounds into revitalising Gregory's Ballybough constituency as the price for his vote. Fr Brendan had initially been aghast, and then in awe of how much Gregory had wrung out of Haughey for his support. It was all tangible stuff: social housing, community centres and a new medical centre. This was legacy material. Gregory was surely elected for life.

Unsurprisingly, Haughey's minority government was riven with petty rivalries and jealousies. It'd barely lasted six months before collapsing ignominiously. He still cut quite a swathe, though, as he made his way through the parting crowd.

Suddenly he changed course. One TV crew collided into another and a camera crashed to the ground with bits flying in all directions. Haughey was practically on top of them before Fr Brendan realised that Cora was the target of his attention.

'Cora,' he said, before sweeping his arm out in a gesture to the assembled media behind him, 'you're just the person I wanted to meet today. The Irish people have just voted on something that was dear to their hearts. Cora Jameson here came to visit me with this young priest to canvass for this amendment, and she was instrumental in my giving a promise that the people would have a chance to vote on this amendment to the Constitution.

'I am vindicated in that decision, by the debate that took place prior to the vote, by the high turnout and ultimately by the result.

'But this lady here is vindicated in something far more important: her work has ensured that the unborn enjoy a constitutional protection of life in this country.'

Haughey positioned himself between them and held his hand and Cora's aloft. The motorised whirring of cameras and flashes filled the air. With a wink, Haughey turned and headed back on a trajectory towards the studio, the press corps still dutifully trailing after him.

Remembering the story about Haughey's aversion to shaking hands, Fr Brendan had noticed that the politician's hand hung limp like a dead fish when he had held Fr Brendan's hand aloft.

fifty-five

Wayne packed his gear into his kit bag. He'd put in a really good training session. They'd all wanted to put the result behind them. After Padraig had calmed down he'd said it was a wake-up call, and that everyone had to learn from the defeat. He'd been putting them through their paces ever since. It'd been a hard session tonight. They'd won the last three games since then and that was helping.

There'd been a big inquiry into the attack on the Christian Brother, but no one had said anything. He'd damaged Sully's eye, and it had been touch and go on whether he'd lose sight in it. The relief when word came back that he was OK was huge.

His Da had warned him to stay schtum. He thought his Da would be angry, although he didn't know whether his anger would stem from the act itself or doing it in a way that so many people had seen him. His only comment had been to say that if Roche or any other copper called looking for him, he was to remember to say absolutely nothing, no matter what questions were asked.

Having his Da home had turned out much better than he'd thought. Firstly, his Da was doing everything possible to get into his Ma's good books. He hadn't laid a hand on her once, hadn't even lost the head. He spent a lot of time down the boxing club coaching, which was something he hadn't done in years.

The priest had stopped touching him up during the trial. Wayne had put that down to the pervert priest thinking that his Da might be acquitted and be released. Wayne didn't think that the priest would start up on him again. But he still had wanted to give up the music lessons. His Ma had said no way. He'd been delighted when his Da had agreed with him. He knew his Da was trying to keep in with his Ma and that he'd gone out on a limb for him saying that he could stop the lesssons if he wanted.

The guards had come down to Padraig Duffy looking for a statement about what had happened. Padraig said that neither he nor any of the players knew anything about the incident. Then Roche came snooping around. His Da had called to the station and filed a fresh complaint before the Garda Complaints Commission, alleging harassment. Roche hadn't been seen again after that.

Wayne was leaving the ground when he noticed Cathy Doyle hanging out with her mates. Lisa Murphy, her cousin, who lived a couple of doors from him, was there as well. Cathy lived in the flats down by the canal but she spent a lot time up his way on account of Lisa. Cathy had a V-shaped face, and long light blonde hair that fell away in ringlets. She was brown as a berry without a single freckle. She was slim with legs toned up from playing sports.

Last summer Wayne had been happy to hang around all evening when the girls played hopscotch in the hope Cathy would notice him. A couple of words would keep him going for days. Since then he'd taken to standing beside her at the back of the church so he'd shake her hand when it came to the part where everybody offered each other a sign of peace. After a while he realised there was no need: she always came over and stood beside him anyway.

Wayne wasn't good around girls, but he'd found it easy talking to her. She made him feel at ease and good about himself. At first he thought it was just the way she was with everyone. But he couldn't help noticing that she perked up that bit more when he was around her. He was sure he wasn't imagining it. He didn't know why, just that he'd be mad to think that it was anything to do with fancying him.

Lads in school, older than him, were always talking about her. Thomas Crilly, a mouthy little fuck if ever there was one, came in one Monday morning claiming he'd got off with her at the weekend. He said that she'd been well up for it.

The thought of Cathy being with a scaly cunt like Crilly cracked him up. What could she see in him? She was far too classy for a fuckin' eejit like him. Maybe Crilly had only been bragging? Wayne had been in the horrors for days until he'd bumped into her and mentioned that Crilly was saying he'd got off with her. She'd been indignant in her denial, calling him a creep. Wayne had been thrilled to hear it.

He stopped to have a chat. The girls said they'd head down the flats with him. They hung out around the stairwell yakking, him smoking, them chewing gum.

'My Da told me that if any copper showed up I wasn't to say a word, and to get his solicitor to come to the station.'

Everyone had been talking about the attack on Sully, and he was anxious to let it be known he was the prime suspect. Lisa was all wide-eyed but he could see that Cathy had no interest. In fact, he sensed that if he'd told them that someone else was in the frame for it she'd have expressed her disapproval. He still insisted on telling the story in detail anyway. He didn't actually say that he'd thrown the rock, but they got the picture. Cathy made a point of saying she was delighted the injury wasn't serious.

When it got late Lisa's Ma shouted out for her to come in. When Lisa said she'd walk Cathy home, her Ma started shouting and roaring at her to come in now.

'I'll walk you down,' Wayne said.

'If you like,' she replied.

Like it? He'd love it, but he knew better than to let on. He chatted on the way down about playing for Joey's; how Padraig Duffy was training them very hard to make sure they'd win the league.

He was nervous and felt his throat going dry. That still hadn't stopped him taking the shortcut along the towpath. It was quiet tonight, just the usual groups of young lads drinking cans and smoking dope. The cloying sweetness from the smoke heavily perfumed the air.

He kept his hands firmly planted in his pockets. Cathy was prattling on about this course she wanted to do in fashion design when she left school after her Inter. Wayne was trying to keep up with a parallel dialogue going on in his head, the one that was urging him to take her hand in his.

Would she be annoyed? Or tell everyone that he was a weirdo? He was sure that she wouldn't entertain him, that he'd hate himself for being such a gobshite, but he was nonetheless equally sure that the risk of that happening wasn't going to stop him.

He'd heard lads in school getting a lot of slagging about dropping the hand. While he was fairly sure that phrase meant putting it down by her fanny, he figured that it'd still be a bad thing if she didn't let him take her hand in his.

Croke Park loomed high into the sky. The end of the towpath was in sight. It was overgrown with weeds, and cans and cigarette boxes were everywhere. He heard a plop and spotted a water rat swimming across to the other side. After umpteen false starts – moving his hand casually in her direction and then slipping it back into his pocket – he took his hand out one more time and slipped it into hers. She didn't react. He entwined their hands together. Still there was no resistance. She kept talking away, not missing a beat, as if nothing had happened.

Wayne stopped under the bridge. She pulled him along but not very hard. 'C'mon,' she said, but he could tell that she was giddy. He pulled her in towards him. She swung naturally into an arc that brought her face right into his. Her eyes were dancing.

He kissed her on the mouth. She nuzzled her face into his neck. He kissed her again. This time she stuck her tongue into the vast cavern that was his open mouth. His tongue touched off hers and he immediately felt warm and fuzzy. They kissed over and over for what seemed like ages. She got flustered when he started kissing her on the neck and warned him not to give her a hickey.

When they were done he asked her would she go with him.

'It's a bit late for that, isn't it?' she'd replied. But she was smiling, and walked ahead of him still holding his hand.

At the entrance to the flats she kissed him on the cheek, said 'See yah,' and ran off.

'When?' he had shouted after her.

'Soon!' she'd answered and then stopped and added: 'Maybe?'

She was smiling though as she backed away before turning around and heading for the stairwell. He stood there watching to make sure that she got up safely. She looked down from the balcony, waved and disappeared in the door.

Whoever would have thought? What was he to make of her answer that it was too late to ask whether she'd go with him? He'd already decided that it was a good answer even if it stopped short of yes. He wished that he'd made a proper date to see her again. He hadn't wanted to be pushy. But he reckoned that he needed to bring about another meeting as quickly as possible to solidify this into something. Otherwise this thing could slip off the hook and it'd be like it'd never even happened.

Before tonight he'd often imagined getting off with her, safe in the knowledge that it'd never happen. It had always worked out perfect in his head. But that still hadn't prepared him for this. What he'd imagined it to be like hadn't even come close. He'd go as far as saying that he'd never felt this good about anything in his life before. For once, real life had worked out better than something in his head.

fifty-six

Fr Brendan emerged from the darkness of the Adelphi cinema. The daylight hurt his eyes for the few moments it took him to adjust. The release of the new *Star Wars* film *Return of the Jedi* meant that the foyer was packed with kids. A boy bumped into him. The box he was carrying went flying up into the air and popcorn scattered all around. He'd been looking over his shoulder talking to his father when he'd slammed into Fr Brendan.

'Yah fucking eejit,' Christy Clarke said and cuffed Wayne lightly on the ear. Wayne looked sheepish until he saw Fr Brendan. Wayne scowled at him, picked the box off the ground and scurried off into the crowd. Fr Brendan watched them recede into the midst of bodies.

Did Christy know? His body language said not. That, and the fact that he hadn't already arrived at the presbytery and kneecapped him or worse. What was there to tell anyway? It wasn't as if he had coerced the boy – well not much anyway. And no matter what Wayne said, Fr Brendan knew that part of him had liked what they'd done. Wayne would never be true to himself until he faced up to that. He'd do well to remember that.

He'd tried to explain to Wayne that it'd all make more sense when he was older. It had no effect. Wayne had sat there sulkily looking out the window. During the trial he'd told him that he wasn't going to touch him up any more. There was no answer. Fr Brendan had assured him that he meant what he was saying. In response, Wayne had shot him a look of unbridled contempt.

Wayne's copybooks were now covered with 3D graffiti dedicated to the fact that *Cathy loves Wayne loves Cathy*. Wayne had stuck it right under his nose to make sure that he saw it. Was the fact that he was doing a line with a lassie the reason why he despised him so much now?

He'd been hurt by the rejection, and, ridiculous as it sounded, it was made worse knowing that Wayne had a girlfriend. He was twenty-eight and Wayne was thirteen. And he was jealous. How strange was that? It was a pretty good reason to feel pathetic. And while he wouldn't interfere in any way between him and his girl, he willed (he couldn't actually pray) that it'd finish and soon. He would comfort Wayne then.

He'd started to really resent Christy Clarke.

It was no coincidence that Wayne had started missing music lessons wholesale after Christy reappeared on the scene. Fr Brendan had called Wayne out of class in school and virtually begged him to do just one more grading. He'd refused in a very offhand way. There was impertinence in his manner. The balance of power had shifted in their relationship.

He'd even called back up to Lillian to impress upon her what a talent Wayne had, and that there was an obligation on them both as responsible adults to make sure he developed it.

This wasn't a word of a lie. Fr Brendan had no doubt that Wayne could go all the way, provided he was nurtured in the right environment. He'd make something of himself and broaden his mind beyond the perimeter of the courtyard of the flats. She'd just shrugged her shoulders and said she was blue in the face saying it to him and what more could she do? He'd wanted to give her a good shake and say that there were plenty of things she could do. She could begin by forcing him to go back to his lessons and do his grading. He was barely a teenager for God's sake.

When he'd pressed her on Wayne not turning up he'd learned that Christy was now carting Wayne around various pubs, entering him into talent contests all over. He'd even incorporated Wayne's impersonations into his act. He'd won loads of turkey and hams. The highlight so far was a one-week family holiday in the Isle of Man with £100 spending money. Christy was even talking of managing Wayne full time, taking him out of school to do gigs around the country.

Fr Brendan had waylaid Christy coming out of the bookies on his way back to the pub. He'd gently explained to him that Wayne's talent needed to be nurtured slowly. Clarke had stood there, hands folded, face looking down on the ground, his expression bored and dismissive.

He'd persevered. The problem, of course, wasn't just overcoming the man's ignorance. Christy Clarke was naturally suspicious of authority and things he didn't know anything about. Behind the bravado lurked an inferiority complex that insisted on controlling everything. Not understanding what classical music was actually about meant that he couldn't control it, and hence he didn't want his son next or near to it.

Christy Clarke's response to his little pep talk had been to redouble his efforts. He was now dragging Wayne around every dive in town trying to get him work. What could the boy achieve with proper classical training? Or with his ear for voices and accents, learning a language, instead of mimicking the sports commentary of Michael O'Hehir or the gravelly tones of Charlie Haughey for a few cheap laughs?

For reasons Fr Brendan couldn't understand, the man had decided to get involved in raising his son since he'd been released from jail. He wasn't forgetting or overlooking the fact that he was his father. Nor was he discounting outright the rumours that Clarke was going to step away from crime and get involved with his family. That wasn't the point. Clarke was supposed to be smart. Couldn't he see that he'd actually nothing worthwhile to offer? That he was too old to change in any meaningful way?

The idea that Christy would manage Wayne's career had probably been the first proposal the man had ever made to make honest money.

In ordinary course he'd have lauded the change from the rooftops, held it up as a shining example of redemption. But the prospect of Wayne spending his life covering non-descript pop music in smoky bars and doing impressions so outraged Fr Brendan that he'd have been happy for Christy to dedicate the rest of his life to committing serious crime if it meant that he'd let Wayne reach his true potential.

fifty-seven

Daly was not delivering up quality intel that could move things on and Roche's patience was wearing thin. He'd made it clear to him that he didn't want any more guff about Clarke retiring from the scene, or acting on a consultancy basis to other established criminals. The final straw was the suggestion that Christy was going to make a living managing Wayne's fledgling musical career. He'd wanted to kick Daly out of his car there and then.

And what the fuck did 'consultancy' mean? There weren't too many ways of making a living getting other people to do your dirty work. The Provos got kickbacks by controlling who worked on the building sites. They'd set up a protection racket extorting contributions from small businesses around the city. But Clarke didn't have the muscle or smarts to sustain or organise anything like that. Besides, Dublin was far too small for that kind of thing. Here, you blagged for yourself or you starved.

There was another impediment. Clarke might well be an evil and prolific criminal with a penchant for good organisation, but he wasn't a team player. He didn't let his right hand know what his left hand was doing. He was incapable of delegating. It was one of the reasons why for all his successes he hadn't been able to build an empire.

He'd got onto the collator's office after his last meeting with Daly and requested that they provide him with every sighting of Clarke, and any mention of him in dispatches. Incredibly, the responses only seemed to confirm what Daly was saying. When he wasn't acting as Wayne's impresario he was down the boxing club helping out and bringing on young lads or going to Wayne's GAA matches.

The only thing remotely connected to criminal activity was a visit he'd paid to the local pawnbroker to reclaim his Liverpool stuff that Lillian had pawned. He'd apparently given an ultimatum to old man Gearty that if his stuff wasn't back by the end of the week he'd kick the bollocks out of him. Gearty had meekly obliged. Roche had sent a couple of detectives down to take a statement from him. Gearty had run them out the door, saying you could never find a policeman when you needed one and that if he made a complaint against Clarke he'd need one alongside him forever.

Roche wasn't buying any of it. He'd known Clarke for too long.

Clarke had never actually worked, at least in the conventional sense. He was unemployable. Clarke had applied to join the British Navy after he'd been released from reform school. He'd apparently ticked the box 'bugler' under preferences. The bold Christy had thought it had read 'burglar'. Roche had initially assumed that the story was part of the folklore but he'd seen Clarke's face colour red when he'd ribbed him about it.

Clarke wasn't the type to pension plan. He'd never retire. Like an old fox or badger in the forest, he'd keep going until he keeled over. Meantime, Wayne's novelty act would fizzle out soon enough. And what would Christy Clarke do then? The chap couldn't lie straight in bed at this stage.

'So, Jimmy, what've you got for me?'

'I got something alright.'

'Go on.'

'Look, are you guaranteeing the gun charge will go away? I can be killed for even being here. I need to know where I stand.'

'You know very well I can't make any promises, particularly when I don't know what you've got. You're going to have put your cards on the table, face up, simple as that.'

Daly had to believe that he needed Roche if this was going to work, and he wouldn't believe he needed Roche if he thought that squaring the charges was straightforward.

Daly said nothing, chewing on his upper lip, and began talking.

'Cocaine. Clarke has access to a big quantity. It was through a contact he made in prison. He's asking around to see if there's anyone who can take it off his hands.'

'Drugs? Christy Clarke? What a load of bollocks. He's a scumbag alright, but I don't believe for one moment he'd be a dealer.'

'It's a one-off. Twenty kilos. He can live with it. It's not smack, it'll be going up the noses of rich kids from Mount Merrion. He got it for next to nothing for a favour someone owed him so he's gonna make a good turn on it. I told you already, he wants to step back from things for a while and work out a few things with his life. Doing this deal will give him cash to do that.'

'Seems very unlikely to me. What stage is this deal at?'

'He's taken delivery and looking to offload.'

'How much is he looking for it?'

'£250,000. He's making it a condition of sale that anyone who wants to deal with him pays fifty grand upfront to even see the product.'

That was some discount – open wholesale market value would be closer to a million quid.

'He knows that once word gets out that it's available you guys will be all over him. That's partly why he is inisting on getting money upfront. It'll keep chancers and messers at bay. But he's getting anxious: he wants this deal done discreetly and done yesterday.'

'Keep me posted, do you hear? This transaction isn't to happen without me knowing about it, and I want word as much in advance as practical. Do you understand?'

'Really? Just like that? Is there a tout's widows and orphans fund?'

Daly was turning into a real whinger and it was getting on his nerves.

'It's not as simple as that, and you know it,' Daly continued. 'He's only brought me into the loop because I know the takers for product like that, in that type of quantity and who'll trade without any fuss. Clarke has his own network of contacts. He mightn't need me. The only way I'll know anything about the deal is if he asks me to set it up. And I'm doing nothing till I know what you're going to do for me.'

It'd be sweet to bust Clarke in possession of a hard drug like cocaine all the same. Aside from never having dealt in drugs, Christy had made a point of spreading out his largesse among the community he lived in. He'd paid for a good few weddings and funerals over the years and helped people out of tight corners when they'd been stuck for a few bob. Apart from the big sentence he'd get going down for cocaine, it'd put paid to his Robin Hood image once and for all.

When you thought about it, drugs were the only way a criminal like Clarke could make serious moolah with minimal risk. He could hire mules to move the product. But there was no way he could stay in the community if he was selling gear to kids who were going to die from an overdose or AIDS. He could manage a one-off deal though. Particularly when the drug was cocaine and not heroin. Maybe the whole thing wasn't as daft as it sounded.

Daly waved the envelope with the cash he got from Roche back in his face. 'A few quid isn't in here if I'm going to jail or I get a bullet in the head up a back alley. Do you know what I mean?'

'Leave it with me, Jimmy. I'm sure that we can work something out. You get Clarke to deal and the gun charge will go away. Meantime, stall any transaction if you can.'

Daly nodded in agreement.

'There is something else you should know. If this deal goes down and I'm not part of it, there's going to be trouble. The kind of trouble that will make the gun charge you're facing at the moment look like small potatoes. Do you understand?'

Daly grimaced in acknowledgement, stepped out of the car and slammed the door hard.

fifty-eight

Wayne hurried down Blessington Street, not daring to be late. Cathy had got annoyed when he'd turned up late before but that was mainly because he'd been pissed. He'd only been trying to impress the lads. They couldn't believe that he was going out with her in the first place. It increased his stock even more, or at least it had felt like it at the time, when he said, 'Fuck her, she can wait, give us another can.'

In his inebriated state he'd even convinced himself that it was good for her to know that there were other things out there competing for his time. And then he'd remembered that he was the son of Christy Clarke, a man who stayed in the pub getting drunk and then came home and ruined it for everyone. And he'd copped on.

The Basin was their secret meeting place. It was far enough away to avoid people they knew, but near enough that they could get to it without too much hassle. It'd been built in the early 1800s as a reservoir to supplement the city's water supply. Up until a few years ago it had been used by the Jameson distillery to make whiskey. Some of the auld lads down the pub swore the whiskey didn't taste the same after it changed.

They'd spend the next few hours on one of the benches by the water, feeding the ducks and chatting. It was private. They never met anyone they knew. Some days he'd slyly look at her watch and see that they had been in each other's company for less than an hour, and it'd seemed like ages. It even seemed a bit of an effort. Then several hours would pass without either of them really noticing.

He saw Cathy walking towards him with a big smile on her face. Wayne spat out the mint gum he'd been chewing and stood up from the bench. His Ma said that Cathy, with her angular face and high cheekbones, was gonna be a model. She made it sound like a boast.

He kissed her lightly on the lips: they sat on the bench. He monitored her every movement right down to the way she sat and where she put her hands. Would she sit up straight with her hands together on her knees? Or would she lie back with her arms outstretched over the back of the bench. He'd tell everything in those first few moments about where her head was at, and how the rest of the date would go.

'Me Ma wants to know will you come away to the Isle of Man with us?'

'And your Da? What's he say about it?'

'He is cool with it, he said that none of us would be going anywhere if it weren't for me.'

It'd be the first holiday that the family had gone on since the time they'd hired a caravan for a long weekend in Bettystown when Wayne was little.

His Da had taken Maurice, Orla and himself to the beach and they'd built this enormous sandcastle. They'd spent hours decorating it with shells under his Da's direction. They finished up every evening with a single of chips and a ninety-nine. It'd been great. There hadn't been a cross word the whole week, until his Da had got mouldy and she'd locked him out of the caravan. He'd practically pulled the door of the hinges in his rage.

'I'll ask my Ma. I'd love to go. Could we stick each other all the time?'

'I wonder will Da be able to hold it together.'

Lately his Da took his Ma out to the pub every Friday night and Sunday morning, just like when they'd got married first. He'd bought her a new washing machine and an appliance that peeled potatoes. It was like a pot with a rough surface. You put the potatoes in and they spun around off the rough surface and it scraped off the skin. He said it was his contribution to women's lib.

Wayne had been suspicious at first, watched for any tell-tale signs that it was an act. There was the odd row when he came in tanked up. He still hit her an occasional slap. But any fool could see now that he was hitting her because he saw that she didn't really care for him anymore. His Da couldn't understand why she was turning away from him and rejecting his offer of amends. In fairness, he just kept trying harder, even though his Da knew better than anyone that once she made her mind up about anything she wasn't for turning.

'He'll be grand.'

'I'm getting a right slagging about all the time I'm spending with you,' she said. 'The girls are really getting on my case. Lisa Murphy says we're like an old married couple.'

'Would you like to be married?' Wayne asked. He said it for a bit of a laugh, it wasn't a proposal or anything, but his heart was racing waiting for her reply.

'I'd like it.'

'Me too,' Wayne replied, doing his best to be casual. He was jumping for joy and excitement inside his head. And the best part was that, at that moment, he knew she was feeling the same way he was. That was the way with them.

'We'll get your pervert priest to do the job!'

The mere mention of him was a jolt. It was odd to hear someone else describe him as the pervert priest. His Ma had got onto Cathy to get onto him about giving up the lessons. In the end he'd told her that the priest was queer, all Roman hands and Russian fingers. Not that he'd ever tried anything on him; he'd burst him if he did.

She was looking at him expectantly, her face, as usual, on the verge of a smile.

She was so lovely. It was such a relief to find out that he liked being with a girl, that he wasn't a puff. He still felt like a freak some days. Did she know? Not a chance, he decided. She'd break it off with him straightaway for sure – and who would blame her?

The pervert priest was forever lurking around corridors in school, trying to find opportunities to talk to him. The confrontation at the Adelphi cinema had been spooky. He'd been glad that the spilt popcorn had acted as a distraction. He'd had a pained look on his face like he was hurt that Wayne didn't want to stop and shoot the breeze with him. He'd made up his mind then: it was time for the priest to go, the sooner the better.

fifty-nine

Fr Brendan lifted up his trousers from around his ankles and zipped up. The man he'd just had sex with gave him a cursory nod and walked through the bushes to re-join the path.

The Phoenix Park had its limitations. There was no afterglow. In the cold light of day he always felt debilitated. Criminalised, despised and laden with guilt. The aftershock had been so bad the first few times he'd been suicidal. He got some relief from confession. But a few mumbled words about unnatural acts in the park, as he'd referred to it, were no substitute for being able to talk about it. But there was no one he could talk to and if there had been he didn't believe that he'd have the courage to broach the topic anyway. He'd put it all down to God's way of reminding him that what he did up here was wrong.

He'd enjoyed the liaisons here much more in the early days. The guilt that descended afterwards notwithstanding, it had been a much more carefree experience. But coming here repetitively cast a gloom over him. It was getting harder to do this without asking what he was getting out of it. He didn't like thinking about the answer.

Anonymous sexual conflagrations behind the hedgerows still served a purpose though. They were opportunities to share something with a like-minded human being that they kept hidden from the rest of the world. The trips here kept the lid on things he didn't fully understand, and that ultimately he might never confront. His sexuality was making him miserable. But he was determined, for now at least, to stay locked into a pattern of sin and confession that he hoped one day might lead, if not to his redemption, at least to some resolution to his dilemma

He watched the shape of the man meld into the twilight. You could still make out the ruggedness of him by the evenly contoured shape of his shoulders and the firm pace of his strides. They'd hardly spoken. He was in his early thirties, non-descript country accent, well spoken. No wedding band or circular mark around his finger. His hands, like Fr Brendan's, were impossibly soft. 'Pen pusher's hands,' the man had observed *sotto voce* and with what Fr Brendan thought was sadness. He probably worked as a lawyer or an accountant or some high-ranking civil servant. He was another shadow leading a double life.

He'd sensed that the man – they hadn't swapped names – was here out of the same sense of frustration, loneliness and desperation as he was. Today this had translated into good sex. It had felt good to connect with someone who was in the same place. The clandestine and sordid nature of their meeting had added spice to the experience. Intimacy brought about a state of ecstasy, however fleeting.

The two of them would be mortified if they ever met again in a traditional social setting. Some of the guys he met up here wanted to hang around chatting afterwards, or to meet up in the George for pints. One fella had wanted him to come to his house for dinner. He found the thought of this repulsive. In the midst of all the isolation he'd never contemplated having a relationship with someone else. Partly it was because he couldn't live with the disapproval that would go with it. But he wasn't really drawn to it either if he was being honest. He often felt lonely but never imagined a relationship filling that void. He wondered did this make him sexually promiscuous and not just frustrated.

Once he'd seen a bloke he met up here at an international rugby match in Lansdowne Road. He'd been a face in the crowd several rows down from him. Afterwards, about half a mile from the stadium, he'd walked around a corner and bumped right into him. He'd muttered an apology and kept going.

The whole thing had been instantaneous but long enough for each of them to see a flicker of discomfort appear on the other's face. He'd been wearing his clerical clothes and had fretted for days afterwards. It was a small coterie of people who came here and some of them were shameless and liked to gossip. It only took one person to see him wearing his dog collar and he'd tell everyone.

He patted down the outside of his clothes and set off. He had to be careful not to leave any debris that would suggest that he'd been out in the woods or that would invite any queries.

He didn't relax until he exited the park down by the Conyngham Road bus station. He paused at Heuston Station to look into the Liffey. The tide was low and the riverbed was a dark green sludge and smelled of rotten eggs. Bikes, shopping trolleys and a rusty bed frame jutted out of the mud.

He hadn't seen Wayne since that night in the cinema when the only acknowledgement had been a scowl. Christy hadn't even given him a second glance. He was in civvies, so he mightn't have recognised him. Fr Brendan had spent more quality time with Wayne than Christy ever had or would. He wasn't his father of course. He wasn't even a father figure, at least in the way that word was traditionally understood. They were connected though. He'd done things for Wayne that would stand to him later in life that went way beyond a trip to the cinema.

The father's casual profanity, and the accompanying clip on Wayne's ear when he'd spilled the popcorn, had actually underscored the natural bond of affection between father and son, and the huge gulf that existed between Fr Brendan and Wayne. He wouldn't be able to replicate the easy intimacy of that exchange in twenty lifetimes.

Men had been drawn to having sex with boys since time immemorial. It was a practice that was practically venerated in ancient Greece. He'd read a scholarly text in which it was argued that it wasn't always exploitation. Men and boys did it because they liked it, because it fulfilled some need, was the argument. Sometimes he thought – or more accurately, fantasised – that in time he and Wayne and others in the same position would face up to what they were doing and acknowledge that it was real.

Try as he might, he wasn't able to draw any lasting comfort from this. He knew that what he did with adult men at the park was different to what he'd done with Wayne. He knew in his heart that sort of thinking wasn't just heresy, it was perverse. Besides, he'd never go against the Church on matters of dogma.

He knew, had always known if he was being truthful, that when it came down to it Wayne had only endured sex with him. He could never justify what he'd done to him, not in any objective sense. But that didn't mean that what he had with Wayne was only lust either. He'd still felt a bigger connection with Wayne than any of his willing accomplices in the Phoenix Park. He missed having Wayne around. It wasn't just that he was a good pupil. Or his modesty – the boy genuinely had no sense of how good he actually was. There was a likeability about him. Being in his company always gave him a little lift, and the good Lord knew that was something he could do with right now.

sixty

Wayne caught the ball just outside the square and hit it hard and low into the corner. The crowd roared its approval. The score put Joey's back into the lead. As a corner-back he didn't get many chances to score. He ran over to the sideline to celebrate. His Da was jumping up and down punching the air and bear hugging the lad beside him. Wayne was on a high, but the sight of his Da and his unrestrained joy pushed him onto an even better plain.

They played out the final couple of minutes. Two more precious points in the bag. The manager had drilled it into them that if they won today they'd get the chance once and for all to put the defeat by Coláiste Caomhain behind them. Coláiste Caomhain were still unbeaten but had drawn two matches, one of them to Joey's when they'd played them in their ground. Today's score meant that the sides were level on points, and the championship would now have to be decided by a play-off at a neutral venue. This time it would be different. He was sure of it.

Afterwards his Da was all over him saying how proud he was. It was the same reaction with his music. He'd been delighted and full of encouragement. Wayne couldn't remember his Da getting enthusiastic about anything he'd ever done before. In fact, the pervert priest aside, he couldn't remember anyone getting excited about anything he'd ever done. The fact that it was his Da made it special. It all felt good.

His Da's time down the club was paying dividends. The youth teams were winning every tournament in sight. There was even talk about naming the annual Dublin Under-16 Youth Cup the Christy Clarke Perpetual Cup. His Da laughed it off, but you could see that he loved the idea of it. It was one of the few times he'd seen his Da get flustered. All of this was new; Wayne couldn't remember his Da laughing at anything before he went to jail.

He walked back to the flats on his own. His Da had gone to Madigan's to meet Jimmy Daly to talk a bit of business. Jimmy was his new best friend these days. Wayne worried. The only reason his Da could be spending so much time with him was that there was some class of a job in the pipeline. A few months ago he'd wanted his Da convicted of attacking Reynolds. But now he didn't want him going anywhere. He liked having him around, liked that he was interested in him and his Ma even. He liked that he wanted them all to be doing well, that he was looking out for them.

Jacinta Dobbins and Mary Kelly were drinking tea in the kitchen with his Ma. These women had been coming around for years. They were so used to Wayne they talked away like he wasn't there. Wayne made a fresh pot and helped himself to a few Marietta biscuits.

Jacinta was putting pressure on his Ma to give Christy a break.

'Will you wise up, Lillian? You said it yourself. He's devoted to yah now. You stuck by him. Why're you not up for it now?'

His Ma sat there smoking and saying nothing.

'She's got a point, Lil,' Mary Kelly said. 'It's not as if he is beatin' yah, or messin' around, or anything.'

Wayne, who was drinking a cup of tea and leaning up against the counter, put his head down and scrunched himself up smaller. His Ma hated comments like that. The only thing that killed her more than the idea that his Da might have been having it away with someone else was other people talking about it.

'Christy, Christy, fucking Christy. It's all I ever hear about. Must be great to be a fuckin' bollocks all your life and then havin' everyone bat for you when you stop for a while. He's not the only one who's changed you know. Not that anyone here'd notice. I'd have to stand on my fuckin' head with an eye patch before someone took a bit of notice of me.'

The women were taken by the vehemence of her tone and seemed unsure how to respond.

'I can see the difference in him. I can even see the goodness in him again. God knows he hid it well over the years. It was one of the reasons I fell for him as bad as I did. Wayne worships the ground he walks on now, and it's mostly even for the right reasons. Maurice worships the ground he walks on for all the wrong reasons. And he's trying to get on with Orla's chap even though he hates him.

'I just don't love him anymore. Is that so bad? Is that a crime? It wasn't the last time I checked. I didn't miss him when he was locked up. Before he was arrested, I was mad jealous that he was with someone else. But now I couldn't give a shite.'

On the night his Da was released Wayne had been disgusted that his Ma had given into him so easy. She'd seen how life was without him. She had a life independent of him. And yet she'd allowed him to walk straight back into her life with no questions asked. It'd felt like she preferred his Da to the relationship she had with Wayne. He felt, in some way that he couldn't put his finger on, that she'd been disloyal.

But circumstances had changed, hadn't they? Even his Ma said so. There'd actually be nothing wrong with the two of them getting on like other couples. But she wasn't for turning. He didn't see why she wouldn't give him a chance. Everyone saw the effort he was making. Hadn't he earned the right to be taken back into the fold? Wasn't that what family was about?

And what did all this mean for him and his Ma? Shouldn't he be steering clear of his Da? Wasn't he being the disloyal one now?

What was he supposed to do, say, 'No, Da, don't come to all my matches, don't find gigs so that we can get free holidays, don't be happy when I've done something well because it stops me feeling like shit?'

He didn't like the way she was treating his Da. He'd always loved his Da – he just hadn't wanted him around when he was giving his Ma a hiding. But now he wanted him around all the time. And it was killing him that just when everything was coming right his Ma didn't want anything to do with him. Why did everything always have to be upside down, to be so fucked up, as his Da would say? There had to be a way around all this. It was no more than the family deserved. But a sense of entitlement wasn't a magic wand. He knew that. He hoped that the pair of them would realise that they had something and that his Da wouldn't give up fighting to keep it.

sixty-one

Roche descended the stairs into the basement of the Forensic Science Laboratory to the vaults where exhibits for pending cases were stored. Jimmy Carney, the exhibits officer, was at the counter doing the *Evening Press* crossword. Carney was the man entrusted with ensuring that items seized during an investigation remained under lock and key until the trial took place. It was a cushy number but you needed a certain temperament to survive it. He looked as he always looked – pale and wan, a side effect of seeing so little daylight.

Roche had approached Flannery again and hinted that there might be a possibility of running a sting on Clarke. He mentioned that he'd need a bit of seed capital to get it going. Flannery listened politely but it was plain that he had no faith in any project formulated by Roche. The next morning there'd been a letter from Flannery on top of his in-tray referring to the meeting and instructing him to get prior written authorisation for any covert operations involving Clarke.

He'd gone to Mountjoy to lodge a prisoner picked up on a warrant later that day and bumped into Reynolds in the yard. The two men had stood looking at each other for a moment before Reynolds starting talking.

'I'm glad I'm at work. I didn't think I'd ever come back. The lads have been good to me. I'm starting to put the other business behind me.'

'Sorry we didn't get your man. There'll be another day.'

Reynolds looked at him the way he'd done in the hospital bed when Roche had been trying to persuade him to give evidence against Clarke.

'Yeah right,' he'd observed with a sigh and went on about his business.

The blistering sarcasm had stung. He understood Reynolds' frustration and contempt. He'd felt the same way when Flannery had dismissed his plan to pursue Clarke after the case had collapsed. It wasn't just the put down that had irked him. It was the realisation that he'd never get any official backing to rein Clarke in. The role of the force was to be passive. There was a tacit acceptance that Clarke would just keep on committing crimes until the law of averages dictated that his number was up.

That was the moment he'd decided to go it alone, and came up with the idea of borrowing the money seized in the Prendergast drugs bust and using it as a lure to reel in Clarke.

There was no room for fuck-up. In addition to dismissal he could be charged with a misappropriation offence. His job could still be on the line even if the whole thing came off. But he didn't really care any more. There was a bigger issue at play now. Either his job meant something or he was just clocking in for wages.

'What can I do yah for, Dick?' Carney said.

'I'm looking for the cash seized in the Prendergast case. I need to get some tests run on it.'

Carney disappeared into the vault to retrieve the item. Roche prayed that he wouldn't be long. The last thing he wanted was some other colleague coming down looking for an exhibit and asking him what he was doing there. Carney reappeared with an evidence bag. He held it up to the light and squinted at it. Not for the first time he wondered how so much money could take up so little space. Money couldn't buy you love and a whole host of other things. But you could kiss goodbye to a lot of life's little problems with fifty grand in your back pocket all the same.

'You on this case, Dick? This is drug squad.'

'Nah, but I got a little bit of tittle tattle about prints that might be on the notes. I'm following that up for myself for now. I'll keep everyone posted though if anything comes out, don't you worry.'

Carney stuck his tongue deep into this cheek and considered the matter.

'It's a bit unusual, I'm sure that there's something about it in the rulebook, but hey, I suppose you're not going to run off with it, are you?'

Roche smiled. 'Tempting as that is, no, I'm not going to run off with it,' he replied.

He signed off on it and left, promising he'd have it back before the end of the week and got out of there before Carney changed his mind.

He drove straight out to the Hunter's Lodge.

He'd gone through the plan with Daly several times already. Daly had looked totally incredulous when Roche explained that he'd come up with the fifty grand cash to get the ball rolling. Daly had kept on asking him where it had come from, no doubt wondering whether there was money he could tap into.

It was an effort to keep Daly focused on the task in hand. There was no point in Daly doing a drugs deal with Clarke, walking away and Clarke being the only one arrested. Daly would be a dead man walking. He'd spent a good part of last night explaining to Daly how he needed to bring other criminals on board to spread risk and protect himself.

At first, Daly had been sceptical. But he'd come up with several helpful amendments, which Roche had been happy to take on board. Daly still kept whinging that it was all too complicated. But Daly had also accepted that the plan needed to be layered up to stop Clarke working out that he was being scammed. Eventually, Daly said that he'd approach the Brennan family, who were vying to become the biggest suppliers of drugs in Dublin, to see would they come on board. They'd agreed to meet today to iron out any remaining creases.

When Daly sat into the car he looked tense. He had none of his usual poise.

Roche had almost felt sorry for him. The whole thing had got personal and turned everything sour. He didn't like the acrimony any more than Daly did. The pair of them had gotten on very well over the years but that didn't make them friends, he reminded himself. This was a commercial arrangement. Tit for tat. For now, Daly wanted to avoid jail. Roche wanted to get Clarke and if he had to break a few eggs to make an omelette then so be it. The relationship was entering its death throes. The tacit agreement was to get through this transaction and have a parting of ways.

'You got funds?' Daly asked.

Roche nodded and gestured towards a leather satchel on the floor. It was hard to read Daly's expression. It seemed to be a mixture of surprise and disappointment.

'Shane and Frank Brennan are going to buy the gear,' Daly said. 'As real purchasers?'

'They're itching to take delivery at that price. They're good to go.'

'Did you say it to Christy?'

'Yeah. He's cool about it. The Brennans are nasty bunch of fuckers but they pay.'

'Why doesn't Clarke do the deal with them himself?'

'I don't know. The less he's involved, the less chance he's goin' to get nicked, I suppose. He's paranoid, trusts no one since he fell out with Harry and Liam. That's why he's carrying the drugs and going to close the transaction himself'

'And what about you, Jimmy? Are you happy with it?'

'Sure, I'm over the moon. Delirious. Course I am!'

'Jimmy, if you're not onside, there's no point in moving this thing along. It won't work if you're not behind it.'

'I do this, we're quits. The firearms charge gets squared.'

'Done.'

'I'm too old for jail.'

Neither spoke for a few moments.

'OK, Jimmy, run it by me again,' Roche asked.

'Christy's young lad Wayne plays for Joey's. They're in the league final and the match is being played on the pitches in Dolphin's Barn. I'm meeting him there for two o'clock. I'm giving Christy the fifty grand. He's going to give me a sample of the coke. I'm going to take it to Shane and Frank Brennan. Christy's going to follow me from a respectable distance with the gear. Christy is working on the basis that the Brennans will pay over the balance of the money once they're happy with the sample.'

'Has Clarke asked why you're the one putting up the deposit?'

'No. He knows I'm churning the coke on to the Brennans for a profit. The way he sees it, I've a big stake in the deal and have to make it work. So he's comfortable with that. '

'What's to stop him just ripping you off?'

'Well nothing, I suppose. I've done a lot of business with him over the years. He's never left me short before. He needs the money from the sale. He's not going to get it fucking around with me. He'd suffer ripping me off for that kind of loot. There'd be a lot of people who wouldn't like it and who'd be happy to use it as an excuse to take him out.'

'Why does he need the deposit? It's making the deal complicated at his end.'

'I'm done explaining this to you,' Daly replied, his anger getting the better of him. 'Why do you keep asking? Do you think the answer is going to change? That I'm going to slip up and you'll catch me out? The man's paranoid. He wants the money as a declaration of intent. It weeds out tyre kickers is what he keeps saying. Now you either give me the money and I try and move this along or fuck off out of here and stop melting my head.'

Roche reached down to the passenger footwell, picked up the satchel and dumped it into Daly's lap. It quickly disappeared inside Daly's jacket.

He'd officially passed the point of no return.

Roche would do the stop himself. He'd look right into Clarke's eyes in a way that would force him to react. He'd watch Clarke squirm when the money and cocaine was found on his person. It might get messy if he started blabbering that he'd got the money off Daly. That was unlikely though. He'd be too preoccupied with working out how many years he'd get for the cocaine to think straight about anything else.

sixty-two

Fr Brendan was pleasantly surprised to see Monsignor de Bruin's Mercedes parked outside the presbytery. He had acted as his personal assistant in the seminary. They'd got on very well. What's brought him down here? he wondered. It had to be important for him to come in person. Perhaps he was to be moved on to someplace else where his talents might be better exploited. If so, it was not before his time. Fr Peter would, at last, see the respect in which he was held.

His expectations were heightened when Mrs Hendricks told him he was expected in the study. The Monsignor was sitting around the table flanked by Harry McGovern on one side and a priest he didn't recognise on the other. Fr Peter was stood by the mantelpiece. They were drinking tea and eating biscuits from one of the assorted boxes they got as presents at Christmas. The best bone china and silverware had been excavated from the presses at the back of the pantry to mark the occasion.

The Monsignor stood up when he entered and pointed for him to sit down at the table.

'Harry McGovern you already know,' he said and then, pointing to the priest, 'Fr Curtis is a canon lawyer with special knowledge on matters as they pertain to the clergy.'

Fr Brendan was impressed. That section of the Church was incredibly secretive and very few people even knew of its existence.

He knew from the summer he spent working in the Archbishop's palace that they were engaged only in the most sensitive of Church affairs and were a very powerful group.

The papers had been full of how he and Cora had bent Charlie Haughey's ear to the pro-life cause and had credited them with being such creative and effective strategists. In truth, the articles had grossly exaggerated the significance of the meeting. Still, the exposure had done him no harm. He was intrigued and flattered that they had come here to see him.

He'd received a cheque from Harry during the campaign. It'd been made out to cash, with a handwritten message of support on the firm's compliments slip. It had asked him to note that the contribution was made in a personal capacity.

Fr Brendan had immediately realised that the solicitor had been keeping his options open, aligning himself incognito behind someone who might be going places. Harry looked a bit sheepish. Was Harry worried that he'd be indiscreet and say something about the donation? He'd no worries on that front.

'Right, gentlemen, what can I do for you?' he asked.

Everyone stared back at him. There was silence. Fr Peter, who was usually happy to play the court jester, looked uncharacteristically po-faced. Fr Brendan then noticed a cassette recorder on the table. Monsignor Brown nodded at him in an officious manner and pressed the play button. The sound of piano music filled the room. He immediately recognised it as one of Shostakovich's sonatas. It was Wayne Clarke playing. His trademark natural dexterity was easily recognisable.

'That's Wayne Clarke, a prodigy, sadly, whose potential will never be realised for as long as he remains under the tutelage of his gouger father.'

No one passed any comment.

Suddenly the masterly clank of the keys gave way to grunting sounds. What little was left to the imagination was banished by the sound of an out-of-breath voice uttering profanities about fucking the little tight-assed boy. The voice sounded just like his. Except it wasn't. Nor was anyone buggering Wayne or anyone else either in the recording. Fr Brendan instantly recognised the voice, the one that sounded very like his, as one of Wayne's near perfeect impersonations.

He had to think quickly, before panic set in. Highlighting that the voice was really Wayne imitating him was only going to get him so far. The first question that'd be asked was why on earth Wayne would do this. It also occurred to him that Wayne had probably thought this through. This was the kind of deviousness for which Christy was renowned. Wayne hadn't licked it up off the ground. If push came to shove Wayne might agree that he'd simulated the scene on the tape. But if he were asked whether he had been abused he was likely to say yes. Why make the tape if he wasn't going to follow through?

They sat there waiting. Waiting for him to speak, to explain himself. Waiting for him to confess. They were using silence as a tactic on him. They were banking on the oppressiveness of it acting as its own pressure, forcing Fr Brendan to break.

'What on earth is that?' Fr Brendan asked with as much nonchalance as he could muster.

'It was posted to the school principal. An anonymous note said that it was, quote, "Fr Brendan, the pervert priest, buggering Wayne Clarke".'

'That's ridiculous,' Fr Brendan replied indignantly.

'Maybe so,' said the Monsignor. 'At present, it's only an allegation. The question is what is to be done about it?'

The Monsignor removed the cassette from the tape deck and ostentatiously placed it in an envelope marked: *Evidence: child sexual abuse allegation. Status: Inactive pending identification of complainant and suspect abuser.*

His mind began examining the permutations. An enquiry, police maybe. There'd be publicity, and jail if he was convicted. His mother would die of shame. How would he cope with the humiliation?

And he'd have to deal with Christy Clarke.

'An investigation might result in charges and would be very damaging to the Church, to you, to the boy, to all concerned.'

'Investigation? You're not serious? It doesn't even sound like me.'

The only one who dared to look him in the eye was Fr Peter, and he was glaring at him as if daring him to deny it further. What, he wondered, had he said about him before he'd got here? He'd probably poisoned them against him.

Fr Curtis spoke.

'At present, you're under the control of the Archbishop of Dublin. The identity of the complainant hasn't yet been ascertained. Wayne Clarke looks like a candidate. Strictly speaking, there's no complaint made against you yet. That might well change, particularly if you remain here.'

'What are you saying?'

'There's an opening in the missions in Nigeria. We think there'd be major jurisdictional issues conducting an inquiry if you took up that posting.'

'And when am I expected to take up this opening?'

He couldn't believe what he was hearing. The idea that he was some sort of parasite that needed to be spirited away was almost as big a shock as Wayne exposing him. And it was truly appalling that they were approaching the whole thing on the basis that the complaint was true.

'Time is of the essence. As soon as the paperwork is done. It's not a good idea to hang around, believe me,' Curtis replied.

Harry passed him over a sheaf of documents.

Fr Brendan leafed through them. There was a letter outlining how the matter would be investigated if a complaint were received, referring to arrest, charge and prosecution. Buggery, he noted, carried a sentence of up to life imprisonment. There was an agreement for him to sign. It was full of legal phrases like. whereas, freely and voluntarily, irrevocably consents, hold the Order harmless, assigns power of attorney, indemnity and third-party claims.

He had no doubt he'd be signing away his life.

'You can pack up here now, today. Take a little holiday with your family and head off early next week, say,' the Monsignor said.

'So that's it?' Fr Brendan asked. 'Sign and go.' There was yet more silence. 'I'd have more rights as a factory worker.'

Fr Peter spoke for the first time. 'You could always go down to Christy Clarke and explain that there's nothing to it. That Wayne, who he thinks the world of these days, is making it all up. And if you're believed, you never know, maybe you could even stay on here.'

Today had started out just like any other. By rights he ought to have resented that it'd fallen on Fr Peter to deliver the coup de grâce. But now, in this moment, he knew that everything had changed. The prospect of what lay ahead was terrifying and beyond his control.

Fr Brendan signed and dated his signature, and went to pack his things

sixty-three

'We are gathered here today,' Roche began and looked down at the expectant faces. He'd picked the exact same team as he'd used in the original investigation. None knew why they were there. They'd simply been told to report at 06.00 to the conference room for a briefing.

'We are gathered here today,' he began again, 'to deal with some unfinished business.' The group of men looked around at each other, breaking out into smiles. They knew what was coming. And he gave it to them straight up.

'Here's how it's going to happen: Christy Clarke has come into some high-grade cocaine and he wants to offload it at a good price. The quantity is twenty keys.

'Jimmy Daly is going to be the buyer. Or more accurately, Daly is acting on behalf of the buyers. The ultimate destination is Shane and Frank Brennan. But we'll be stepping in long before it gets that far.

'The initial handover will take place behind the changing rooms at the GAA pitches at Dolphin's Barn. Joey's are in a playoff for the junior cup. There'll be a good turnout. Wayne Clarke is on the team. Christy is going to use that as cover.

'The purchase price is £250,000. Jimmy will meet Clarke at the ground and pay fifty grand upfront as a declaration of intent.

Clarke will sample him the product. The full exchange will take place half an hour later down near the flats. Once Clarke has got the down payment, he'll personally bring the cocaine to Jimmy to complete the transaction.'

He could see the men digesting the information, parsing and analysing, and reaching the same conclusion he had. The making and breaking of this case was within their control. They weren't dependent on an ACO Reynolds, or how a jury might interpret something, or vulnerable to some rabbit out of a hat.

'The stop and search is to be made under section 23 of the Misuse of Drugs Act, 1977. He is to be taken to the station for immediate processing. Questions?'

'What about Jimmy Daly?'

Wally Drennan was a pain in the arse sometimes but, to give him his due, he was, as usual, on the money.

'What about him?' Roche asked non-committally.

'Is he going to walk off with a big lump of coke in his back pocket?'

'Daly will be kept under surveillance from a respectful distance. He is to be allowed proceed to meet up with the Brennan brothers.'

'And what then?' Wally persisted. 'We move in on the three of them?'

'Clarke is the target of this operation. I want Clarke guessing where we've come from, and about how much we know. If we scoop up Daly and the Brennan brothers it'll indicate to Clarke how much information we have about the transaction. I want Clarke guesssing.'

It was as near as he dared come to telling them that Daly was to fall between the cracks.

He went down amongst them and handed each one a sealed pack. Inside there were sheets of paper showing where everybody was to be positioned. It was headed 'Operation Driftwood'. He'd christened it that on the basis that it pretty much summed up Clarke and the name seemed appropriate.

The men studied it carefully.

'OK – listen up. A lot of work has gone into this. We've commandeered a house that overlooks the back of the changing room at the GAA pitch, and which will give us a birds-eye view of the players and more importantly their interaction.

'Each of you has been issued with a walkie-talkie tuned to its own special frequency. Radio silence is only to be broken to report something specific to the operation. There's to be no small talk. Understand?'

Several nodded.

'The match is scheduled for 14.00 hours. The most up to date information suggests that the down payment and sample will be exchanged at halftime. Once Daly is satisfied that the product is legitimate, he'll make his way down to the Brennan brothers. Clarke will follow him at a distance. There'll be no hanging around. Clarke has made it clear that he wants to be back on the sideline before the match finishes.

'Please look at the enclosed sketch map carefully. There is a laneway from the main road that goes up to the pitches. There are high walls on either side. We'll have men posted at either end. Once Clarke enters the laneway carrying the holdall we'll seal it. That's where the stop and search will take place.'

The men were studying the documents intently and conferring with each other.

'Is there anyone here who doesn't understand what this operation is about and more importantly his own role in it?'

The men shook their heads.

'Right then, let's get cracking.'

sixty-four

Wayne was marking Ryaner again, the long streak who had scored the winning goal in the first match. Even with all the extra training and improved fitness he was still half a yard short. Wayne tapped Ryaner's ankle as he bent down to pick up the ball. Ryaner let out a little piggy squeal, which he belatedly tried to disguise as a grunt, but he still managed to scoop up the ball and turn towards goal.

A sly elbow from Wayne into his ribs caused Ryaner to lose focus just long enough for Wayne to hammer-punch the ball out of his hands and it bounced away harmlessly. The two of them bailed down the pitch after it, Wayne's hair stuck to his scalp with sweat.

'Let it out!' their manager Sully screamed.

A few moments later the ball came back out over their heads. The pair of them ran after it. Ryaner got there a fraction of a second before Wayne, long enough to catch the ball and turn so that he was facing the goal. They were a long way out, just on the halfway line.

Ryaner kicked the ball high and hard and let the gusting wind do its work. The ball bounced into the square just in front of the Joey's goalkeeper, who'd stepped off his line to meet it. The height from which it fell, the strength of the kick and the wind all combined to ensure that when it hit the ground it bounced high again over the keeper's outstretched arms and into the net.

There was a huge cheer. The ref blew for halftime. The scoreboard read: *Coláiste Caomhain* 2-6 – *St Josephs* 1-15.

As Wayne trudged off the pitch he looked to the sideline but his Da was nowhere to be seen. Where the fuck was he?

'C'mon lads. You've the beating of them,' Padraig said in the dressing room. 'Just one push, that's what we need, a goal and a point, it'll change the game. Not only will we get back into the match, the match will be ours for the taking. They're shitting themselves, I can smell it.'

They hadn't made the mistake of underestimating the opposition this time. But it was slowly beginning to dawn on them that the reason they couldn't take this team apart like other teams was that Coláiste Caomhain was simply better than them. Not just on the day, but all the time.

As if to reinforce this sense of inferiority, they could hear Sully shouting next door. 'Each one of you is a better player than your opponent. Collectively as a team you are better. But you'll have to hold your nerve if you are to win. Concentrate. Fight for every ball. Prove your worth, prove you're true champions. And avenge this!'

Wayne conjured up a picture of Sully on the other side of the wall pointing to the scar below his eye. He heard them trudging down the corridor, the noise from their studs echoing around the building. It felt like the game had already slipped away from them. Fellas around him muttering 'bunch of cunts' and 'we'll do them' wasn't doing it for Wayne today and he suspected he wasn't alone in this.

The gym bag that his Da had left in the dressing room before the throw-in was still there, so he clearly hadn't gone far. It would have been nice to hear a few words from him before they went back on the pitch.

Wayne went behind the dressing room for a quick pee before the game restarted. He saw his Da talking to Jimmy Daly. The two men were so caught up in whatever it was they were doing that neither of them noticed him. He saw his Da hand Daly something wrapped up in plastic. Daly cut into the corner of it with a blade. He put his finger inside and then sucked on his finger when he took it out. Daly nodded his approval and gave his Da the thumbs up. The package disappeared into his inside pocket. Daly, in turn, handed his Da a small black cloth bag. It was like the bag you'd keep a pair of football boots in. His Da dug his hand into it and pulled the contents to the top. Wayne saw that it was a wad of notes. It disappeared down his underpants.

Wayne was gutted. Normal service had resumed. Or worse. That looked like drugs. If his Da got into that the IRA would kill him. It'd only be a matter of time before he became a bollocks all over again and was back in prison. He'd said only the other night that he'd used up all his luck. He'd even talked about going straight. He'd all these plans for managing his gigs and all. Why was he doing this now?

Wayne was tempted to shout over to him. His Da didn't like distractions when he was doing business. Just then his Da looked up and shouted for him to wait up. He ran over to him.

'Sorry, son, I'm just doing a bit of trade here. I'll be out in a couple of minutes. You'll have the makings of that lanky cunt in the second half. I'm sure of it. Do you get me?'

Wayne nodded. 'What business, Da? What was in the package?'

His Da ignored him.

'Another thing. Make sure to bring home your kit bag after the match. Do that for me, right, and you'll be my friend for life. Do you get me?'

'Sure thing, Da.'

'One more thing?'

'Yeah, Da, come on, I'm back out.'

'You're a great man, do you know that? Go out there and show us what you're worth. Go out and enjoy yourself. I'll be watching. I'll be behind yah, no matter what.'

He ruffled his hair and gave him a gentle slap on the face.

Wayne ran onto the pitch. His Da was at the top of his game. He'd get on top of Ryaner no matter what it took now. Not just because he wanted to win, but because, for a reason that made no sense, he wanted to be the man his Da was now.

sixty-five

The radio crackled into life with the news that Tango 1 had exchanged gifts with Tango 2. Tango 1 had stuffed the package down his jocks. Tango 2 was now exiting the ground and would come into view of the watchers outside in a few moments.

After what seemed like forever the radio crackled, 'Tango 1 gone into dressing room.' Was Clarke retrieving the holdall he'd brought to the ground with him? A pause and the seconds ticked by agonisingly slow. And then on cue: 'Tango 1 out of dressing room carrying a black gym holdall bag, making his way to the exit.'

Roche watched him every step of the way after that. He began to relax. Worst-case scenario now he'd get his money back. Anything above that was a bonus. Clarke stepped into the laneway. Plain-clothes men had taken up their agreed positions at either end. There were now six people in the stop and search corridor and five of them were guards. Roche kept his head down on his approach until he got right up to him.

'Afternoon, Christy. Are you not staying for the second half?'

Clarke stopped; he made no eye contact with Roche.

'You mustn't have much confidence in the Joey's lads to make a comeback. Wayne will be disappointed.'

Clarke went to walk on. Roche put his hand across his chest.

'What's in the bag?'

'Am I under arrest?'

'No, is there any reason why you should be?'

'Well then go fuck yourself.'

He pushed past Roche's arm. But Roche had anticipated this move and stepped into him to block his path.

'The immovable object and irresistible force meet again. That's us don't you think, Christy?'

Clarke stared downward and made no reply.

The plainclothes had made their way up to see this unfold for themselves. Roche was in no hurry. The pincer was complete. This was a moment to draw out for as long as possible. Clarke was at the point where every second that he wasn't rumbled would seem like an eternity and in which there was still hope of making the final denouement all the more unbearable for him.

'That was a very lucky escape you had down the Four Courts recently. Jesus wept. I said to myself that was it. We'd never see Christy Clarke in the dock again. We'd had our chance and blown it. Life's strange, don't you think, all the same.'

Clarke just stood there, staring ahead.

Roche used his foot to lift up the bag Clarke was carrying. He felt the reassuring presence of weight on the toe of his shoe. Twenty kilos of mass, he'd say.

'Fairly bulky, Christy. It's not football or gym gear whatever it is.'

Clarke stepped forward again as if to walk on down the lane. Two of the plainclothes squared up to him and he stepped back.

'Throw it up there Christy and I'll take a quick look and you can be on your way in no time.'

'What power of search?'

'Section 23 of the Misuse of Drugs Act, 1977.'

'I don't do drugs and you know it.'

'Then you've nothing to worry about, have you? Now put the bag down like a good man and step back please.'

Clarke did as he was told. Roche pulled the zip of the bag across, peeled back the flap and peered inside.

There was something in it but he couldn't make out what it was. It was wrapped up in a red jersey. He looked at Clarke and wondered what he was thinking. His face was expressionless.

He pulled the jersey away and held it up. It was Liverpool, number 7, autographed by Kenny Dalglish and the crest on the front said European Cup Final 1978. He rummaged inside the bag. There were hundreds of Liverpool match programmes. That was it.

'That's private property, my property,' Clarke said.

Roche gestured to the plainclothes to do a body search. The money. Where the fuck was the money? Not a word was exchanged between them now as they methodically searched his person. Nothing. They searched a second and third time. The searchers finished up and said, purely for the record, 'Negative.'

They could take him back to the station to do an internal. But there didn't seem to be much point. There was no way Clarke had got fifty grand in cash and or twenty kilos of coke up his arse.

The realisation hit him in an instant, and it hit him hard. There was no cocaine and there never had been. There'd been something not right about Daly sucking his finger. What the fuck did Jimmy Daly know about cocaine? The sample was probably icing sugar or glucose. He hadn't wanted to spook Clarke so he hadn't put any men into the ground. The only time he'd been out of sight was when he'd gone into the dressing room. The money – his money that he had to account for to Jimmy Carney, exhibits officer – was gone, passed over to one of his runners and spirited far away from here by now.

Was Jimmy Daly in on it?

The silence was broken by the static of the radio.

'Man down at bridge in Rialto. Shot three times in the head from close range. Armed suspect bent down and took an item from the pockets of the victim and fled the scene as a pillion passenger on a waiting motorbike.'

He'd just got the answer.

'Always was a pushy little fucker,' Clarke said under his breath.

'What'd you say?' Roche said to him, unable to conceal his rage. 'What'd you say, you fuckin' scumbag?'

The plainclothes stood with their hands in their pockets. Roche was rooted to the spot, one arm as long as the other. Clarke stared straight ahead. The radio crackled incessantly with updates.

When had Clarke got onto Daly? Probably the moment he'd turned up at his release party. And for what? Surveillance could put the two men exchanging packets a few minutes before Jimmy was executed. He didn't even have enough to arrest Clarke. It'd only make him look even more foolish.

It was over. The fallout would be huge.

Management would appoint senior men to anonymously brief against him in the media. There'd be stories planted in the newspaper quoting anonymous sources explaining how much pressure he'd been under and how personally he'd taken it when Clarke had been acquitted of causing Reynolds GBH. Flannery and the others he'd excluded from the operation would take great delight in highlighting the holes in it and how it would never have been approved if they'd been consulted. It would surely come out that Daly had only participated because Roche had strung him along that he'd have non-existent charges dropped. And then there was the missing fifty grand. He'd be suspended immediately. Thrown out ignominiously from the force.

He'd never shake the feeling that Daly's blood was on his hands. The guilt would embed itself in him and fester.

sixty-six

In the dying minutes of the match Wayne went up to catch a ball. It slipped through his fingers and bounced straight into the path of the streak of misery. Ryaner picked it up and headed for goal, Sully's exhortations to let it out ringing in their ears as Wayne gave chase. Padraig had hammered it into them during training: 'When you're running and you can't get any air into your lungs, that's when you try harder, push yourself and get up to the next level.' He'd tried it a hundred times. Sometimes it even worked. But not today when it really mattered: try as he might, he couldn't make up the distance. The gap was widening to the point where Ryaner had that vital half-second to steady himself before he made his kick.

The goal Ryaner had scored at halftime had come at a critical time. It'd knocked the stuffing out of Joey's. They'd done really well to maintain the deficit at four points at half-time. It had risen as high as nine in the second half and the gap would have widened but for the fact that Joey's had scored a lucky goal and a point in the one short phase of the game that they'd actually played.

The crowd had got behind them. For a few minutes there was rhythm and flow. Wayne had hoped that his team would take the match to them. But it hadn't happened. They'd stalled, plateaued.

Coláiste Caomhain had banged points here and there from long-range play and it'd taken everything for Joey's to stay in touch. You could feel that they were running the game down now.

Ryaner kicked the ball high for a point. It was going over from the moment it left his boot. He had ground to a halt so as to enjoy the trajectory of its flight. It increased their lead to six points. They'd now need at least three scores, two of them goals, to get into the lead.

Wayne kept moving. He slapped Ryaner right across his face with the open palm of his hand just as the ball was level with the crossbar. He didn't know exactly why he'd slapped him as opposed to giving him a box. That was almost a girly thing to do. The slap had been spur of the moment, instinctive even. It felt like the right thing to do.

The sound reverberated around the pitch so loudly that it inhibited any celebration of the score. Ryaner put his hand up to face. It was red and stinging, and for one moment Wayne was sure he was going to cry. Sully appeared on the pitch out of nowhere, and furiously wiped Ryaner's face down with a wet sponge. Wayne saw – they all did – that Sully was doing it as much for the team as Ryaner's personal dignity.

Wayne was suddenly aware that the referee was beside him, asking him what did he do that for. Wayne shouted back at him that it had been a fuckin' accident. The more the referee remonstrated with him the louder he said it, as if his repeated insistence made it true.

Padraig ran out onto the pitch and pulled him aside. 'You can fuckin' kill them afterwards, Wayne. After the game – get them then.' Padraig hadn't kept his voice down. In fact he'd said it at a level that meant everyone – even the ref – could hear him. He kept saying, 'Afterwards, Wayne, wait till then.' Wayne expected the ref to intervene, to run Padraig off the field. But the ref just stood there waiting for Padraig to leave.

The goalkeeper kicked the ball out high and up into the centre of the field. A Joey's lad jumped in the air. He ran up the pitch and kicked it out to the corner-forward. He ran towards goal and fisted the ball over the defenders approaching him. Another Joey's lad got hold of the ball just outside the square and drilled it into the net. There were massive cheers echoing around the pitch.

The Coláiste Caomhain keeper stepped back from the ball, picking out his players in the midfield to whom he might aim the ball. Maybe it'd been the sound of the smack, or the incongruity of an adult encouraging a kid to beat up his opponents. The event had created a void. It was instantly filled by fear. Joey's smelt it. They drove the ball back into the goal from the kick-out. Joey's played liked a team possessed. Coláiste Caomhain receded into themselves like introverts. Joey's banged in two goals and four points without a reply by the time the referee blew up for full time.

The Caomhain lads left the pitch without shaking hands. Wayne glanced at Ryaner. He didn't make eye contact. He didn't just look defeated. He looked scared and ashamed.

They lined up for the presentation. Wayne hung his medal around his neck. The captain raised the cup. It was filled with Fanta orange. It was passed around for everyone to get a drink from. They did a lap of honour around the pitch and posed for a picture for the paper. They stood in front of the supporters who cheered and sang 'We Are the Champions'.

Wayne scanned the touchline but couldn't see his Da anywhere. How come he'd come to all the training and mickey-mouse games but had missed today? It didn't make sense, or did it? Wasn't he the very one who had said of his Da that a leopard didn't change his spots on the night his Da had come home? And then his Da had seemed to change in so many ways, not least in the interest he'd shown in Wayne.

Wayne hadn't known how to respond. He'd been bamboozled by the random acts of kindness and encouragement. At first he'd been flattered. And then suspicious, until he got to the point that he'd enjoyed it and needed it. It was like an addiction. He'd come to rely on his Da's attention. Most of the other parents were there to see their lads pick up medals and hoist the cup. Where was his Da when you needed him?

sixty-seven

Fr Brendan waited for the final boarding call for flight BA412 to Lagos before he joined the queue. Last night he'd attended a hastily convened orientation meeting at the Mission Centre. An elderly priest (he looked about a hundred) had shown him slides depicting life in Africa. A disproportionate number featured women with drooping breasts. He spoke in a repetitive didactic tone that had drained the life out of him.

He'd been up at five in the morning to catch the first Aer Lingus flight to Heathrow. His anxiety trumped any tiredness.

He was still reeling from shock. He'd been virtually forced to pack up his things in the presbytery and leave under cover of darkness. He'd been sent home while arrangements were made. His mother had cried incessantly, and had kept on saying, in an accusatory tone, how she didn't understand why he was being sent away when he was accomplishing so much here. His father didn't say much: he couldn't shake the sneaking suspicion that his father knew that he'd done something terribly wrong and the indecent haste with which he was going on the missions was a cover-up.

It was hard to make sense of the last few days. He'd bedded in, at last, in the parish. His latest pet projects – getting young couples to look in on elderly neighbours, and drawing up a register of skills, so that if anyone needed a tradesman the work would stay in the parish – had all been roaring successes. The picture of Haughey holding his and Cora's hands aloft at the Simmonscourt Pavilion had been the front-page picture in *The Irish Times, Glasgow Herald* and *El Pais*. His upward trajectory had seemed unstoppable then.

How had it come to this? He didn't just mean his disgrace and banishment. There was a big void in his life, which he didn't know how to fill.

His mind drifted back to the open air Mass. The house and neighbours had been so welcoming. Cornfields was a place where *The Word* and *The Catholic Herald* sat casually beside *Homes & Gardens* and the *Farmers Journal*. This was heartland territory, a place where he could feel at home. But something had not been right.

At one point he'd surveyed the room and noticed that almost everyone present was much older than him. He'd asked himself why he wasn't out celebrating life with people his own age? He'd avoided the answer: it only made him feel uncomfortable. He believed in God. He wanted to help people. He believed sex was for procreation, that sex between men was unnatural and that a desire to have sex with children was perverted. The Church in its own limited way provided him with some reason for being, That was why he had become a priest.

He'd really enjoyed chatting to Siobhain Cassidy on the night of Marie's removal. It was nothing sexual but he found her easy to talk to. They were worlds apart in background and didn't have much in common, but it had felt good to be hanging out with someone his own age. It'd been one of the few moments in his life when he'd felt carefree.

There were certain men of his own age in the park he'd been with on a few occasions. The sex with them was better for that. The familiarity made the whole business easier. But he had never been drawn to any one person with whom he wanted to have a relationship. He'd often wondered why. He had also wondered, if he ever did experience such feelings, whether he would leave the priesthood. He did not believe that he would have the courage to do that.

He felt that if he could get to the bottom of how it was that he didn't crave a soulmate or even an ongoing sexual relationship with one person, he'd resolve a lot of things. He'd come nearer to it with Wayne than he had with anyone else. It was disastrous for all concerned, but he hadn't been able to stop himself.

Had what occurred in the potting shed with the gardener when he was a boy stunted his ability to form relationships with adults? Even with men? You didn't need to be a psychologist to see that there was something quite infantile about the casual, anonymous groping sessions in the Phoenix Park.

His first schoolboy crush had been on a boy called Dominic. It'd been in the year of his Inter. He'd invented ways to be in his company, had been excited when they were paired together for a project for the Young Scientist Exhibition in the RDS. There were lots of young ones chasing him but he'd never seemed interested. Their project on solar energy had won a commendation. They'd had their picture taken and were interviewed by a journalist from the *Irish Press*. Afterwards, when they were alone savouring the moment, he'd blurted out his feelings, knowing the opportunity to spend so much time exclusively in his company was about to end.

Dominic had quietly informed him that another boy in the class had told him the exact same thing. Brendan could guess the boy's identity easily enough – he'd been his hangaround earlier in the year. But Dominic's refusal to confirm his identity had infused him with jealousy and rage.

He was still totally unprepared for what came next.

'We experimented.' Experimented? What was he on about? He and Dominic were the ones doing the experiments. Building solar power for the future. The words hit him with the force of a sledgehammer.

'Sex, like, I mean,' Dominic had added quite unnecessarily.

'How do you mean?' he had asked, trying to quell the hurt in his voice, the feeling that he'd just been betrayed, cuckolded even.

'We wanked each other off.'

There was a lot he wanted to ask, but knew he wasn't permitted.

'It was awful,' Dominic added.

'Sometimes that happens,' Brendan had found himself replying, trying to sound knowledgeable. 'It could be different between us, really nice.'

'I'd never do it again. Never.'

Brendan knew he meant it. It hadn't stopped him pestering Dominic for months afterwards though. He'd begged Dominic to try it with him just once.

'Look,' Dominic had replied. 'I know how hard it is for you people. I like you, and we can still be friends. But I won't ever be doing anything with you. I'm not queer.'

The apartheid – 'you people' – had cut him to the quick much more so than the label of being queer.

And so he'd gone to the seminary and thrown himself enthusiastically into preparing to be a priest. He met plenty of others who were in the same boat. Many priests couldn't control their sexual urges and were the subject of tittle-tattle. What they did was tolerated provided it was all done discreetly. But they were despised too. He didn't want to be like them.

He'd poured his heart out on the eve of his ordination to one of his lecturers, riven with fear that his homosexuality meant he was unsuited to the priesthood, that he was using the celibacy of the cloth as a cover.

'Not at all,' his confidant and mentor had replied airily. 'What is confession for but to obtain forgiveness for our sins and in particular the sins of the flesh? Nobody's perfect, you know, least of all priests. It isn't sinful to want something that is wrong. It's the act itself which is wrong. You're young. In time your desire will wane. You'll grow out of this. It's a phase. Do you understand? Meantime pray and keep going to confession.'

In his heart he'd known that it was nonsense. But like a drowning man reaching out for a lifebuoy he'd latched onto the comforting words. He'd slept well that night knowing that he didn't have to break the news to his Mam that he wasn't going through with his ordination.

After his ordination he'd been sent to a scattering of parishes before ending up at the Archbishop's palace. It was a peach of a job. He'd spent time reading up on files dealing with complaints made by the parents of children who alleged their children had been abused by priests. He'd been shocked to discover that his mentor was himself a paedophile and had been a teacher at a national school where he preyed upon vulnerable prepubescent children. He'd been constantly moved from parish to parish, always with the same result, leaving a trail of destruction in his wake. He'd eventually been moved to a teaching post in the seminary, where it was adjudged that he could do no more harm The guards caught up with him eventually. Harry McGovern had made an appointment for him to go to the station and make a statement. He hanged himself the night before.

Fr Brendan found his seat and settled down for the flight. The plane taxied slowly down to the apron where it remained stationary until it was cleared for take-off. It hurtled down the runway gathering unstoppable momentum. He liked the feel of the forward thrust of the jet engines just before the plane rose off the ground.

He'd reconciled himself a long time ago to the existence of the bricktappers, and his ongoing need for sexual release. His old mentor had reached the point where he could no longer cope. He didn't want to turn out like him. There had to be a better way. And he was determined to overcome his cowardice and find it. But he was not optimistic that he would succeed.

sixty-eight

His Ma screamed with delight when Wayne came home with the medal around his neck. She danced him around the room. She sat down and lit a fag, opened her purse and gave him a tenner.

'Tell me all about it.'

And so he did. How they had been trailing throughout. How it looked like they were beat. And then he'd hit Ryaner a slap, and after that the other team had crumpled. The way he said the word 'slap' made it sound like he'd given him a box or a dig. He didn't want her to know that he'd slapped him on the face like a girl.

'And where's your Da?'

'With Jimmy doing a bit of business.'

'When?'

'Earlier.'

'Before or after the match?'

'Half-time.'

'Poxbottle! *Business?*' she sneered. 'The fuckin' pub more like.'

He sucked in his breath and felt his chest go tight. Waiting for the deluge that was sure to follow. No one had been more disappointed than him that his Da hadn't stayed. But she wasn't being fair. She was unwilling to give him credit for the things he did, and was down on him for the things he didn't.

His Ma ran a bath for him and loaded it up with Radox. It felt all girly to have the oily suds on his skin. But it was just the thing for a footballer after a hard match. It felt good to lie there and plan the night ahead.

He was going out with Cathy later to the flicks. It was a toss-up between *Trading Places* and *Flashdance,* some mushy story about a factory girl who wanted to be a dancer. He'd wanted to see Al Pacino in *Scarface* but she'd vetoed that outright.

He and Cathy were getting serious now.

They were having sex. The first time they'd tried had been a mess. He'd been really nervous. And then to make matters worse the things he'd done with the pervert priest had come flooding into his mind just as he was about to put it in and his thing went soft.

His thing that went hard with the priest when he didn't want it to went soft just when he needed it to stay hard.

He'd freaked out, and went around kicking and punching things. She'd tried to reassure him, saying it was grand, that they'd do it another night. That'd only made matters worse. He'd completely lost it, said it was her fault, and then they'd had a big row. And then made up.

He'd done the voiceover on the tape as soon as he got home and posted it to the principal's post box in the small hours before he could change his mind.

He'd sort of got the idea from his Da. A couple of months before his Da had found out that a guard was having it off with the missus of a detective inspector. That the two men were great mates added spice. They were Man U supporters and went to games a couple of times a year together. His Da had staged a photo of a man wearing a Man U top climbing out of the window of the inspector's house. He'd then plastered it all around town, under the heading 'Sergeant Jimmy Doran playing away at home – home of Detective Inspector Dan Crowley that is'.

His Da had explained that there was nothing wrong with a bit of dramatic licence once the core of the story was true. Denying it, he explained, would only make the pair of them look even more foolish.

The next day he'd seen a big Mercedes car pull up outside the presbytery and a load of priests getting out of it. They'd only gone and sent the pervert priest packing to darkest Africa. A result or what?

Downstairs he heard the door open. It was his Da. Straightaway his Ma was tearing into him. Wayne could tell he was mouldy, and that he was making a right hash of the story about doing some business.

'One lousy fucking game. But no, it was the pub with a waster as big as yourself.'

His Da did what he did best: he changed the subject.

'Incidentally, missus, when I was down the pub, the place where nothing useful happens according to you, I heard that my daughter has been away on weekends with Derek Behan. Why wasn't I told?'

'And why would you be told? So that you can fuck it up like you fuck up everything else?'

'And when she's up the pole, what then?'

'Oh yeah, you're real worried. That's why you're in and out of her room at all hours. Giving her a talk about the birds and bees no doubt.'

Wayne sank under the suds. Even sober, that wasn't the sort of thing that his Da was going to take lying down. He held his breath for as long as he could. When he surfaced he heard the sound of digs. Just the noise of the impact. The blows were hard, but apart from the odd grunt she didn't react.

Wayne stepped out of the bath and wrapped a towel around his waist. Then he heard two sets of footsteps scampering up the stairs, the lighter step ever so slightly in the lead. He was belting her with a brolly. Whenever she put her hands up to protect herself he'd slip in a sly dig in the stomach with the tip of the brolly.

'Yah fuckin' bitch. I hate yah.'

His Ma lay in the foetal position, hands over her face and top of her head. He beat her all over. 'You watch your tongue, woman. You ever say that again and I'll do yah.'

By now, his Da was all puffed out and his breath was coming in fits and starts. His voice trailed off. He tossed the brolly on the ground and walked into Wayne's bedroom.

Moments later he emerged carrying Wayne's kit bag. He was rifling through it as he walked. He pulled out the black cloth bag that Daly had given to him behind the changing room at half time. He must have stuck it into Wayne's kit bag during the second half of the match. His Da tucked it under his arm and discarded his kit bag onto the ground.

Wayne watched his Da cross the landing. His brow was furrowed in anger. Then it relaxed, and he looked worried, slightly lost. He looked up and saw Wayne standing at the bathroom door. His expression changed again. He looked ashamed or embarrassed before he gave the gentlest shrug of the shoulder and arching of his eyebrows, as if to say you know what she's like. All of this had taken place in an instant. It was like watching the essence of him outlined in a series of snapshots.

His Ma was still lying on the ground. Casual as you like, she lifted the brolly by its pointed tip and pulled on his right ankle with the handle just as he went to step out onto the staircase.

His Da tumbled forward headfirst.

Wayne ran onto the landing. His Da was lying at the bottom of the stairs. A pool of blood was forming beside his right ear. It was crimson in colour, a much darker hue than the dribbles that came out of his own little cuts and scrapes. It was the same colour as the red wine used by the pervert priest in Mass.

The blood was slowly pooling outward. The perfect circumference was broken by a large wad of notes sticking out of the bag he'd got from Jimmy. The corners of the notes turned red as they absorbed the blood. His Da's eyes were utterly still, and the life was gone out of them.

His Ma crawled over alongside Wayne and looked over the top step of the staircase.

'He lost his footing, son,' she said.

Wayne didn't answer. He hoped that his Da had found out that they'd won the match.